If it lead her to activity in searching out and
alleviating the wants of the neighbouring poor.

Drawn by H. Corbould.

Eng.d by C. Warren on his prep.d Ste

Page 242.

Forgiveness

The life and murder of
Bessie Caroline Goodwin

A sensation novel
by
Simon Hobbs

THE CHOIR PRESS

First published in the United Kingdom in 2025 by
The Choir Press

ISBN 978-1-78963-469-3

In memory of my father, Tony Hobbs, (1932–1973), who never got the chance to realise his full potential.

'A noble jilt, my dears,' said Mrs Carbuncle eloquently, 'is a contradiction in terms. There can be no such thing. A woman when she has once said the word, is bound to stick to it. The delicacy of the female character should not admit of hesitation between two men. The idea is quite revolting.'

Anthony Trollope
'The Eustace Diamonds'
1873

GRIPPER:
One moment, if you please! I wish to speak to you about my fate –

AUTHOR:
Oh, you're too late! We've settled everything.

W.S. Gilbert
'A Sensation Novel'
1871

Contents

I

A Betrothal

❦

23rd April 1863

Captain Francis Goodwin, the current custodian of Wigwell Grange, has come to regret the presence in his library of a scarlet velvet chaise longue. It had been a surprise birthday present for his granddaughter, Bessie. However, he would be the first to agree that it has never really fitted in. It sits awkwardly against the dark oak panelling that dominates the room, like a high-spirited child placed in the care of an unwilling elderly relative. The library itself features huge leather-bound volumes on topics of special appeal to the Captain such as hunting and fishing, ferns and fossils, and freemasonry and God. None of these interest Bessie one iota.

Bessie's true passion is the countryside which surrounds her adopted home. She will happily stride out from the Grange in any direction. To the right the new turnpike to Alfreton takes her past pale cows, and then past ancient beeches that tiptoe down to the edge of the River Derwent. Here vibrant green weeds, caught by eddies, imitate a young woman's hair being stroked by a moderate breeze. In winter this gentle soul of a river is transformed into a more frightful creature altogether as the surrounding hills pitilessly offload their rainwater. Then the Derwent turns, in a heart's beat, from would be seducer to determined abuser. The river churns against the bridge's cutwaters, repeatedly seeking a weakness in its defences. Bessie gets as close to the insurgent torrent as she dares, relishing the chilly mist it generates and the sensation of her face tingling with the cold.

Uphill to the left leads her past an ancient standing stone, then off towards the gritstone outcrop of Black Rocks, which stand aloof from their limestone cousins across the valley. As she makes her way along Barrel Edge, Wirksworth is spread out beneath her. The town's stone dwellings cling desperately to each other round the holes that Man is currently engaged in gouging out of the valley, in the name of 'Progress'.

On a fine day St Mary's is clearly visible; next to that the Tudor Gothic folly that is the Gell Grammar School and, next to that, a modest, but elegant, stone mansion. This is the vicarage, home of the Reverend Robert Harris, Bessie's mentor and friend.

⁓

This particular spring day Bessie turns left out of Wigwell but heads down past the Malt Shovel Inn, instead of along the ridge. Cloud sits low in the valley as she follows the snaking track down to the town. Little of Wirksworth is visible at first, other than the tip of St Mary's dagger-like spire.

Bessie is alone this morning, and her gait is more halting than usual. From time to time she stops, for no apparent reason, and then, having paused for a few moments, resumes her trek downwards. She meets Reuben Conway halfway down the hill, near Mill House, but she barely acknowledges him. She immediately regrets this. Reuben will be troubled by her apparent coldness and will wonder what he can have done to upset her.

Soon the vicarage, surrounded by unfeasibly high stone walls, comes into sight. The Reverend Harris' housekeeper, Mrs Turner, a severely thin and plainly dressed widow in her late fifties, but with remarkably dark and plentiful hair and a face seemingly untouched by the ravages of time, admits Bess into her house. She does so reluctantly. Mrs Turner leads Bessie to the Reverend's study, even though Bessie could very easily have found her own way there. They find the Reverend engrossed, typically, in a formidable-looking ecclesiastical tome, with his head bent forward and his chin thrust unnaturally onto his chest in order to try and get a better look at the text. With his long legs, bushy eyebrows and permanently puzzled expression he looks, Bessie fancies, like a troubled grey heron.

'How lovely to see you, my dear. Come and sit down.' He indicates a worn leather armchair which is her favourite. He replaces his book in precisely the correct position on the bookshelf. 'You will have some tea, I am sure?' Mrs Turner stomps off to the kitchen to fetch it. The Reverend stokes the fire and comes back to perch opposite Bessie on a most uncomfortable-looking straight-backed rattan chair.

Bessie sits back in her allotted armchair, affecting a relaxed state. She briefly meets the gaze of the Reverend but then quickly looks away, feigning interest in a small watercolour of a lady riding a horse which is one of the very few concessions to decoration in her friend's austerely furnished room. They sit there in silence for a few minutes. Then, without altogether meaning to, Bessie lets out a deep sigh. The Reverend makes no reference to this but follows up on it.

'How are you, my dear? Is there something troubling you?'

Bessie has anticipated the question but is nonetheless still unsure how to answer him and, because of this, a sense of panic begins to rise up in her. She feels her cheeks begin to burn red. Fortunately at that very moment Mrs Turner returns with the tea. The arranging of the crockery gives Bessie valuable thinking time.

Mrs Turner eventually departs, and Bessie begins to speak. In preparing for this meeting with the Reverend she had decided on taking a circuitous route to the main issue. But now she wonders if this strategy had really been the right one. Her speech seems more contrived than it had done when rehearsed in front of the oval mirror in her bedroom at the Grange, where she had addressed the flock of mermaids which flank the mirror's gilded frame.

'I have been reading the Gisborne book you lent me. You know the book I mean; it is about the so-called duties of the female sex.' Bessie wrinkles her nose in disapproval. 'I have it with me here.' Bessie fishes the small book out of her prettily beaded reticule and holds it out in the palm of her right hand but makes no attempt, as yet, to return it to its owner.

The Reverend nods encouragingly.

'Yes, I have been reading this book,' Bessie continues. 'I have not finished it yet, but I am quite a way through it. It's a book even my grandfather would likely approve of me reading – which is saying something as I don't think he much approves of the female sex reading at all.'

The Reverend smiles, wanly.

Bess realises she is already getting off her topic. After all, it's not her grandfather she has come to discuss. She makes a determined effort to bring the conversation back on track – she can feel the potential for further panic on her part and needs to get her dilemma across as soon as possible. She also knows that Robert will find the discussion that she intends to have with him something of a challenge and this makes her even more nervous.

'There is a passage that ... I want to read it out to you. To seek your counsel, I suppose. If you don't mind, that is?'

The Reverend nods again.

She has tried to learn the passage in question by heart. Unfortunately, when practising in front of the mermaids, she found herself doing it in a singsong voice which was most inappropriate. She has therefore scribbled the page number – 167 – on a piece of notepaper which she produces from her dress pocket. She fumbles for the correct page in the book. Eventually she finds it and reads out the following:

'A young woman is sometimes led to contract a matrimonial engagement without suspecting that she does not entertain for her future husband the warm and well rooted affection needed for the conservation of connubial happiness.'

She reads the words slowly and deliberately, stumbling slightly over 'connubial'. She then falls silent, failing to give any indication as to the type of advice she wants. She knows that her silence will only increase the pressure on Robert. She realises also that he may not know the exact state of things. But he does surely have sufficient knowledge to enable him to put two and two together and make four? Satisfied of that, she does not feel that there is any need to add to what she has already said. She is confident that Robert will be able to help. After a few moments he breaks the silence.

'So you want my advice, about a betrothal?'

Bessie nods but says nothing.

'So you are betrothed presently?'

Bessie shrugs her shoulders.

'And you don't want to be betrothed?'

There is no response.

The Reverend eases the Gisborne book from Bessie's by now tight grasp and finds the passage she has been referring to. He studies it for a few moments. It is located in a chapter entitled 'Considerations Antecedent to Marriage'. He reads on, aloud:

'She beholds him with general approbation; she is conscious that there is no other person she prefers to him; she receives lively pleasure from his attentions; and she imagines that she loves him with tenderness and ardour. Yet it is very possible that she may be unacquainted with the real state of her heart. Thoughtless inexperience, susceptibility of early youth, and chiefly perhaps the complacency which all persons, whose affections

are not preoccupied, feel towards those who distinguish them by particular proofs of regard, may have excited an indistinct partiality which she mistakes for riveted attachment. Many an unhappy wife has discovered this mistake too late.'

Robert looks up and is surprised to see that this passage has reduced Bessie to tears. There is something child-like about her, in spite of her height and her bearing. She is almost, but not quite, 22 years old, with that compellingly luminous complexion that is peculiar to young women of passion. Her dark hair is tied back severely but, even so, her tresses are only just restrained. They are determined to be liberated as soon as circumstances should permit. Whilst often lowered in company, her eyes are a piercing blue and, once fully engaged, can unsettle the most worldly-wise member of either sex. Her lips are full, perhaps slightly too full for some people's tastes. Now, though, it seems as if, temporarily at least, the child has triumphed over the woman. Robert moves closer to Bessie, as if he intends to take her in his arms and provide some comfort. He cannot do this, of course, for reasons of propriety. Instead, he places a tentative hand on her shoulder. She stares at him as if she still expects him to divine, by intuition, the exact nature of her predicament. Revelation then strikes the vicar.

'You want to be betrothed – but not to whom you are presently?'

Bessie both nods and shakes her head in turn.

'And you want my advice as to what to do – how to ... how to end any obligations and free yourself, for someone else, someone else you are fond of, maybe even somebody that I know?'

Bessie once more gives way to tears, but this time her crying is more in relief than in sorrow. She lunges towards him, being much less inhibited than the cleric is, and holds fiercely onto him for several minutes. Once he has extricated himself from this unexpected embrace, Reverend Harris hesitates, again apparently at a bit of a loss as to what to do next. He reads on, aloud again:

'It is highly desirable that a young woman as soon as ever she receives particular attention from an individual of the other sex, should communicate with perfect openness the circumstances to their parents. And every young woman ought habitually to reflect, that her first object

should not be to be happily settled in matrimonial life, but to be prepared to do her duty in any situation in which Providence may design her to be placed.'

This time Gisborne's words have a very different effect on Bessie. Her face has turned ashen, and her features distorted. She stares at Robert. Then she starts to berate him, her arms flailing around as she does so.

'My duty. My duty? Who on earth are you or your beloved Providence to tell me what my duty is? What experience do you have of the world hiding away in this fusty presbytery of yours? What makes you qualified to tell me what to do about anything, let alone what my so-called duty is? Don't just sit there, please. Answer me. I need to know. This is urgent. I need to act. And soon. I have already let things go on for far too long.'

Her tirade at an end Bessie slumps back in her chair. The Reverend Harris also remains impassive and silent, staring into the middle distance. Then Bessie gets up and, without a further word, departs for home. The Reverend Harris is left on his own. But, as the front door is slammed shut, Mrs Turner appears as if from nowhere, anxious to learn the purpose of Bessie's visit and the reason for her raised voice and noisy departure. Reverend Harris chooses to keep his own counsel on both counts. He picks up the book Bessie has just abandoned and studies its content for a few minutes. The frontispiece depicts a gentlewomen ministering to the sick. With a sigh he returns the book to his shelves. He wonders if he should have told Bessie everything he knows.

II

A Challenge

ぐんへ๛๑

Sadler's Gate, Derby
16th March 1872
To: Frederick Leech Esq.
<u>Barrister at Law</u>
Gray's Inn
London

My dear Fred,

Heartfelt congratulations from your mother and myself on your being called to the Bar. Your success is well deserved. It is especially pleasing to see you entering the senior branch of the legal profession rather than the more junior office of attorney in which capacity your father has laboured away for so long.

I see that you have taken advantage of our enormous pleasure and pride at your achievement to renew your long-standing request that I set down for you my reflections about the Townley case. You say you want to benefit from 'any lessons that I may have learnt'. You strongly imply (or is this just my imagination working overtime?) that this is my opportunity to admit to any mistake(s).

I have tried hard to take your comments in the positive spirit that I am sure they are intended. With the presumption that only a child can contemplate towards a parent, you have also stipulated that I should be entirely truthful as to my role in the case. You say you would 'expect no less'. This does, however, make me wonder why you felt the need to specify it in the first place?

Be that as it may and having considered your request further I have decided to do what you ask. Your mother, my Lydia, with whom I have, naturally, consulted, supports me in this but has also put her own two penn'orth in by reminding me of the virtues of brevity and modesty.

7

However, I cannot, realistically, promise to be either on a consistent basis.

A word of warning before I begin. You cannot ask for candour on the one hand but not expect some uncomfortable surprises on the other. If mine is to be a true account, which is certainly my intention, then disclosures will need to be made which would not normally figure in a father's communications with his child, and so may feel most uncomfortable, however adult and worldly wise that child may now believe himself to be!

My first disclosure is not a difficult one to make. It may, I dare say, add some degree of credibility and substance to what follows. I have preserved my own personal collection of papers at home dedicated to the Townley case. It is a comprehensive archive of letters, copies of witness statements and attendance notes produced in the course of my investigation. It also includes public material – eye-witness accounts of the trial, press cuttings, ballad sheets, cartoons and the like. I have kept these papers concealed from prying eyes in a secret drawer in my desk. I do not think even your mother has discovered them yet – not that I am accusing her of having prying eyes; she has beautiful verdant eyes as it happens ... But to get back to the subject. You may think, quite reasonably on the face of it, I suppose, that the accumulation of this material is purely an exercise in personal vanity on my part, even though I have not – until now – divulged even its existence to another living soul. If that is what you think then so be it. In truth I am puzzled myself as to why I have kept material that might, in the final analysis, prove highly damaging to my own cause. Notwithstanding this I intend to quote freely from my 'archive' as our correspondence proceeds. But I will still need, in some instances, to rely on my own recollection of events to supplement these written resources. I believe my memory to be reasonably sound, but errors may creep in, most especially, I suppose, where they concern my own actions or omissions. I am, after all, playing a lead character in this drama. I have a good deal invested in the script.

In providing this account to you I will trust to your absolute discretion. Some of what I will tell you in the coming weeks is confidential. It had better stay that way. By reading on you are deemed to have accepted the requirement of absolute discretion I am placing upon you. If you cannot do this then please return this letter and we need never speak of the matter again, nor will I think any the worse of you. How could I when I approach your request with such trepidation? It would be a blessed relief. But, knowing you as I do, I think it unlikely that you will want to fall at this first hurdle.

My second revelation will immediately engage the aforementioned duty of confidentiality. It may, or it may not, come as a surprise to you as well. I am an attorney, a solicitor, by profession, yes, but I am a worrier by nature. I commenced worrying at the tender age of fourteen having by then lost my faith in the existence of a loving and caring God. That this followed hard on from the sudden and untimely passing of my own dear father is, I am sure, far from coincidental. How I yearn to be like my colleagues who suffer no such agonies in life and who simply entrust their fate to Providence. Not me, I'm afraid. Nor you either? I think of my worries as silverfish. Appearing without warning they rush here and there inside my skull. As my mind reels so my imagination lurches from one potential crisis to another. Each imagined scenario has more and more dire consequences. Eventually these silverfish vanish, just as suddenly as they arrived. But they are always alert and ready to resurface without notice, if required. I find myself at one with Mr Septimus Harding, the protagonist of Mr Trollope's novel, who worries himself half to death over 'a poor 800 a year' and whether or not he is morally entitled to receive it.

But this 'flaw' has not held me back in my chosen vocation. To the contrary. Much to my own surprise I have turned out to be a good lawyer. Not so much at wills and conveyancing and all that dull, dusty stuff. This I gratefully leave to my partner, Mr Gamble. What I relish, like you I think, is the court work, the thrill of litigation, the excitement of the parties squaring up to each other. Like you I am a 'black letter' lawyer, that is, I scrutinise every gobbet of law, every clause and every subclause, to tease out an interpretation which best serves my client. In short, I worry away at it.

No doubt as a consequence of my reputation for bringing hope where there is little or no basis for it, I found myself, in the summer of 1863, urgently instructed by a Mr Charles James Townley of Manchester to attend on, and represent, his eldest son, George, who was by then confined in Wirksworth Lock Up. He was accused of murder.

You will agree with me, I am sure, Frederick, that all clients, however disreputable they present as, or however downright wicked their conduct may have been, are entitled to the best possible legal representation? A man may believe himself to be as guilty as sin, but yet his lawyer may still, if he has grounds, seek to persuade society not to extract the ultimate price. I feel this most strongly – it has been the mantra of my whole professional life. So I had no qualms in accepting Charles Townley's instructions, for and on behalf of his son. Indeed, I accepted his instructions with alacrity and an excited sense that this case might just be the making of me. I had no reason to think, at the time, that I might later come to regret that decision. 'Fools rush in where angels fear to tread' I imagine you muttering. And on that note, I end the present letter – but with the promise of much more foolishness to come! More than you can presently imagine, I'm sure of that.

From your affectionate father
Samuel

III

A Betrothal Revisited

☙⚬❧

23rd April 1863

Bessie hastens back up the hill towards the Grange. She pauses several times on the way up, just as she had on the way down. But this time there is no chance encounter with Reuben, which Bessie is thankful for as she is not sure that she could stop herself from breaking down and confessing all to her friend. She is aware that it would be wildly inappropriate, in some people's eyes, to even call him a friend, given his inferior social standing. But such is her current state of mind that she thinks that she would struggle to hold herself back. In normal times she has no time for stuffiness. In the mood that she is in now she does not give a fig for social conventions and niceties.

On reaching the Grange, and gaining discreet admittance via the back gate, she rushes up to her room, freeing her hair with one hand as she does so. She frantically consults again with her mermaids. This time, sadly, she finds that they have nothing to offer her. She regrets having behaved so badly to the Reverend. She resolves to make it up to him. He will not hold her recent outburst against her for long. But his recently spoken words, or rather the Reverend Gisborne's words percolated through him, keep coming back to her. They hang in the air like the putrefying smell of comfrey tea. She turns over and over in her mind the moral obligations, according to that advice, she is now burdened with:

One – she must communicate with perfect openness the full circumstances to her (grand)parent.

Two – her primary object must not be her own happiness.

Three – she must do her duty and submit to Providence.

She finds herself becoming angry all over again. She half wishes she had never sought Robert's view. It was not fair that a single mistake, or perhaps more accurately one and a half mistakes, should now condemn her forever to an unhappy marriage. Must the past always poison the future? Must our errors always blindly dictate our fate? She had no doubt that her grandfather would be appalled were she even to hint that she may be bound, in any way, to George. She barely remembers now why she had got betrothed to George in the first place. It seems a long time ago and she was so very young. She has a better idea why, having broken things off the first time, she had then allowed a revival of sorts to occur. But this is not really her fault either. There are extenuating circumstances.

She decides she needs to refresh her memory as to why she ever felt that she was in love with George so that she can, perhaps, better understand why she has fallen so out of love with him now. She may then be able to explain this to him? Apart from the obvious reason that is. He need not know about that quite yet. If at all.

She goes over to the small chest in the corner of her bedroom. This cabinet, though modest, has captured her heart. It is made of satinwood and is jauntily decorated with sprays of holly and berries, all carrying a dusting of snow. The pretty chest is raised on a stand by elegant long, tapering legs. It is the piece of furniture that Bessie loves most in the Grange. The chaise longue her grandfather had unexpectedly bought her last year does not even run it close.

Bessie keeps her secrets safely under lock and key. The key is, as usual, hung around her neck. She takes it off and opens the chest. She fumbles around for several stacks of letters and places them to one side. Then she pulls out a slim red leather volume which bears the title 'The Birthday Scriptures Book' embossed in gold letters. The volume contains a week of the year on the right-hand page, on which it is intended the owner will record the birthdays of those dear to her. The left-hand side features improving Bible passages, deemed relevant to the particular day. The volume had been a birthday present from the Reverend Harris for her twenty-first birthday on 23rd June last. On presenting the gift to her the Reverend had pointed out that this book might have an alternative, additional, use as a diary. He had rather lectured her about how he hoped he might be helping her to acquire the habit of keeping a diary which he himself had started at about her age and which he found of great solace now. He had added, almost as an afterthought, that he also hoped the Christian exhortations the volume contained would strengthen her faith.

She is being a bit petty about the birthday present which had been a very thoughtful one. She had adopted Robert's suggestion and started her diary officially from 1st July 1862. She is far from being a conscientious diarist, however, not being overly interested in squirrelling away memories for her old age. However, she does sometimes think an event, or a thought she has, is worthy of recording. When she does write something down her entry often spills over from the allocated day. Bessie glances back briefly at some of the spidery entries she made at the beginning of her diary, before turning to April 23rd 1863. Carefully, in the smallest handwriting she can manage and with her nicest pen, she writes the following, which, on this occasion, fits comfortably into the allotted space:

Morning tea with RH at Vic. Mrs T cold to me, as usual. But RH also rather horrid. RH agrees with TG that I must marry GT. That cannot be.

She finds it has improved her morale to have so decisively rejected, and in writing, the advice she has just been given. She snaps the diary shut and replaces it in her beloved chest.

She then turns her attention to the several bundles of letters. She finds the letter she is looking for and, having shut her bedroom door, whispers out loud as she reads.

5 Hendham Villas, Hendham Vale, Manchester
30th June 1862
My dearest, dearest Bessie,
I can barely hold my pen so full of happiness and 'élan' do I feel myself to be following your visit. I can hardly write the words I need to record for fear that they may float off the paper as soon as I have committed them to the page. At the moment only you and I (and God himself) can know the cause of my great joy. Soon it will be known throughout the county, indeed throughout the world if I have anything to do with it. But for the moment, dearest, I am content for it to be known by us and by us alone. For it to be our precious secret. The fact of our betrothal is more than sufficient for me, the promises we have made to each other, though entered into 'hors de vue' and not before any altar, yet they are as true and binding as if they had been made in the most magnificent cathedral before the holiest of priests and the most distinguished of congregations.

It goes without saying, of course, that I am, in so many, many respects, unworthy of you. Your beauty and grace take my breath away. Your intelligence, whilst differently cast to my own, is as equal as I could reasonably expect of a life companion. But it is your essential virtue that has really reached out and touched my soul. 'L'habit ne fait pas le moine'. That is, 'The clothing does not the monk make'. Fear not I don't wish to be misunderstood – I am not comparing you to a monk or suggesting that you should live like one in the future! What I mean is this. In everything you do you cannot help but show your purity to me. You are not like other women, nor I like other men. I have no desire to see you display yourself in the latest silly, silky fashions. Such things are ephemeral and are beneath our contempt. Rather your goodness shall be your gown, your faithfulness your jewels, and your duty your crowning glory. I, for my part, promise to be a loving and indulgent husband to you. You will never have cause to question my authority for it will always be justly, fairly and yes, benevolently, administered.

I am bursting with pride to break this most felicitous of news to our families. My mother and sister will be delighted. My sister is already your intimate, my mother, I am confident, soon will be. They are the two people in this world who are most precious to me. I have no doubt they will soon become just as precious to you. As for your grandfather, I do not deceive myself. I know he is a far harder nut to crack – but crack him I assure you I will. Indeed, I have a plan to do so. With God's (and, hopefully, also my own father's) assistance I will soon find employment more commensurate with my talents and abilities. It will mean me going away for a short time – you will just have to bear that as best you can my dear – but I have no doubt that I will return a rich and successful merchant. The Captain will then be only too pleased, I am sure, to learn of my existence, and of our betrothal, and to hail me as his kin by marriage, and his successor by entail. But I know also that for now I must be patient and wait. 'Le prix vaudra la peine d'attendre.' I have no doubt that together we stand on the cusp of great happiness and fulfilment. The prize is so nearly within our grasp. We should not, nay we must not, let it slip.

In the meantime, I have just one modest request of you Bessie my dear – at least I hope that you will think of it as modest – that is that you send post haste a photograph of yourself for me to take with me on my forth-

coming travels. Do so on the pretext of needing a carte visite – they are very much 'a la mode' I believe – that way you need not arouse any suspicion of your motives by a visit to the photographer. I am sure your grandfather will indulge you in this. Please do oblige me in this one small thing. I will then not only be able to keep you close to my heart but also I can look at your near likeness as often as I wish to, which will be very often. I say 'near likeness' as I am sure that the photographer, however skilled he may be in his trade, will do you scant justice. Never mind. Each time I examine your image I will wonder anew that we, you and I, are very soon to be man and wife. How exciting it is to commit the words 'man' and 'wife' to paper darling – it is, literally, beyond my wildest dreams!

A bientôt
Your loving George

Bessie reads the letter several more times in silence. She pulls a face at herself in the mirror. The letter does not provide her with the answers she had hoped for. In fact, it only increases her concern as to how things now stand.

She had obtained permission from her grandfather for her photograph to be taken, utilising the excuse suggested by George. Spares of the resulting cartes were dumped in the chest, and she takes one out. She never made use of them, though she was a regular and welcome visitor to houses in the neighbourhood. The reason for this should be obvious to anyone who sets eyes on them. She hates the photograph of her they bore in every way it was possible to hate a picture of oneself. It really did not do her any favours. As George, to be fair, had predicted.

To start with she dislikes the background, if you could call it a background. She would have liked to have been photographed against her beloved rolling hills and wooded valleys, rather than in a small, dank studio in Derby on Sadler Gate where a sharp, bitter smell assaulted her nostrils as soon as she entered the premises and a half-drawn curtain was the only backdrop provided. It was explained to her, at some length, that that this was not possible as it would have meant the photographer, his equipment and dangerous substances being brought to her at the Grange. She accepted this explanation with reasonably good grace. Even so she could not, for the life of her, see the point of that half-drawn curtain.

Some kind of crude allusion to her adult life just beginning perhaps. Who knows? Again, on raising her reservations with the photographer's assistant she was informed, rather shortly this time, that if a half-drawn curtain was good enough for Her Royal Highness, Her Majesty the Queen, to pose in front of then it certainly should be good enough for her.

She would have preferred to have her hair combed and set free rather than pinned back. It made her look pale and ill. But this was not possible either; indeed, the very suggestion was treated as if it were an indecent one.

Last, but by no means least, she hates the fussy jacket selected for her to wear over a bustle dress. This was not her usual style at all and made her look much plumper and shorter than she was in real life, not just shorter but also frumpy and rather mouse-like. It was something she might have worn about the house but certainly not in company, probably not in the house, actually, owing to its impractical full skirt. Still, despite her serious reservations, George had liked the picture. Or had said that he did. And, at the time, that was all that mattered.

Before she can go back to the diary entries again to see what exactly she had said about George in them, if anything, she is interrupted by the familiar sound of her grandfather's bell summoning her. It is a special bell to which she alone is required to respond, not any of the servants. She is not sure how this bell has come into use. Her grandfather, it is true, is now somewhat frail, as befits a man well over eighty, but he is remarkably physically fit for his age and is quite capable of seeing to most things himself, if he has a mind to. She hastily replaces the letters and cartes, carefully locks the chest and returns the key to its place of safety. She hurries down the stairs, taking two steps at a time and pinning her hair back as she goes, to see what her grandfather wants. As she does so she is careful to cast off any trace of worry and to put on a face of happiness and contentment. It would not do for her grandfather to see her upset. It might arouse his curiosity.

IV

A Murder

Derby
All Fool's Day, 1872

My dear Fred,

Thank you for your letter of 19th March in which you generously acknowledge my 'candour' to date, but also express your impatience to know much more, much more quickly. What you would really like, you say, is for me to hand my papers over to you 'lock, stock and barrel'. That is not going to be possible I'm afraid. I have promised to give you a blow-by-blow account and I will be true to my word. But, indulge me, will you? For I wish to do it in my own time and in my own way. Context is everything in this case.

You may not have grasped yet, but I believe I have already told you, just how difficult it is for me to re-live the events in question, at this distance in time. I am revisiting what was a very dark period of my life and doing so entirely for your benefit. Certainly, it is not for my own. I would much rather have let sleeping hounds slumber on. Can you begin to imagine what it was like for your father, a mere provincial solicitor, to find himself, on 8th February 1864, accused by Members of Parliament on the floor of the House of Commons, of irresponsible conduct? It was a terrible shock, on top of everything else that had happened. It took the then Home Secretary, Sir George Grey, no less, to intervene on my behalf in the debate. I say 'intervene' because even he did not exactly leap to my defence. But at least he did make some attempt to call off those 'hounds of hell' also known as our elected representatives. He stated, as per Hansard, that he imputed 'no blame to the indefatigable (sic) prisoner's attorney for taking the course he had done, so long as the law sanctioned it.' You will note that he left it open whether or not the law did sanction it. Hardly a ringing endorsement now, was it? It is left to the jury of public opinion to judge me. It is never a very pleasant thing to be arraigned before the court of public opinion. By the way, talking of arraignment, I looked into the mirror today, something I would usually avoid doing at all costs. I was shocked anew at the dumpy, prematurely wrinkled fellow who stared back at me. The dumpiness you will, no doubt rightly, attribute to my taste for rich food and fine wine. However, the hairline (hairline?) cracks which have begun to open up on my face are directly attributable, I feel, to the case you are now asking me about.

I am sorry, Fred, if you feel that I am labouring this point, but I do hope that my account, painfully extracted as it is, is not just for your amusement, or that of your Inns of Court lunching cronies, but that you genuinely feel it will serve some instructive value. On that strict understanding, as a second (or is it a third? I have lost count!) 'condition precedent', I will continue with my account.

I left you last time with the news that I had, as a bolt out of the blue, been instructed to act on behalf of a Mr George Townley then confined in Wirksworth Lock-up. Accordingly, early on Saturday morning 22nd August 1863, I made my way down by train from Derby to Whatstandwell, following the route George Townley presumably would have taken the day before. This is a scenic trip in winter, but now, in the height of summer, the countryside sparkled in the sunshine. The railway line runs in parallel with the canal which, in turn, more or less apes the course of the glassy River Derwent, gliding unperturbed through the valley. Commerce and country thus live in harmony.

This day I was preoccupied however, with the grave matters that awaited my attention at the other end of the line. I had purchased a copy of the morning's *Derby Mercury* before boarding my train. The object of my trip dominated the news –

Horrible murder by a Gentleman near Wirksworth

*On Friday afternoon at tea time a shocking
murder was committed near Wigwell Hall,
Wirksworth, by George Victor Townley, who
describes himself as a gentleman, residing at
Hendham Villas, Queens Park, Manchester.
The victim was Miss Elizabeth Caroline
Goodwin of Wigwell Hall.*

*The intimate relations between the murderer
and Miss Elizabeth Goodwin, the social
position of both parties, the popularity which
Miss Goodwin had won by her amiability and
kindness, the incidents connected with the
murder, all combine to render the tragedy one
of the most extraordinary we have ever been
called upon to record. Miss Goodwin has, for
four or five years, resided with her
grandfather Captain Goodwin with whom she
was an especial favourite. She was a fine, tall
lady, and was generally esteemed as
accomplished, courteous and, socially, kind to
the poor.*

I shifted uneasily in my seat. The newspaper's fulsome appreciation of the
late Miss Goodwin's virtues was surely the final nail in my client's coffin,
if, Fred, you will pardon this wholly unprofessional observation.

❦

The inquest was held on Sunday 23rd August in the Moot Hall in Wirksworth. This accommodation had been requisitioned at short notice. The
Hall is, doubtless, more than adequate for its normal business of adjudi-
cating on disputes between quarrelling lead miners. But it proved
thoroughly unsuitable for an inquest. There was limited space and no
reserved seats for professional advocates like myself. Moreover, the place
was full to the gunwales with people from all walks of life hoping to see up
close the cut of the man accused of 'dear Bessie's' murder. For it goes

without saying that everyone present had, overnight, become Bessie's dearest friend, even those who had previously been her more vocal critics.

There was a faint, but unmistakeable, odour of sweating bodies, which was hardly surprising as it was another hot August day. The sun streaked in from the tall leaded windows behind the jurors so that they were transformed into mysterious beings from another world fringed in light, like silhouettes fashioned by Edouart. You have come across his work, I imagine? Mr Cox, the coroner, similarly short and rotund but slightly older than myself, and with less hair, entered the room and made his way onto a small wooden dais to commence proceedings. On being seated, Mr Cox gave me a solemn nod of recognition. It was a nod, I realised, that acknowledged our shared responsibility for clearing up this terrible and bloody mess.

George was brought into the Hall last of all in order to minimise the chances of him being threatened, or even assaulted. I would have advised him not to attend at all, had I been consulted on the point, and I was surprised that the constabulary had seen fit to facilitate it. Cries of 'shame' went up, accompanied by loud hissing, as, escorted by the constable, George was slowly paraded through the Hall to a seat beside me. He was restrained by manacles to his wrists and feet, hence his and the constable's painfully laboured progress. I did not notice whether any members of the jury participated in 'greeting' George in this way. I would not be at all surprised if they did. George, however, did not react. He stared straight ahead. Once seated he read, apparently with great interest, from the roll of Barmasters and Stewards of the Soke and Wapentake of Wirksworth engraved on a marble plaque opposite his seat. It was, quite possibly, the one and only time that these local worthies have been the subject of such intense scrutiny. Whilst he was doing so I had a chance to study him. He was taller than I had imagined, his short dark hair had ambitions to be parted and he sported a large untamed beard. His black eyes were set far back in his skull – sunken I suppose you could describe them as, if one were being unkind. His whole features – his eyes, his nose and his mouth were easily accommodated in the upper part of his elongated face leaving plenty of room for the aforesaid beard to flourish below. He was, in short, a very unattractive fellow. Not someone who you would have taken a second glance at if you had encountered him in the street. But these were far from normal circumstances. His (alleged) deeds had already promoted him from nondescript to notorious and, therefore, endlessly fascinating.

The inquest eventually got underway. The coroner's officer read out the report of the medical examination that had been conducted 'in situ' at the Grange by a Dr Newton Mant.

'I examined the body of the deceased at Wigwell Grange.

'There were three wounds on the right-hand side of the neck. One stab below and behind the right ear. A second one, in front of this, but superficial. A third wound, three inches long and extending within half an inch of her chin.

'On closer inspection this last wound was produced by a stab directed downwards and backwards. The transverse process of the vertebrae was entirely separated, as also were the carotid artery and jugular vein. The long wound did that.

'In my view the stab at the back of the ear was done by someone standing close behind. It was the long wound that produced death. It was done with superhuman force and there would have been much blood. It is my painful duty to add that, in my opinion, death would not have been instantaneous, but somewhat lingering.'

The officer was understandably nervous in front of such a large and raucous crowd and struggled, at times, to read Dr Mant's report out. He delivered the last sentence in a near whisper. The attending citizens again let their feelings be known, this time by pointing at George and chanting 'Murderer, Murderer, Murderer' at him in unison. He did not react. The chanting was so inappropriate in this forum that it seemed to me almost comical. The coroner eventually restored order.

On the basis of Dr Mant's report, the cause of death was never in doubt and the finding by the jury of unlawful killing was a foregone conclusion. What disturbed me, however, was the manner in which the jury reached its decision. After the coroner and the jury had viewed the poor corpse of the lady in the next-door anteroom, which in itself was a pointless and unnecessary ordeal, the jury foreman showed a salacious interest in the identity of Miss Goodwin's friends and acquaintances, including my client, but not limited to him. This juryman seemed unhealthily interested in a mysterious clergyman admirer of Bessie's, pressing the Reverend Mr Harris, the local vicar and headmaster and one of the last people to see

George before the murder, as to whether he was aware of this other clergyman and how he had responded to George when asked about him. The Reverend answered the question in the following terms.

'Mr Townley said he called upon me as Miss Goodwin's friend to see how matters were. I said anything I knew was in confidence. I declined to tell him, though he asked me more than once, in a very pressing manner. He asked me if another clergyman had been staying at Wigwell Grange and what his name was. I told him that I believed that there had been a clergyman staying there but I declined to give him his name.' He turned to the coroner at this point. 'I do not propose to give the name now either unless you require me to do so, sir? I would be surprised if you chose to require it of me, but I would not, of course, resist your ruling.' Mr Cox, to his credit, showed no inclination to pry further into Bessie's private affairs. George, who had briefly sat up when the identity of the clergyman was referred to, now slumped back into his chair as it became apparent that this line of questioning would not be allowed to proceed further.

⸙

I had the briefest of conversations with Mr Townley in a private room in the Moot Hall after the hearing and before he was returned to the Lock Up which is located a short distance away in North End. Oddly he gave every sign of being quite keen to get back there even though the accommodation it offers is none too comfortable. I had thought he might show at least some emotion during our meeting, bearing in mind that Bessie lay lifeless just a few yards away from where we were holding our conference and that he had only just had the misfortune to hear, as we all had, a detailed account of the grim injuries that he had inflicted upon her. But he did not. He slouched at the table that had thoughtfully been provided by the Trustees of the Moot Hall for our use. I had to move back in order to avoid his protruding legs which had temporarily been liberated from the manacles he had worn, as indeed his wrists had been from their cuffs. His clothes had obviously been held over since last week and so he probably looked more dishevelled than would normally have been the case.

The most disconcerting thing about him, however, was not his appearance or his deportment but his attitude. Despite the obvious immense vulnerability of his position, he displayed such 'sang froid' that he clearly regarded even talking to me, his own attorney, as a tiresome inconvenience. He used the short time that he was generously able to spare to give me the benefit of his own legal analysis, a role reversal that I found extraordinarily galling. He was much more animated than hitherto. He relished the opportunity to show off his knowledge. It was not so enjoyable for me. It was an unwelcome novelty to find myself being instructed in the law by my own client!

After being told that the basis of a criminal charge was establishing the mens rea (which he, most patiently, explained to me 'was commonly called the motive') and the actus reus ('the action taken in furtherance of the motive') he then sought, still without a hint of emotion, to apply this analysis to his own dire situation. In doing so he consistently referred to himself in the third person. This added to the impression given that he was an eminent law professor, and I was merely his attentive, if not very able, student.

Thus said Townley:

'The mens rea, Mr Samuel (sic), I have just explained to you the meaning of this term and I trust that you were paying attention, will inevitably be found in Townley's strong, but justified, resentment of his displacement in Miss Goodwin's affections. The actus reus is the unpleasantness that Townley and Miss Goodwin had subsequently, and consequently, been involved in on the turnpike. There it is – actus reus and mens rea richly satisfied. It is an open and shut case if ever there was one.'

Townley went on thus:

'As to sanctions, Townley will most certainly be hanged. Accordingly he cannot see why his father has seen fit to fund even second-rate legal representation, given that his son's cause is so evidently hopeless and devoid of merit "il sera passible de la peine capitale". If you want my opinion, Mr Leech,[1] Townley Senior is only going through the motions of supporting Townley Junior when, in reality, he is perfectly indifferent as to his fate. George's indictment of his father reads as follows:–

---

[1] Let it be noted Frederick that I had not, at any point, asked for it. I must add that I did not appreciate the reference to my legal advice being second-rate.

One.

Said Father did little or nothing to help George when he could desperately have used some help – to advance his career and help him to become established in life so that he was then ready and able to take on a wife.

Two.

Said Father had given up on George years before that. Said Father had told George on numerous occasions that he was good for nothing.

Three.

Said Father had accused George, in the presence of his work colleagues and inferiors, of falling asleep whilst at work and of being a wastrel and a layabout.

What do you think that did for George's reputation or his confidence? I will tell you, Mr Leech, it destroyed both, utterly, irrevocably. Accordingly, whilst Townley has no objection to your presence per se Mr Samuel (sic, again), neither does he embrace, endorse or welcome it.'

With those words he summarily terminated our interview by calling out for the constable. It was, I suppose Fred, refreshing to be instructed by a client who has such low expectations of a positive outcome. I still had my professional pride in doing a job well, or at least to the best of my abilities. I wondered if that would be enough to see me through the challenges that surely lay ahead.

I have taken enough of your time for now my dear Frederick having gone on for far longer than I had originally intended. No doubt you will be able to contain your excitement until the next episode, which I expect to be able to furnish you with shortly. I am not yet so senile as to compare myself with the famous author, but it occurs to me that this must be rather like Mr Charles Dickens feels as he solemnly issues the next sensational instalment of a new novel to an expectant public. I'm only too aware of your likely derision at my last remark. Leaving to one side the many other differences my story is, after all, a true one!

Yours affectionately (and paternally)

Samuel

V

A Dinner

❦

September 1862

It is 25th September 1862, the day of the annual Volunteers' Dinner at the Grange. A final desperate rally by summer has, for the moment at least, postponed any thoughts of the colder and darker days that lie ahead. The Grange's park trees have yet to develop even a hint of an autumnal stain.

Final preparations for the dinner are underway and spirits are high amongst the staff, it being a much-anticipated local event. Bessie has been busy planning for it for several months. She has had a hand in everything – from the choice of a hearty and substantial menu to the white lilies that festoon a modest marquee, which has been erected for the occasion. Working with Reuben, her 'Assistant Gardener' for these purposes, she is delighted to have timed to perfection the production of several bunches of delicious black dessert grapes – a 'taste of paradise' she calls them – which have been grown in a ground vinery constructed for the purpose in the Grange's grounds. The grapes are prominently displayed on a circular silver salver at the entrance to the marquee for the admiration of guests as they enter and to whet their appetite for the feasting to follow. So 'fine and dandy' is it all that the Captain is heard to remark, more than once, unnecessarily loudly, that it is as if Bessie has been planning her own wedding breakfast, but with none of the inconvenience of having to take account of the groom's wishes, never mind those of her prospective in-laws. Bess overhears this remark. She finds it vexing but chooses to ignore it.

The Captain, seeing the relish with which she has set about the task, has given Bessie free rein to do as she pleases. An innovation for this year is the hanging of red and blue bunting and candle lanterns (at a safe distance from each other) from the trees in the park. As per the Captain again, it is as if 'the trees are transformed into an exotic species from a far-off land.'

He is so proud of the acuity of this observation that he is later to repeat it more than once to groups of his guests as he slowly makes his rounds of them to welcome them to Wigwell.

In advance of the guests' arrival Bessie is to be found checking that the staff, augmented by the services of the dependable Reuben, his wife and their two daughters from the farm opposite, and also Reuben's nephew, James, are well-versed as to their respective duties. But she also wishes to secure tasks for herself. 'Now what can I do to help? There must be something for me to do, however menial? Do make good use of me, please,' begs Bessie. 'That is what I am here for. To help you. I don't want to be just a useless spectator, a spectre at the feast. Where is the fun in that? So tell me what I can do and it will be done. Please?' Her heartfelt plea falls on deaf ears. There is only an embarrassed silence. The servants are instinctively reluctant to identify any tasks for their own mistress, dear though she is to all of them. So Bessie is forced to act on her own initiative and busies herself polishing glasses, folding linen napkins and laying tables. Even so, Margaret Poyser, a maid, whispers to James Conway that 'Miss Goodwin is in danger of doing both of us out of a job.' James only grunts in response. He is a man of few words. It is one of the things that Margaret likes most about him.

At six o'clock sharp the Volunteers, preceded by the band of the Corps, march into the park to be greeted by the rapturous applause of guests. A beaming Captain Goodwin, now resplendent in full ceremonial dress, leads the parade, with the help of a stick. His troops are also dressed for the part, sporting smart scarlet coats with yellow facings and white trousers. Once the Captain has briefly taken his men (who vary in their aptitude for marching) through their paces, all concerned gratefully retire to the marquee for an early dinner.

The dinner is excellent and substantial and, having taken their fill, the Volunteers eventually settle down to hear speeches. Upon removal of the cloth, Captain Goodwin takes the chair, ably supported by Reverend Robert Harris, the Guest of Honour. The usual loyal and patriotic toasts having been observed, along with a toast to the Guest of Honour, the Captain, in eloquent terms such as only he can muster, then wishes health and prosperity in this Golden Age to the Rifle Volunteers of Great Britain. The Captain remarks that he has no fear whatsoever of Napoleon the Third – 'or sorry, should I say *Emperor* Napoleon the Third,' (cue jeers and boos) 'attempting an invasion of this county ('hear hear'). He would be mad to attempt such an ill-advised expedition and would be loath to do so if, like the Captain, he had just witnessed 'such a fine body of marching men dedicated to the defence and protection of our hearths and homes.' (hear, hear) The Captain goes on to give generous praise to his grand-daughter, Bessie, for her efforts in organising the dinner, stating that, 'without her, the dinner would not have been the roaring success it has been. The credit, which is considerable, all belongs to her'. The company indicate their unanimous agreement by banging the table with anything that comes to hand, including in some cases their own boots which they have removed for the purpose. They cheer her to the echo. Bess modestly hides her face in her shawl.

Further toasts are given, and graciously received. Then, as most of the members of the Wirksworth Corps consider themselves to be musical, the singing begins, tentative to start with and then more raucous and, finally, becoming a little bawdy. Bess again hides her face in her shawl to conceal her blushes. She decides that at this stage she can safely leave her guests to it without her withdrawal being remarked upon, or even noticed. Besides, Bessie has good reason to temporarily absent herself.

The songs, accompanied by band members of the Corps, whatever their musical merit, have indisputably enlivened the proceedings and added much pleasure to the evening. Eventually the citizens of Wirksworth, reluctantly and slowly, depart for their homes and hearths, replete in belly and soul and admiring the sight of the park's trees which, by then, are illuminated by a score or so lanterns, sparkling like captured stars.

But that is not quite the whole story of the dinner for Bessie. In fact, it is hardly the start of it. Bessie had met the Reverend 'William Young', (not his real name – but it will serve for our purposes) when 'William' stayed earlier in the summer with the Reverend Harris, from whom it had been arranged that he would receive some theological tuition. He visits the Grange with Robert to meet Captain Goodwin and is introduced, albeit briefly, to Bessie. He is immediately intrigued by her. The feeling is mutual. William, by hook or by crook, secures an invitation to the Volun-teers' Dinner at Wigwell, along with the Reverend Harris. Since Robert is the Guest of Honour at the dinner, William is also allocated a seat at the top table. Bessie ensures, also by hook or by crook, that she is seated immediately to his left. She is delighted that she has successfully engineered for them to sit together but also nervous as to whether he will like her or not. She thinks he will.

'So how do you find us in Derbyshire, then, Reverend?' Bessie initiates a conversation with him casually enough. 'I suppose you are accustomed to a more refined and civilised way of living down there in Surrey? Compared to us simple country folk in Derbyshire, I mean?'

'Please do call me William, or, even better, Will,' he responds. 'And please, Bessie, if I may call you that, don't make me sound ancient before my time. But in direct answer to your question, I find both Derbyshire and its inhabitants very good, very promising indeed. Though it is early days. I am hoping to see more of it, and more of them as well. Only then will I be able to give you my final verdict. But from what I have seen so far, I would say that the situation is very promising, very promising indeed. There is very good . . . raw material to work with.'

'Well, I very much hope so, Will. How gratifying! Good raw material, eh? I'm so very glad to hear that. We, in our turn, hope to convert you to the people and the hills and the moors of this beautiful county of ours, however desolate the county and heathen the people might appear to you presently . . .'

William ignores her last remark and continues, 'And then there are your great houses – Chatsworth, Haddon, Kedleston and the like. I would very much to like to visit some, or all, of them if that is possible, if the appropriate introductions can be obtained, that is?'

'Yes, William, I can see you are well informed. And keen to impress? But in your hurry to mingle with the grand and the good please don't neglect attractions nearer to home, in our own humble neighbourhood. Not only the church of St Mary's, which I assume you are already very familiar with, but also the Moot Hall, the old Cottage Hospital on Greenhill, and best of all, in my opinion, the ancient wood at Shining Cliff.'

'Ah yes the woodland, the woodland – permit me, dear Bessie, to recite a short verse on that theme, if you will?'

Bessie nods, she hopes enthusiastically.

'There is a pleasure in the pathless woods,
There is a rapture on the lonely shore,
There is society, where none intrudes,
By the deep sea, and music in its roar.

You are familiar with the work of the poet the late Lord Byron, I'm sure?'

'Of course,' said Bessie, rather surprised, but also rather encouraged, at his willingness to quote poetry to her so early in their acquaintanceship. 'We have pathless woods here … plenty of them … and solitude if that's really what you desire most – but we can't offer either sea or shore here in Derbyshire, I'm afraid. That's one thing that is most definitely not available. I must say that we rather rejoice in our distance from the sea. We relish being thoroughly enclosed, embraced, if you like, by the land – it is comforting to us. We are not at the mercy of the sea's capriciousness … our men are not away braving its moodiness and so we can sleep soundly in our beds at night without fearing the tolling of the bells. It's one less thing to worry about. We do have plenty of rivers, if that is of any interest to you, part compensation maybe? The Dove, the Derwent, the Wye –

Her velvet turf, stretches on either side to view the streams,
of those fond rivers hurrying to blend, their glassy tides.

That is all a bit tame for your tastes methinks? But we do have scenery here as noble as anything you might find in Greece or Switzerland. I believe that your very own Lord Byron may have shared this opinion?'

Bessie is conscious that she has rather monopolised the conversation thus far. She is distracted by the unsettling thought that Will bears more than a passing resemblance to Lord Byron, with his dark tightly coiled hair, prominent nose and full lips. But is he a bit too good to be true, she wonders? She decides to further test his mettle.

'Anyway,' she continues, 'without wishing to speak ill of the dead, Lord Byron was a man of questionable morals as I understand it, and so I am surprised to find that you, an aspiring man of the cloth, are to be found promoting his work so enthusiastically. And to an innocent young lady like myself at that. I was rather hoping that you were more of a gentleman.'

Will is stung by Bessie's last remark but shows no sign of abandoning the field to her just yet.

'I am a gentleman, least I hope so anyway. I try to be … a poor gentleman it's true, but a gentleman, nonetheless. But I do fervently believe that one must distinguish the man Byron from his poetry just as we should always sever in our minds the artist from his art, the composer from his tunes, the chef from his culinary *pièce de résistance*. Well not the latter, maybe. That may be taking things too far. But you understand what I mean, I think? It's an unfashionable view, I know. Take Signor Caravaggio. He's a good example, or a bad example, of what I am talking about. Should we not separate out in our minds the artist Caravaggio from Caravaggio the murderer and ne'er do well – even if his paintings do seem to us rather alarming, evil even? Even in his extreme case it is for God to judge his sins rather than for us mere mortals to do so. Do you not agree? But it is for us mere mortals to appreciate, or indeed despise, the art that artists have produced. Do you follow me, and do you not agree with me? Judge not lest ye be judged.'

Bessie has never heard of Caravaggio. As far as she can remember none of his paintings had graced the pages of her grandpa's pristine copies of the Art Journal which she has occasionally flicked through when it was raining and she was stuck in the house, bored. She did not know that he had a murderous past, either. But, although she does not feel theologically equipped to take on William on this territory, she does feel that for him to suggest that it requires God to judge the manifestly evil conduct of a murderer, if that was what he is saying, is nothing short of preposterous. She changes the subject. She decides to test his knowledge of public affairs instead, and, by doing so, to gauge his sympathies. 'So, tell me, William, sorry, Will. What do you make of events across the ocean in America, the terrible war that has begun there. Are you with the South or with the North . . . or do you not have any view? Maybe you are just not that interested?'

'I most certainly do have a view. I am with the North,' William answers unhesitatingly. 'I detest slavery with all my heart, and I stand squarely with all its opponents here or abroad . . . including, it is said, our glorious queen. As that noble and god-fearing man William Wilberforce has said, "Christianity is not satisfied with producing merely the specious guise of virtue. She requires the substantial reality." I very much hope to live up to Mr Wilberforce's injunction as I progress in my own life – both my divine life and that as a man. I want to actually live a Christian life, not just to instruct other people how to live one and then to luxuriate in their inevitable failure to measure up.'

Bessie is pleased with this answer, which is both pretty and pretty nearly what she herself might have answered. Bessie reflects that he has passed the tests she has set him with, more or less, flying colours. By way of a reward, she smiles warmly at him. Will colours up slightly in response, which Bessie also finds rather charming.

Bessie and William continue to chat away incessantly for the whole of the dinner. Once the speeches are concluded and the songs are in full swing, the duo manage, at a signal from Bessie (including a rather hard kick of his shins under the table) and despite William's expressed reluctance to offend his host, to sneak out into the garden, ostensibly to admire the lantern sparkling trees that Bessie has told Will about. Their conversation quickly turns to the beauteousness of the real stars high above in the dark sky. William stands daringly close to Bessie as he helps her to point to the North Star with its surrounding constellation, the Little Bear. He is so close that she can feel him begin to shiver. It suits Bessie to allow him to believe that he is assisting her. In reality, she is well aware what she is looking at and is quite capable of locating the North Star on her own. Then, to impress him, Bessie tells William, in strict confidence, that she has been on several night-time expeditions with her neighbour, and 'accomplice', Reuben Conway, from the farm opposite. She says that Reuben has taught her the pleasure to be found in standing in an empty field at night and just listening and breathing, whilst gazing heavenwards and contemplating the stars. She quickly realises this is something of a miscalculation on her part as William seems to be rather put out on hearing about Reuben and their joint exploits. Could it be that he is already a mite jealous of Reuben? She deliberately touches his jacket sleeve, intending to communicate to him that her connection with Reuben is innocent and harmless and so not one he needs to be in the slightest bit concerned about.

Bessie then announces that they must return to the house, as the guests are now beginning to depart, before her grandfather notices her absence and comes to look for her. William trails slowly behind Bessie as they go back inside. Having been reluctant to take the risk of sneaking out and having then been emboldened by Bessie to do so, he now drags his feet, seeking to prolong their time together alone for as long as he can. Eventually he follows Bessie back to the marquee. He is welcomed back by the Reverend Harris who asks him no questions about where he has been, indeed he barely seems to have registered his absence.

Bessie, light-headed after her encounter with William, is unable to sleep that night for more than a few hours, or for several nights afterwards. She is, already, allowing herself to contemplate excitedly a future vastly different than that she had hitherto resigned herself to.

Her entry in her birthday book for 25th September 1862 reads as follows – *Met young Revd 'W' again, he likes Lord B and Signor C and, most esp., Revd W (i.e. himself) – but q. promising raw material overall.*

VI

An Eccentricity

ᴄ∿ᴅᴄᴏ

6th April 1872

Fred,

A file note for you to examine. A few observations first for context.
Father *aka* 'St Jude'.

I had chosen to spend the nights before and after my interview by
George in the basic but adequate accommodation offered by the Bull's
Head Inn. Your mother had expressed doubts as to whether the expense of
one overnight stay, let alone two, was really justified. But I had put my
foot down and, given the modest cost, the expense was, reluctantly,
approved by the powers that be, i.e. your mother. It was good of her.

The hotel was located a mile or so from the Grange, next to a robust
little arched bridge crossing a bend in the River Derwent. Not relishing
being cooped up in my room for a second night I went for an evening
stroll along the river. It was a lovely summer's evening, as I recall. The
sunset was extraordinary, pink-tinged, but with a menacing grey framing
the whole. A pair of herons flew over. I was struck by the awkward grace-
fulness of their flight. During my walk I chanced across workings of the
Duke of Devonshire dug in the cause of extracting sandstone for commer-
cial sale some years ago. A few of the quarries had, through recent neglect,
quickly reverted and become a natural feature of the landscape in their
own right. Ferns had begun to take over and, being now exposed to the
elements, the remaining, rejected rock to darken, so that the whole could
have been taken for a small jungle rather than simply another man-made
intrusion into the countryside.

Returning to my lodgings, and ruminating on the day's events, I was
struck anew by the utter strangeness of my client's behaviour in the aftermath of the murder. It was really most peculiar. He had not sought to cut
and run as would have been the natural, indeed the expected, thing to do.

His failure to do the expected thing, to flee from the scene, only added insult to injury as far as the public was concerned. He had stayed to brazen things out rather than to end his own life in a ditch of his choosing. Having now met George in the flesh I could not help thinking that the ditch might have been the better option for him.

I ordered a large glass of brandy and pondered on George sitting alone in his cell in the Lock Up. Unless I was able to pull off a miraculous intervention then his life was, to all intents and purposes, over. This rescue was a tall order, even in my burgeoning role as the patron saint of hope and lost causes. That's St Jude, of course. I presume you looked up my earlier reference, if indeed you did not know it already? You certainly should have done, you are a fully fledged lawyer now, after all? Allegedly.

I mentally steeled myself for the struggles to come. I anticipated the blast of war sounding in my ears. I stood ready to stretch every sinew on my client's behalf, completely indifferent though he was to my efforts. Anyway herewith, for what it is worth, is my recollection of the events of the following day. You may well disapprove of some of my comments regarding Mrs and Miss Townley – but then excluding all emotion is not always the way to go, and you did agree warts and all, did you not?

꩜

File note for Townley file

24th August 1863

On 24th August 1863 I accompanied Townley, escorted by the redoubtable Constable Parnham, as he was brought by coach and four from Wirksworth to the County Gaol in Derby where he is to remain until the day of the trial. This, I judge, will be sooner rather than later if the 'powers that be' have anything to do with it. In my experience, justice administered with such undue haste can very often be justice denied. His mother, Mary, and sister, Caroline, had arrived from Manchester the same morning by train and were to reside, I learnt, at the County Hotel near the railway station, a pleasant but rather too prominent an establishment. I met them there by prior arrangement. They both immediately made a favourable impression on me, despite the most awful, indeed unimaginable, circumstances they found themselves in. Both mother and daughter were intelligent, but scrupulously polite and well-mannered. Both were slight in stature, and both were, incidentally, strikingly pretty, the mother giving away little or nothing to her daughter in that department, despite the difference in their ages. Their long dark hair, though pinned back, provided, in both cases, a perfect foil to their pale faces and fine features. Being dressed, as they were both, in deep mourning only enhanced their appeal. They will make exceptionally good witnesses I think, judging from their demeanour alone. In my experience if there is one thing that jurymen warm to it is a pretty female witness on the edge of despair. It brings out their sense of chivalry.

After the usual courtesies, rather a strain in the circumstances, we quickly got down to business.

'So how did you find my brother?' said Caroline, on the edge of tears. 'Is he still disturbed in his mind?'

'It's hard to say, Miss, as he spent most of our first meeting giving me a lecture on elementary legal principles and most of the journey here berating the constable for having handled him too roughly!'

Caroline looked faintly cheered. 'That sounds like George, to be sure. It's good to hear he still has some measure of fight left in him.'

'He has resilience, of a kind,' I said carefully. 'He regards himself as doomed, but he is also unrepentant of his actions and says so openly to anyone who will listen. It is a bad combination – defiance on the one hand and resignation on the other. I should not disguise from you that I am afraid that he is, in his present mood at least, at significant risk of fulfilling his own prophecy and paying the ultimate penalty for his crime.'

Caroline responded, 'But Mr Leech, this is why we are here now. To tell you the whole story. You need to understand, everyone needs to understand, that my brother is a very sick man. He has been a sick man for a long time, he was always sick maybe. A strain of insanity runs strongly and deeply in our family, I fear. Tell him mother – tell Mr Leech about our sad and damaged ancestry.'

Mary then spoke. To begin with she avoided looking at me whilst she spoke, and she spoke so quietly that it was hard to make out what she was saying, and I had to lean forwards to do so. She will have to learn to speak up if she wants the court to take any notice of what she has to say.

'It is true that our family has been so afflicted, Mr Leech, at least ten family members have succumbed to a greater or lesser extent to mental distress. That is the sorry reality. The worst, Aunt Mary, my father's sister, died by her own hand and was then found, on enquiry, to have been insane. Other relations have found themselves confined in asylums for a greater or lesser period of time. My mother's brother had a family of nine children of whom six went to an early grave having showed traits of madness. So you may understand why I say that I have always feared for George. Some say he carries the family curse, do you see? I do not myself believe in curses, any more than I do in witches or wizards. But there is no doubt in my mind that my son is different to other men and that he carries the burden of this difference heavily. It overhangs him.'

'But there is more, much more than this. Tell him, Mother, about George's strange behaviours. He must be told everything. Now is not the time to hold back.'

Again the mother was taciturn but, under further prompting from her daughter, gave me the following additional information.

'You mean his eccentric behaviour, dear? Yes, well once, about a year ago, he bought seven white hats all in one go and then cut different size squares out of each of them so that he could tell one from the other and then wore them on successive days of the week. But that is not mad, is it, Mr Leech?' she added defiantly. 'Strange yes, eccentric yes, but not mad? Another time he plunged into a bath with all his clothes on. I do not know why he did not undress before doing so but he may have had his reasons, I don't know. Perhaps he was in a hurry?' (She looked at me as if she was daring me to laugh.) 'But as I say these are examples of his eccentricity rather than of madness.' She became more assertive. 'After all, how can each of us really, honestly know whether we are mad or sane? We only know what we know. Perhaps we are all a little bit mad and a little bit sane as well, both together, at the same time? Or maybe we are more or less sane more or less all of the time but also have occasional spells of being mad? I, for one, do not place much store on outward manifestations. It's too easy to label, label things, label people – do you not agree, Mr Leech? It is the easy thing to do. The lazy thing to do?' She looked directly at me again as if she detected that I myself might be prone to such indolence. I did not rise to the bait. Instead, we agreed that we would meet regularly henceforth to discuss any developments in the case. I counselled them not to expect any immediate progress – this was going to be a long haul.

I should add that I did not respond to her challenge straight away, as my mind had shifted to worrying as to the ultimate fate of the two people in front of me, most especially the mother. Although noble concern for her son does her great credit and the news as to familial insanity does at least provide the suggestion of a hook for a defence to be hung on, I fear for her, as much as for George, once the trial begins. They (mother and daughter) will be as much on show as circus animals, their every move and gesture will be scrutinised and, no doubt, the subject of sanctimonious comment by the 'gentlemen' of the press. One false move by either of them, and the whole moral edifice could come tumbling down on top of them: 'It was the mother's fault. She should have done more to contain him' … 'What did the sister think she was doing in advising her brother to come to Wigwell at all for that final, fatal interview? What business of hers was it anyway?' And so on. And so on. No stone will be left unturned. Putting to one side the vulgar public cant and clamour, how does a mother cope with knowing her son is a killer? Can a mother's love survive intact after such a terrible blow? How can a son's love for his mother have any meaning when he has, by virtue of his own deliberate actions, cast himself and his family so far out of decent society? Yet she bears herself with such dignity and poise that I cannot help but admire her.

I roused myself from my musings and managed to mumble a few words in response to Mary. I was then embarrassed by my inadequate response, and left hurriedly under cover of having another client to see. I spent the cab journey to my office berating myself for not having answered her very pertinent question more fully, and more honestly.

I felt a sense of relief once I got back to my office and found that the trial date was now fixed – it was to commence on 11th December 1863 at the Derby Assizes.

VII

A Judgment

໐ᚭᚷᚋᚭ

16th October 1862

Bessie sees William again some weeks later when she and her grandfather make the arduous journey south to visit an ex-army comrade of his
in Surrey, close to William's parish. It is a considerable way to travel just to
enable her grandfather to rekindle an old friendship, even one, as here,
forged in the heat of battle. But Bessie knows she cannot refuse to go and
so leave her elderly and infirm grandfather to travel such a long distance
on his own. So she resigns herself to the prospect of having to play the part
of a rapt audience member for endless after-dinner military anecdotes, no
doubt considerably exaggerated in the re-telling.

The reality turns out to be different, and much more to her liking.
Though she knows that Will's parish is within a stone's throw of where
they are staying, she has not allowed herself to imagine that they might
actually get to meet again so soon. Well, in truth, she has imagined it
but not with any expectation that her fondest wishes would be realised.
Picture her excitement then to find Will in attendance at a dinner party
held to honour Captain Goodwin's visit. The two young people lose no
time in rekindling their friendship. They soon discover they have a
mutual love of walking. Surprisingly to Bessie, her grandfather, who has
listened in to their conversation, sanctions, without hesitation, a
walking expedition that William proposes for the following day to see
a recently re-discovered ancient mural. Will feels obliged, as a matter
of good manners, to issue an invitation to all of the assembled dinner
company, without discrimination. But he is far from displeased that it
is Bessie alone who turns up at the appointed time and place the next
morning. No one has apparently given even any thought to the question of a chaperone.

And so it is that William and Bessie now stroll alone together over
Farthing Downs in bright autumnal sunshine. As they reach the crest of

38

the Downs, William points out the bulges in the hillside that apparently contain the mortal remains of Iron Age warriors – an unsettling revelation. On they walk through the delightful but modest Happy Valley to reach the church where a medieval mural has recently been unmasked by surprised workmen. The workmen, as William explains to Bessie, fortunately had had enough common sense to alert the vicar to their discovery, thus preventing its permanent destruction and preserving the mural for future generations.

Along the way the two young people laugh and joke. William's liking for Bessie is immediate and obvious and, despite being slightly embarrassed on his behalf, she revels in the joy of his unalloyed admiration.

'I am struck by how easy I find it to talk to you, William,' said Bessie after they had been walking a short while. 'We fit together so well.' She blushes, adding quickly, 'What I mean is we are perfectly complementary, as friends . . .'

'I agree, my dear. It is like we are two sides of the same coin. Well, I am considerably more intelligent, more handsome and generally more of a catch – but, leaving that aside, we are more or less identical, cut from a common cloth, would you not say?'

Bessie plays along.

'I agree, my dear William – apart from the fact, surely too obvious to state but I will do so anyway. Just for the record. Apart from the fact that I am prettier, cleverer, and kinder than you. And better off, of course – let's not forget that, shall we? Apart from all that, leaving all that to one side for one moment, I would say that we are as two peas in a pod – would you not agree?'

'My dear Bessie, it is true that you are almost perfect and indeed might be mistaken for being so were it not that you have the misfortune to be currently comparing yourself to me and, in the final analysis, as I am sure you will accept, there can, sadly, be only one winner. As for being richer, well, I would have thought better of you than to plead this in your cause. Do I need to remind you what the Bible says about the rich man, the camel, a needle and entry into heaven?'

Bessie thinks she detects a smirk and pulls a face at William in pretend outrage.

So keen are the pair to outdo each other that this increasingly competitive conversation lasts several more rounds with each claiming parity with, but at the same time vast superiority over, the other. The game eventually results in them both having an uncontrollable fit of the giggles when William claims, with a straight face, to possess the courage and intelligence of the late Duke of Wellington, the compassion of Florence Nightingale and the wisdom of Her Majesty the Queen all rolled into one – whilst at the same time claiming Bessie and himself as a pair of identical parakeets contentedly sitting side by side on a single perch!

The glow of their mutual admiration is marred, but only slightly, for Bessie, by sudden pangs of guilt as to what George would make of seeing the two of them together like this, playing the fool. She tries to put this out of her mind. After all, she and George are now no longer tied in the way they once may have been and so she was really under no continuing obligation to him. She tries to take herself in hand. She reminds herself that she is now free to behave as she wishes, with whoever she wishes to, within the constraints of good manners and common decency, naturally.

They cross the threshold and enter the small, squat and gloomy church together. Despite the gloom there is no need to search for the mural that is the purported justification for their outing. Still William points it out proudly, almost as if he himself was the artist. Bessie stands in awe before the pinkish, brown and white monstrosity that occupies the whole of the back wall of the church. It is obviously ancient, but it still looks freshly done and this only serves to accentuate the horror of the scenes depicted. William embarks on a long explanation of the mural's narrative, speculating as to the identity of the devils and sinners portrayed, and detailing the bright colours that had originally been deployed to heighten the painting's impact. Bessie ignores him. Suddenly she speaks. 'I cannot believe the cruelty of it. Death was all around them; it had seeped into their very existence. And then this – the final insult – death, it turns out, might provide no relief at all. Instead, they are confronted every day by this awful spectacle. All those poor souls being judged, convicted and tossed by toady-headed monsters into a furnace to be consumed alive by the fire. Where is God's pity and compassion here? Where is your precious merciful and loving God?' asks Bessie.

William treats the question as a liturgical challenge and not, as it could have readily been interpreted by him, a personal affront. 'It's . . . Catholic . . . I grant you that, but God is here all right, look, there, at the top of the picture, above the ladder – He is doing what He does best – judging souls, sorting the sheep from the goats if you like.'

Bessie ignores him and continues, 'Those devils with their horns and gruesome expressions – they are enjoying the whole thing a little too much if you ask me. Look at those desperate wretches crossing that serrated bridge of fire. And those devils, I assume they are devils, they are poking them with forks. They are truly horrible as well. They're also far too enthusiastic for my liking.'

'But be reassured, Bessie, it is only the sinners that are getting their comeuppance, not the decent and moral people like us. We are resting in purgatory, if we accept for a moment that there is such a thing, until the time comes for our redemption. And those others, the wicked ones, they deserve what they are getting, don't they? After all they are the unrepentant – the usurers, the swindlers, the rascals, the liars, the adulterers—'

Bessie interrupts. 'It's not them I am worried about. I expect that they can take care of themselves. It is the poor peasant who was confronted by this awful vision day after day, week after week, month after month. This painting, for all you say about its pretty colours, was intended to put them firmly in their place, wasn't it? Never mind the just deserts of sinners, this was just intimidation, pure and simple, wasn't it? You do what we say, or you will come to a gruesome end, like those doomed bridge-crossers in the painting. So, what did the peasants do? They did what peasants normally do, they toed the line and put up with their lot.

> The rich man in his castle,
> The poor man at his gate,
> God made them high and lowly,
> And ordered their estate.

That's it isn't it?'

She looks fiercely at Will, waiting for a reaction.

'I do see your point, Bessie dear, and I do sympathise with you, I do, up to a point anyway. I admire your humanity, I do. But I still say the wicked must get their just deserts, their dose of fire and brimstone. Where would we all be if we did not unconditionally condemn evil and punish sin?'

Bessie, still disturbed by the vision and its implications, sways slightly. 'I need to get some air,' she says and, followed closely by William, she makes her way rapidly out of the church. Once out into the sunlight it is as if she herself has been spared and she quickly regains her composure. Her equanimity returns as quickly as it had previously vanished. 'Let's go back, William. I am sorry that I snapped at you. I know it's not your fault. You can't be held responsible for a medieval artist's choice of subject matter after all, can you? We can agree to condemn both the art and the artist on this occasion I think? Maybe the artist just did as he was told and was paid to do but, if so, he certainly put his heart and soul into the task, didn't he? He didn't hold back. I also think, Will, that behind that determinedly conventional and grumpy exterior of yours, you agree with a lot of what I am saying. I hardly know you yet but that part that I do know is not vindictive. Well, we don't need to get into a debate again about that now. I can see that you are itching to get the last word!' (Will starts as if to respond but bites his tongue.) 'Let's just agree that we have had a lovely and interesting day – and leave it at that, shall we? There will be time enough to debate these issues hereafter.'

Will smiles at her. Bessie wonders whether he has noted her reference to further opportunities of talking with her and if this is the cause of his pleasure. She hopes it is.

So it is that they leave the church graveyard arm-in-arm and in almost as high spirits as they had entered it. They make their way back across the recently stubbled barley fields, gleefully spotting a fox skulking on the margins of one of the fields, his fur burnished gold by the weak sun's retreating rays.

VIII

A Viscount

⚬⌇⌇⚬

Derby
14th April 1872

Dear Frederick,

Please do not be too alarmed by the second of the two incidents described below. At least you can be sure that I lived to fight another day! The damage done was strictly superficial and chiefly to my pride.

As evidenced in my file I spent hours preparing for trial but not to any great effect. Never had the difficulties of making a silk purse out of a sow's ear been more apposite. As if that were not bad enough the full implications of being seen to be George Townley's defender-in-chief had also begun to dawn on me. I have never courted popularity and have represented some out and out scoundrels in my time, but my association with this particular client made me increasingly uneasy. Whether it was because of the sheer brutality of his crime, or the saintly personality of his victim or the shameless whipping up of emotions by the popular press, the strength of feeling against George was unprecedented in my experience. And such was the strength of feeling that, again uniquely in my experience, this vitriol spilt over into hatred of anyone who was perceived to have any connexion with him – principally his mother and sister but also me. My determination to do a good job, or as good a job as I could manage, was unaltered, the cause being greater than the individual. But yet I did worry about the implications for my family of me being seen to be George's doughty defender. Doughty had its limits after all. I was determined to do nothing to besmirch the name of Bessie. I have nothing but admiration for her. I hope you agree, Frederick, that it is the men who are the problem here. The women are, more or less, beyond reproach.

⚬⌇⚬

My new-found notoriety was brought home to me, in a small way, when your mother and I were invited at short notice to an evening soiree held in the Palladian splendour of Kedleston Hall. It was an invitation I would, for myself, have been happy to politely decline but Lydia thought differently. So it was only fair that we went. In all the finery we could muster.

Shortly after our arrival at Kedleston, in fact more or less as we entered the magnificent pink and white marble hall, I was accosted by our host, the Reverend Alfred Nathaniel Holden Curzon, JP, 4th Baron of Scarsdale. The current custodian of Kedleston was a spindly, gaunt man with intense blue eyes. He had an aristocratic air which suggested that he was accustomed to deference and was not inclined to brook dissent from his social inferiors, regardless of how well qualified or informed they might be. Our brief exchange is reprised below word for word, or at least as accurately as I can remember. Whilst the adverbs included in brackets are, of course, my own invention, there is not really too much scope for interpretation.

Lord C (pleasantly enough): 'Ah, Leech, isn't it? Welcome to Kedleston.'

Me (nervously): 'Thank you, my Lord. Thank you for inviting my wife and myself. It is an honour to be included in such … distinguished company.'

Lord C (slightly more menacingly): 'Well, Leech, never mind about that. I invited you because I particularly wanted to speak with you directly. We are both men of the world, so I'll not beat around the bush. You represent that egregious villain Townley, I believe? I can't say I approve of you assisting him in any way at all, but I suppose you legal functionaries have to earn a crust somehow, eh?'

Me (pleasantly): 'Indeed, my Lord.'

Lord C (patronisingly): 'I assume, as his attorney, you have had opportunities of seeing Townley, in the flesh, so to speak. So tell me now, Leech, man to man, is he sane or insane?'

Me (hesitantly): 'I could not rightly say, my Lord, not being medically qualified and—'

Lord C (pugnaciously): 'I will tell you then. He is as sane as you or I, Leech – that much is certain.'

Me (persistently): 'That may be so but that is, potentially, a matter for the court to decide, my Lord, not for me … or (more assertively), I respectfully suggest, for you either.'

Lord C (angrily): 'Is that right? Mark my words – to a certainty he will be, and he must be, hanged. An eye for an eye, eh? No milk and water intervention by you, Leech, or anyone else for that matter, can save him now. He is a Derby duck is he not? A Derby duck, I say. His fate is well and truly cooked, is it not? Just as a Derby duck – being a local man yourself you are familiar with that expression, I am sure?' (He laughs uproariously) 'We want no more lunacy from you and your mad doctors, Leech. You know the ones I mean, those so-called medical experts? We've had our fill of them and their half-baked opinions, quite enough. You know who I am talking about, Leech? The ones who believe a man can be insane but can still play a decent hand of whist, eh? What do you say to that – it's poppycock, yes?'

I was sorely tempted to correct his Lordship on a point of jurisprudence. A premeditated attempt to stab the monarch with a bread knife bought for the purpose (the case that I assume he was alluding to) was scarcely comparable with my case. But he had, by then, turned his back on me and so there was no more to be said. The interview having come to a natural, if abrupt, conclusion, I returned to your mother's side.[2]

If certain of my social superiors were contemptuous of my role in defending Townley then that was as nothing compared to the out and out hostility of some members of the public. I was increasingly unable to make my way down from my home in Duffield Road to Sadler Gate where our offices are situated, normally a pleasant enough level stroll, without being accosted by one or more of these fellows anxious to give me guidance on how I should conduct the case, or alternatively, to reprimand me for having the temerity to raise any kind of defence on behalf of 'that murdering scoundrel'.

Other names I was called were similarly far from pleasant – 'Townley's Lackey' and the 'Lunatic's Whore' being two that stuck in

---

[2] I did not hear from him again until he accused me, a full year later, in a letter to the Derby Mercury, of having all the time subscribed to his own opinions as to the sanity of George. I can only assume that he misheard me. Either that or he was indulging in a flight of fancy. Without wishing to be unfair to his Lordship the latter does not seem very likely as he does not strike me as a man of great imagination. SL

my mind. But I was mostly able to brush this abuse off as the price to pay for being a jobbing lawyer required to defend anyone to the best of my ability.

Nothing that had been said or done before, however, prepared me for the incident that occurred one morning as I made my regular way down towards Sadler Gate. I was feeling enlivened by what was a bright early autumnal morning. My troubles lifted, temporarily. I passed All Saints Church on my left, a stump of a building which had a guilty conscience as to its past, but which was no less loved by Derby's inhabitants for that. I proceeded rather more quickly past a couple of ale houses of doubtful repute and entered the Market Place. As I did so I noticed a well-dressed, young gentleman, whom I did not recognise, striding towards me apparently intent in engaging me in conversation.

I felt a sense of apprehension as he got nearer. Something did not feel right about this encounter. I was not sure what. He was about five yards away from me when I saw his face was puce with anger. By that time I had ceased to want to find out what it was that was bothering him. I decided to ignore him, keep walking and hope for the best. He also kept advancing but, as I passed him, he suddenly brought up his arm and elbowed me full in the face. I felt a searing pain in my eye and staggered blindly for a few moments. I was briefly convinced, of course, that I had lost my sight, but this quickly returned. I crumpled to the ground, more out of shock than out of necessity. I curled into a ball, fearing a further attack might be imminent. I lay there for a few seconds. I was on the verge of tears, partly because of the pain but mostly because of the humiliation that had been inflicted on me, right on my own professional doorstep, so to speak. My assailant, I assume, kept walking straight ahead. I swear I heard him chuckling. I never saw him again.

Having recovered somewhat, my priority was how to restore my dignity. A small crowd had gathered around me by this time, more sympathetic than I expected. I was helped to my feet, dusted down and, my intended destination having been ascertained, I was escorted to the door of my offices, at which point I thanked my would-be rescuers warmly, wished them 'Good Day' and stumbled through the door. Matthew, shocked by my appearance, quickly recovered himself and having dabbed at my eye with cold water, in a rather perfunctory manner, then offered me a glass of brandy, which offer I gratefully accepted.

On my return home later that day you will not be surprised to hear that I was subject to extensive cross-examination as to the cause of my, by then very prominent, black eye by your mother, who was becoming ever more concerned about my role in the Townley case. She was particularly unhappy, given her total lack of sympathy with Townley. She wanted me to give the case up there and then.

'I know that you are always for the underdog, it is one of the things that first drew me to you, Samuel, your strong sense of right and wrong, and not only that but your determination to turn thoughts into actions – it is admirable, Samuel, it is,' she said. 'But do you have to defend a man who by his own admission has committed such a vile crime? And if you do have to do so then do you have to do it with such enthusiasm?' She went on to point out to me, forcibly, that our daughters, your sisters, were more or less of an age with the late departed Bessie. How would I feel about any prospective murderer of theirs being defended so assiduously? I agreed that I would not like it. It was something that I had already worried about, but, stung by her criticism, I chose not to admit this to her now. Instead I referred, in rather stirring language to the importance of justice for all. This, understandably, only further infuriated her, particularly when I added that I was simply doing my job in compliance with the ethics of my profession. Your mother retorted that that was what Magistrate Hulton had said when ordering the terrible massacre of innocent people on that blackest of days in Manchester. I said we could not conduct a civilised discussion on the basis of her outrageous comparison of myself with the satanic Hulton.

You will not be too shocked, I hope, if I confirm that, at this point, all communication between the two of us ceased for the rest of the evening and for most of the following day. I was confident that normal relations would resume sooner or later, and you will be relieved to hear that no lasting damage has been done, as far as I know.

I hope you have found my latest missive sufficiently 'educational' Frederick? I am sure I will hear soon enough!

Kind regards

Father

IX

A Mountain

෬〜໓〜෭

24th October 1862

Despite the trip to see the mural not having been an unqualified success, Will persuades Bessie to stay on in Surrey for a while longer after her grandpa has unexpectedly returned to Derbyshire alone. William plans another outing. They both agree to give ecclesiastical sites a wide berth this time round. This time the question of who will accompany them has been properly raised and discussed. They are to be chaperoned, by Will's sister, Emily. Emily has already made it clear when the arrangements are discussed that she interprets her chaperoning role most liberally. A visit to Leith Hill is mooted by Will and agreed upon by the three of them. 'A lot more interesting than Box Hill, with better views,' he claims. This means very little to Bessie, who has no idea where Box Hill is or what its particular attractions may be.

The day of their jaunt is disappointingly damp and cool. Autumn has arrived with avengeance. But, despite the weather, they feel elated to have escaped from under the feet of their elders and excited about the day ahead. On the way there Will, as Bessie is increasingly coming to expect, explains in some detail the history of the tower at the top of the hill and how it had been built with the intention, and the exact dimensions, of converting modest Leith Hill into superior Leith Mountain.

'It was built about a hundred years ago, by Richard Hull, a local squire, as a place for the common people to come and enjoy the glory of the English countryside. I thought you would enjoy seeing it, Bessie, especially as you are so fond of the common people.' Bessie was going to ignore this mild jibe at her expense but Emily pricks up her ears and immediately takes up cudgels on Bessie's behalf. She is having none of this patronising nonsense even from her elder brother, least of all from him, and she intends to nip it firmly in the bud.

'What do you mean, Bessie is so keen on the common people? Why should she not be? What on earth is wrong with that? Are you setting yourself up apart from the common man now, superior to him? You know I love you but does your arrogance know no bounds? And you a so-called "man of the cloth" and all? You should be ashamed of yourself.' Whilst Bessie does not need Emily to intervene on her behalf, being more than able, she feels, to fight her own battles, she is nonetheless touched that Emily has chosen to back her in such a forthright and public manner. Will, meanwhile, does not take the telling off that he has just received from his younger sister at all well. He takes it very badly indeed. He falls silent, apparently indulging in an extended sulk. Bessie makes a mental note to raise this aspect of his behaviour when they are next alone as it just will not do for him to be so moody. And in company as well. In the meantime, she chatters away merrily to Emily about this and that – fashion and such like. For they have entered into an unspoken pact to expose the childishness of William's behaviour by simply ignoring him and carrying on as if neither of them has a care in the world, and certainly have not noticed that one of their company has fallen suddenly and unaccountably silent.

Arriving at the bottom of the hill, it quickly becomes obvious that the ascent is not only going to be a strenuous one, but muddy as well. The local Surrey clay clings to boots and dresses as they begin their climb. Emily is far from enamoured with this but Bessie links arms with her for encouragement, leaving a still silent Will to make his own way, some distance behind them. Bessie and Emily make an odd couple, Bessie is taller than Emily by some inches. But, building on their new-found rapport, Bessie and Emily talk not about trifles, as previously, but about important things. In Bessie's considerable experience walking often lends itself to the discussion of profound topics with one's companion, whoever they may be. This is no exception. Emily impresses Bessie by disclosing, in strict confidence mind you, that she aspires to become a doctor, whilst being fully mindful of the apparently insuperable obstacles that stand in the way of her ever achieving this ambition. She will, she says, do whatever it takes. Bessie doesn't doubt her determination and would not be surprised if, in due course, she succeeded, in spite of the overwhelming odds stacked against her. That is not all. For Emily goes on to express admirably advanced views about women having more say in public affairs and even having the vote – the more respectable ones at least. Bessie decides she likes Emily a good deal and finds herself in agreement with much of what she has to say. But, after going a short distance further, Emily suddenly makes an announcement, standing with her hands on her hips as if to add emphasis to her words.

'I have *no* wish to go on any further in this beastly mud. But you two youngsters carry on. Don't let my feebleness spoil your day.'

Addressing Will, who by that time has caught up with them via some discreet acceleration on his part, like he was engaging in a game of 'grandmother's footsteps', she adds, 'And you need to behave a lot better if you expect the lovely Bessie to take you seriously.' And then, addressing the pair of them again, 'I am going back to our coach but I do not expect you to return for some time. I have a novel by Mr Thackeray with me to read. It's rather turgid but I will persist with it. I do not wish to see you young people again before it begins to get dark. I will be very disappointed if I do. Now shoo and mind you make your way right to the top.' She waves the couple off with a dismissive hand gesture, turns and begins to make her way gingerly back down the hill.

The couple do not need a lot of persuading to push on up the hill alone. But, despite Emily's strictures, Will's recent moodiness hangs over them to begin with. Bessie thinks Emily's reference to their youth is slightly condescending – Emily, she judges, being not much over twenty herself. But it is also in her character, as Bessie now knows, for Emily to be simultaneously both forthright, and generous. Besides she cannot really resent being called 'the lovely Bessie' now, can she?

Once Emily has retreated out of sight Will offers his arm to Bessie and, after a moment's hesitation, Bessie accepts it. Bessie takes this gesture to be an unspoken apology from Will for his earlier behaviour. So Bessie and Will now link arms as they continue to make their way up the hill.

They traipse on up to the top only to find that the tower at the summit, whose merits Will had earlier so warmly extolled, is now near derelict and unsafe to enter. So, instead, they sit down on a grassy bank under fir trees that have colonised the upper reaches of the hill. Will, ever the gentleman, provides his jacket to Bessie to protect her from the damp grass and fallen pine needles. Together they admire the extensive, if still misty, views of Surrey and Sussex and talk about their respective hopes and dreams. Says Bessie, 'I want to do some good in the world. I feel I have so many good things in my life. Everything I could reasonably have asked for, except one. Some may look at my situation, and the only too early passing of my dear mother and think otherwise. But I have inherited her strong desire to help people. That is her legacy to me. And what a legacy it is! People may pity me living with my grouchy old grandpa, but the truth is my father was never really cut out to look after me and he was even less so once he had lost his wife, my mother. I have so, so, many advantages that I should be thankful for, and as for the rest, well I must make the best of it. I live in a handsome house in a beautiful place. I am well loved, though not necessarily by those I might have most expected love from. But what of that? I am still loved. What do I have to complain about? Nothing at all. Very little.'

This time Will does not tease her but listens respectfully. He is genuinely in thrall not only to her long limbs, lithe body and soft fresh skin but also, more importantly he assures himself, to the goodness of her soul. Now it is William's turn to speak from the heart. William speaks of his passionate desire to serve God in whatever role God might call upon him to do. He dreads, he says, becoming a reputable parson of a respectable parish at the beck and call of whoever he happens to owe his living to and not able to speak out as to what he thinks is right and Christian. He wants to do much more than that, to make full use of his God-given talents. As they talk, Bessie comes to realise that, whilst they approach the world from different standpoints, yet their ambitions are not so very different. If, as Bessie points out to him, one substitutes William's 'God' for Bessie's 'Man' (and 'Woman') the similarity of their ambitions becomes obvious. They are, it turns out, she says, more or less soul mates.

Bessie feels a rush of feeling towards the good man who stands before her. She fervently wishes he would take her in his arms right this instant. Unfortunately, he does not do so, despite her giving him some very meaningful looks. He is not very sophisticated in that way. But so relaxed does she feel in William's presence that she indulges instead in the phantasy that they are a young married couple out for the day but with the enticing prospect of returning to their cosy inn nearby for a supper in front of a roaring log fire and then the unknown pleasures of their matrimonial bed. She does not share this vision with William, feeling that he might be rather shocked by her frankness, but this does not in any way dilute her imaginings. How she wishes that all this was so. Or could be so. It could, couldn't it? She refuses to believe that it could not. She closes her eyes and wishes as hard as she possibly can. But instead of William she sees only George. He is scowling at her. She does not understand why. He surely has no reason to scowl at her now. He is ancient history as far as she is concerned.

X

An Investigation

Leech and Gamble Solicitors
Sadler Gate

25th April 1872
Fred, I am confident that you will be as incensed as I was when I tell
you that it became increasingly obvious that the prosecution solicitors,
TH Newbold of Matlock, intended to do as little as they could to assist
the defence, even, and I do not say this lightly, going so far as to positively
obstruct me when they felt that they could get away with it. Their whole
approach was astonishingly unhelpful. No evidence had been disclosed to
me despite the fact that we were uncomfortably near the trial. They
already had had the nerve to pinch two of my witnesses from under my
nose. The underlying assumption was that Townley had no defence and so
no assistance need be afforded to his legal representative. It was a waste of
time and breath to do so. I should accept the inevitable, as my client had
already done. I should follow his good example. This was indeed breath-
taking arrogance on their part. I hope that you will agree with me
Frederick that it should be fundamental to English justice that the accused
should know the case they face before they face it in the dock. I, for one,
was not prepared to settle for being fed crumbs by the prosecution as and
when they deigned to do so. There being, as you know, 'no property in a
witness', I decided that I really had no alternative but to instigate my own
enquiries, to investigate the crime myself! I am no Chevalier C. Auguste
Dupin. I have, sadly, no ability to read other people's minds. But,
nonetheless, I would do the best I could.

The obvious starting point was Reuben Conway. I was a little apprehensive about interviewing him as I was aware that he had been on good
terms with Miss Goodwin and thus might not welcome being seen to
assist her murderer's attorney. But he could not have been more helpful.
He returned my letter to him with a brief note saying that he would be

happy to speak with me about what had happened. Bessie's grandfather, Francis Goodwin, who, like Reuben, had not witnessed the crime itself but had witnessed the immediate aftermath, was noticeably less enthusiastic about meeting. Eventually, after several extremely stern letters on this notepaper threatening the issue of a summons if he did not cooperate, he agreed to see me – but on the strict condition that I kept matters brief and to the point. Did he really think I wanted to spend any more time with him than was absolutely necessary?

For reasons of convenience, and to avoid any last-minute backsliding by the Captain, I arranged to call on both of them at the Grange, rather than expecting them to visit me at our Derby offices. So it was that on 14th October I again made my way to Whatstandwell by train and made my way up the turnpike to Wigwell Grange. It was a long and steep walk up to the Grange and, halfway up, out of breath, I wished I had arranged for a cab. Walking up to the Grange did give me the opportunity to visit the murder scene. I had brought with me a rough map to help me locate where the crime had occurred. This was the very same map as had been published in the *Derby Mercury* immediately after the inquest, which publication had led to a large number of morbidly curious visitors to the scene. In fact, the newspaper had felt obliged, a few days later, to express the disappointment of its editor at what had occurred. More than that it had also published an open warning to its readers to desist forthwith from such 'voyeuristic and ghoulish behaviour which is in danger of forever soiling the reputation of Derby citizens in the eyes of the nation'.

I paused to consult this map as I climbed the lane until I was satisfied that I had found the spot where the fatal stab had been administered, just below the hunting gate. Any direct evidence of what had occurred had long since been washed away or been ground into the dust by the boots of the aforesaid ghoulish citizens. There were, in short, no visible blood stains. But I was taken aback to find that despite the lack of any physical evidence of what had occurred, the location was not lacking in a sense of melancholy. Whether it was the poignant beauty of the view down to the river I had just climbed up from, or whether it was the banality of the gate and track that had been the actual scene of the attack, or whether it was just my own imagination working overtime, I am not sure. But I was moved to stand in silence there for a few minutes and to pay my own respects to Bessie. I must confess that the images of your sisters again trespassed into my thoughts. It made me very sad. I pulled myself together and hurried on up the hill, pausing only briefly to view the other key locations that figure in the 'lamentable chronology of Bessie's last moments' as supplied by the *Mercury*. By this time I was running late, so I increased my pace.

Having arrived somewhat breathless at the Grange I was escorted to the library by a servant. Reuben was waiting for me there, looking slightly anxious, perhaps intimidated by the grandeur of his surroundings, though they were not unfamiliar to him. More likely it was the unknown nature of the legal process that he now found himself inextricably caught up in.

'Good afternoon, Mr Conway. I am very pleased to make your acquaintance.'

'And I yours, Mr Leech.' He greeted me with a formal, but warm and hearty, handshake. He was not at all as I imagined him to be. I could not now tell you what I had imagined. He was, in reality, a short, beefy man with a ruddy complexion and even ruddier large nose. He wore his hair long and this was bleached blond by the sun so that he had a bit of the look of an amiable scarecrow about him. I kept my opinion on that to myself.

'How have you enjoyed the late unseasonably good weather, Mr Conway?'

'Please do call me Reuben. The fact is, sir, that I have neither enjoyed it nor endured it. My thoughts have all been about Bessie, do you see, sir. I am not meaning to be rude to you, sir, but I have had no room in my head for anything else, such as the weather. It has been such a terrible loss for us all, you see sir?'

'Yes Reuben. That was crass of me. As for Bessie I know she was your friend as well as your mistress. I can see how much pain her death has caused you and I am most reluctant to cause you any further pain. But it is my job to understand what happened and why. You may not think that to be important, Reuben, not in the scale of things that is, but there it is. That is my task.'

'I have no issue with you or your calling, sir. And I bear you no ill will. I do not think your role trivial. Though I loved Bessie with all my heart I love the truth also, even more so if that does not sound a stupid thing to say? So ask me your questions and I will answer them as best as I am able.'

'Again, I owe you an apology Reuben. I never intended to question your motives.'

I believe that of you, sir, and thank you for saying it, sir, so ask away please. I am ready.'

I then asked him about the events of that fateful day. I furnish you below with a copy of his statement which I drew up based on what he told me and which he subsequently approved, without amendment. What perhaps does not come across in this statement was the sheer effort that it took Reuben to describe what he had been through. Here was a man who was shaken to the core but who was desperate, at the same time, to be as fair and accurate in recounting his memories as was humanly possible. The effort involved in so doing was overwhelming and he frequently broke down in tears. I had to lay my pen down to give him time to recover himself. I gladly did so. But it was notable that he was straightforward and honest – for example, he made no bones of having entertained doubts about some aspects of Bessie's recent conduct. These added an extra layer of intensity to his feelings of guilt that, as he saw it, he had failed to help her when it really mattered. He asked me if I felt that he had done all that he should have. I assured him that he had, that it wouldn't have made any difference what he had done – but I can recognise a fellow worrier when I meet one – so I rather doubt that my few words were anything like enough.

Statement of Mr Reuben Conway of Wigwell Farm, Wirksworth lodged at Derby Court on 28th October 1863 by Gamble and Leech, Solicitors, of Derby, in the trial of TOWNLEY, George, charged with murder.

I, Reuben Conway, **WILL SAY** as follows:

I live and work at Wigwell Farm, opposite the Grange. I am a tenant farmer, that is I grow anything on the land that is asked of me by Mr Bowmer, the gentleman who manages the Goodwin's estate. I will not be being vain however if I say that I do know what grows well here.

Our cottage overlooks the entrance to the Hall and so my wife and I see something of the coming and goings to the Hall – but we do not gossip about what we see. We are a God-fearing family and my girls attend Sunday school at St Mary's every week without fail. I am friendly with the staff at the Grange. I know the Captain, by sight, as I work at the Hall

56

from time to time, mainly in the gardens. I also knew Miss Goodwin.

I have not always liked what went on at the Grange where Miss Bessie is concerned. Last winter a young reverend from the south of the country, I will not give his name here, it is not for me to do so, stayed at the Hall whilst Captain Goodwin was away somewhere. He preached one Sunday at St Mary's. I trudged through the snow, curious to get a look at him. I was not the only one whose curiosity got the better of them. There was standing room only in the church. I judged him a handsome man who preached a good sermon. He used words well. But I cannot think on what terms he stayed at Wigwell alone with Miss Goodwin either then, or when he returned later in the year. It is odd that the Captain had approved, if indeed he had. I know Captain Goodwin to be a God-fearing man, like myself, and I am sure that he would do nothing to harm Miss Goodwin. He has always had her future at heart. I am not sure that everyone round about here would agree. I myself witnessed the two young people together very late one night walking back down the turnpike. But I have nothing further to say about this. In fact, in the light of what happened to her, I hope that she did experience some joy in her life.

Sadly, her future was to be far shorter than Bessie, the Captain or indeed myself could have imagined. I was also a witness to Bessie's untimely passing – may God have mercy on her soul.

On 21st August this year of our Lord 1863 at about half past seven in the evening I was coming along the turnpike, returning from harvesting. The sun was setting. It had been a long day, and I was dog tired. I was aching for my supper, and my bed.

I walked up towards Wigwell Lane End. When I had got about halfway up I heard a low moaning noise. It came from near the top of the hill, but I could see little or nothing from where I was. The sun was by now low in the sky and squinting or even covering my eyes did not help. I thought at first the noise was coming from a cow that had fallen into the ditch or got itself stuck fast in a hedge. But this noise sounded different somehow, more terrible, more unworldly. I dreaded what I might be faced with if I continued up the lane. It crossed my mind to turn round straight away and return home by a different route – to go across the fields rather than carrying on up the turnpike. To leave someone else to discover whatever it was that was there. But could I in all conscience, simply pass by on the other side of the valley? What kind of man would that make me – a coward and a hypocrite. It was, I realised, a test of my faith. I could not let myself or my God down.

I ran forward as quickly as my tired body would allow. I saw someone standing by the wall near the ditch. I still could not make out who he or she might be. As I got closer, I realised it was Miss Goodwin herself who was standing by the wall. She was only just standing. She was unnaturally leaning over and was trying to guide herself back towards the Grange, using the wall to hold herself up. I went to her straight away and, terrible to say, found her lace dress covered all over with blood. She was groaning, groans that came from deep inside her. She was lamenting the terrible pain she was in but also bemoaning the terrible injustice of what had been done to her. I could not make sense of everything she was saying but I managed to make out some of it. It is hard for me to write her words down now, knowing where they would lead ... but not as hard as it was to hear them at the time.

She said in a quiet voice, almost a whisper – 'Home.'

Then, 'Take me home Reuben.'

Then, 'A gentleman is a murdering me.'

Then, 'I fear I'm going to die.'

Then, 'Not now Reuben, not yet. It's not my time.'

Then, 'Please help me Reuben, please don't let me die. I beg you.'

Then she fell silent. She had given up with words for now. I put my arm around her and led her about twenty yards further up the road. It was slow progress. Just putting one foot in front of the other was clearly agony for her. Then she spoke again – 'Are we being followed, Reuben?'

I looked down the road and saw a figure about a hundred yards or more away, striding towards us. I nodded. 'Can you carry me then, Reuben? We must get away from him.'

If truth be known, I was pretty desperate to get away, as well. On the second attempt I managed to pick Bessie up and we started off again, more slowly this time but at least I felt we might now make it safely back to the Grange, with God's help.

However, when next I looked back, I saw that the man concerned was now only about sixty yards away and gaining on us all the time. I had a hard choice to make. I did not want to desert Miss Goodwin in such a terrible state, even for one moment. But I felt that I must confront the murderer man to man and, if there had to be a struggle, to meet him on as equal terms as possible, given that he was very likely armed, and I was not.

I made my choice. I laid Miss Goodwin as gently as possible on the turf at the side of the turnpike. She became distressed again and said, 'Please don't leave me Reuben.' I told her that I had no intention of ever leaving her.

I walked rapidly towards our pursuer and then paused in the middle of the turnpike, trying to look as intimidating as I could to show him I could hold my own if it came to a struggle. As he approached closer, I challenged the man directly. I said something like, 'What dreadful deeds have been done here, for God's sake? Are you the fiend responsible for murdering my mistress? What can have possessed you to have done such a ghastly thing?'

I could see him more clearly now. He was smartly dressed, in black, from head to toe. He was tall but slight and scrawny – he did not look like a fighting man. He avoided looking at me directly and stared at the ground in front of him instead. He confessed at once to seeking to murder Miss Goodwin. He said, 'It is true. I have stabbed her.'

He was no threat to me, that much was obvious, but it was not clear to me if he still was any threat to Bessie. I thought that he was not. I asked him if he would help me carry Miss Goodwin to her home. I realised that this assistance might further excite and alarm Bessie, but I saw no alternative if I was to get her back to the Grange alive, and anyway I did not think at the time that he would agree. To my astonishment, however, he readily agreed to do so. He took hold of her shoulders and I her legs and together we carried her slowly towards Wigwell. It might have been better I suppose, thinking back, if I had taken her shoulders and him her legs, but I did not think of this in the heat of the moment. Bessie gave out a muffled scream as his face lunged into her view, but she had no strength in her to do more. In response he called out, 'Poor Betsy,' several times, presumably to reassure her. On one occasion he added, 'You shouldn't have proved false to me.' She was further distressed by this comment. We laid her down at Wooley Bottom's Gate. He began to put something around her neck, her shawl I think, to try and staunch the bleeding, I assume. I probably should have thought to do that sooner. She was alarmed once more, fearing, I imagine, that he was looking for a new method to finish off what he had earlier begun, but again she had no strength to resist. He asked me if I had anything better we could use to stop the bleeding and I said I did not have anything on me but could fetch something from the farm. I told Bessie what I was about – I don't know that she really took in what I had said. I then ran to get something, only too aware that by doing so I was leaving Bessie alone with her would-be killer. But, again, what choice did I have? I was away about four to five minutes at most. It took that time to fetch something, as no one was at home, and I had to search around in the ottoman in our bedroom to find something suitable. He was still holding her shawl around her neck when I returned. I was gasping and out of breath. I asked him if she was still living and he said she was, but only barely. We used the sheet I had brought from home in place of the shawl, but it was not much more use, I'm afraid.

She again said, 'Take me home,' and we carried her a short distance further towards the Grange. We met several others as we went along who each joined our desperate procession – they were Seeds, who I work with, and my nephew, James Conway, and also Mr Bowmer. In each case as they joined our unhappy cortege the man said to them, maybe to avoid any blame falling on me, 'I know and he knows (indicating me) I'm the man who has done it, there is no question at all about that, and I must be hanged for it.'

Miss Goodwin was still groaning piteously and repeating that she was very much afraid that she was dying. She was delirious by this time and asking for her mother, who I knew had long since passed. When we had got only a little further the man said, 'I'm afraid that she is dead now. Poor Bessie.' He knelt down and kissed her on the lips. I was shocked by this. She was indeed dead by then. May God have mercy on her soul.

We carried her body the rest of the short way to the Hall in silence where we met Captain Goodwin and one of his housemaids, Ann Poyser, walking out of the gate. The man told him straight out (as if he could not have seen for himself) it was his granddaughter Betsy that we were carrying swaddled in the sheet, and that she was dead. Her precious blood was, by now, leaking from the shroud she was wrapped in onto the road. He repeated that it was he who had been the cause. They, master and maid, were much affected by the bloody sight. I believe that she took hold of his hand, to comfort him.

Captain Goodwin asked the stranger who he was, and the man replied,

'My name is George Townley.' The Captain seemed none the wiser, which I thought odd in view of previous rumours of a Townley's romantic attachment to Bessie. My nephew and I then carried her body into the Hall and laid her down to rest, as comfortably as we could, on the kitchen table. There was still a good deal of blood. How she had any more to give by then I don't know. Bessie was too tall for the table and so her feet dangled off at one end. As I left the kitchen, I saw Captain Goodwin lead the man Townley by the arm towards his library, a strange sight indeed.

As there was nothing more to be done for now, I went back across the turnpike to my home. I must have been quite a spectacle, spattered as I was with Bessie's blood. But, on my return, I found that my wife and daughters were there and had heard the terrible news already and so were somewhat prepared for my frightful state. I hugged my wife and then both my daughters in turn. Not a word was exchanged between us – none was necessary. I don't mind admitting I was crying myself by now. I felt both a far luckier and far sadder man than I had when I set off for the fields to work.

May God have mercy on her soul

May God have mercy on all our souls.

(Signed) Reuben Conway

26th October 1863

꙲

I must admit to liking Reuben. Never have I met a person who so richly deserved the label 'Christian'. He had not a bad word to say about anyone unless he felt that they merited it, in which case he was blunt to the point of rudeness. But, having said that, I had to admit that his evidence added little to the defence's case. Apart that is from confirming the voluntary aid that George had unstintingly offered after the event and his frank admission of his guilt to everyone he came across. Both might normally have helped his case for mitigation to some small degree. However, this was more than counterbalanced, from a legal point of view, by George's ready admission that he understood that he must be hanged for what he had done. It made George's initial analysis of his legal position only too accurate.

It was with a great sense of foreboding that I then awaited my interview with Captain Goodwin. He did, not unexpectedly, keep me waiting, arriving over half an hour after the appointed time and mumbling something about needing to walk Bessie's labradors – now that she 'was no longer available to do so'. Thankfully Poyser had arrived unbidden in the library bringing with her a welcome pot of tea and so, whilst awaiting the Captain's arrival, I had spent a pleasant enough interlude sipping my tea and gazing out through the full-length windows admiring the rich farm-land and the copse of beech trees beyond.

XI

A Winter

⌘

Early December 1862

On her return to Wigwell in early November Bessie finds that she is both bored and lonely. She continues to play her full part in the local social calendar (such as it is) in Wirksworth and the surrounding district. She still has her beloved walking also to distract her. She will still walk out, stretching her long limbs before her and leaving Ann or Margaret in her wake. Or she will venture out with just her grandpa's black labradors as an escort. The two dogs, relishing their temporary freedom, rush far ahead of her, persecuting squirrels. Then, remembering which side their bread is buttered on, they saunter back to her side.

But, despite these welcome diversions, she is missing Will badly. She writes to him regularly and he does reply, though not quite as regularly, or as fully, as she would like. Then comes Salvation. In late November the Revd Harris is in touch with Will to suggest that he comes on a further visit to Wirksworth as Robert speculates that he might benefit from a little further spiritual guidance. Robert also contacts Bessie's grandfather to see if there would be any objection to Will staying at Wigwell rather than at the vicarage, explaining that Mrs. Turner did not feel that she had the energy to devote to taking care of a staying visitor as well as looking after her vicar. Bessie is not sure how far Robert is engineering the situation for her benefit and how far he does in fact genuinely believe that Will needs further tuition, but she would have hugged Robert within an inch of his life had he been within range when she found out what was planned. The necessary arrangements having been made and Francis' consent obtained, Will arrives back in Derbyshire early in December. Bessie meets him at Whatstandwell Station and they embrace. They decide to walk back up to the house as they both have plenty to say.

'I am so happy you are back in Derbyshire, Will,' begins Bessie as they cross the bridge next to the hotel and slowly make their way up the hill towards Wigwell. 'I really believe that we can make a Derbyshire man out of you. But more than that I think we might make a Wigwell man out of you too. Even better! Of course I didn't set out to do that, and I don't expect you will ever entirely lose your peculiar southern ways but I feel that you have showed splendid potential for integrating yourself with us.'

'I am happy too, Bessie. I feel so at home here with you already even though the weather here is mostly pretty terrible. I feel like we can face anything that fate may throw at us, be that rain, sleet or snow, and come out on top. I certainly hope so anyway...' He laughs heartily as snow begins to fall exactly on cue.

Snow falls and continues to fall around the Grange for the next few days and the next few weeks. The winter of 1862 is a severe one. But Bessie, for one, cannot be happier. She cannot believe her good fortune to be living under the same roof as her beloved – with no distractions and no chaperones. The heavy snow then assists her cause in a most unexpected way. Despite the inclement weather her grandfather goes off to Buxton for a few days for urgent, but undisclosed, business reasons. Before leaving he strongly, if rather hypocritically, cautions the Reverend Young against travelling down south until the weather had settled and this 'damn snow' has retreated. Indeed, he forbids it. Bessie goes out of her way to reinforce her grandfather's strictures and thus finds she has William's exclusive and undivided attention for an indeterminate period.

The happy couple spend these precious days enjoying each other's company, their verbal jousting having developed by now to a form of understated, but knowing, flirtation. As the weather is so inclement for much of the time, they take the opportunity to sit in front of a roaring fire in the library and, when Bessie can drag Will away from her grandpa's books, indulge in various parlour games. Bessie's personal favourite is *The Minister's Cat*, or as Bessie rechristens it, *The Reverend's Cat*. Bessie always makes sure that she starts off and Will goes second – partly because it gives Will a chance to use Bessie's favourite line – 'the Reverend's Cat is a Beauteous Cat and her name is Bessie', but also because it gives Will the near-impossible task of identifying a virtue and a name beginning with X. After a few abortive tries Will becomes wise to her tactics and refuses to play the game again, at least on Bessie's terms, that is until he chances on Xenacious and Xerxes whereupon the tables are turned, and it is now Bessie who is reluctant to play. During this and other parlour games a lot of casual touching of the other takes place – nothing improper or calculated to abuse the privileged position they find themselves in, but enough, a touch on the sleeve for example, to cause a frisson of excitement. They are rapidly falling for each other. What Bessie loves most about Will is not just his physical appearance – is it too much to say that he now bears a startling resemblance to the god Apollo now that he wears his hair longer, as she had suggested he should do, and his curls had elongated and all but disappeared? Nor is it just his high intelligence that impresses her he did read theology at Cambridge and achieved 9th in the final year tripos, as he is keen to mention from time to time. It is his loving and giving nature which really endears him to her. Sometimes, as Bessie is the first to admit, this virtue is well hidden behind a dry, and apparently unforgiving, wit. But this is merely a cover – for he is, in Bessie's estimation, the most generous and positive person that she has ever yet met or is ever likely to. Nothing daunts him. No obstacle, however formidable, fazes him. He sails through life as if the fiercest of storms were entirely to be expected and merely require a temporary battening down of the hatches in anticipation of being able to unfurl the sails and sail on directly into the sunset once the weather has improved. As it inevitably would. For Bessie, for whom every setback is a drama from which the worst is almost certainly bound to happen, this is a refreshing way to view life. She finds that his optimism has begun to infect her, if that is the right word. What is more, by some miracle, her grandfather seems to, more or less, approve of him too. Or at least not actively disapprove.

That should be the death knell to any intimacy that Bessie is considering having with anyone, yet she found to her surprise that here it was not. She found that she could overlook it. She could almost welcome it. It was all most strange. It most certainly merited a specific entry in her diary – *Thank heavens for the snow and for grandpa's absence. I pray for much more of both!*

XII

An Argument

෧෧෩෩

10th May 1872

F,

My account of my subsequent meeting with Francis and the product of same. It will, I think, give you a good flavour of how things stood.

S

File Note

Townley case

14th October 1863

Captain Francis Goodwin JP, DL was even less cooperative in my interview with him than I had imagined he would be. Purely in order to try and expedite matters I presented him, at the commencement of our interview, with Townley's draft statement. He responded with barely concealed disdain.

'What is this then, Mr Leech? A statement that you have written for your client, eh? Words that you would rather like to put into my mouth, if you can get away with it, eh? And you are seriously expecting that I will roll over and simply agree to what he "says". I can confidently predict, even without reading it, that that is inconceivable. I can tell you now that I will certainly not be commenting on anything in here until I have read this whole statement of yours line by line. I suggest that you make yourself comfortable since you most certainly have a long wait in store. Perhaps you might wish to recline on that ghastly sofa thing over there …' he pointed to the red chaise longue. 'I have always hated it myself. It would be more at home in a brothel than in a respectable house like this, don't you agree? But at least now I do not have to pretend to like it, or even to tolerate it. You settle yourself there, if you can. Don't you fret – I will tell you when I am good and ready.'

He took forever to read the statement. After he had read each paragraph he made it abundantly clear that he fundamentally disagreed with the contents. My client's statement had, at George's insistence, been very strongly worded and so I was not altogether surprised that the Captain reacted adversely. Still the manner of him taking exception was something worthy of note. He signified his disapproval by making noises such as whistling to himself, taking a sharp intake of breath or just grunting. He frequently paused, looked over and stared at me as if he pitied me for the lamentable drivel I had produced on behalf of my client.

At last he signalled that he was ready by silently beckoning me over. He remained seated behind his grand desk, and it became clear that he expected me to stand up facing him as if I were the subject of a court martial and he was the disciplining officer. I was only surprised he did not ask me to stand to attention. He then proceeded to take the statement apart, sentence by sentence, paragraph by paragraph, page by page, becoming increasingly angry as he did so. It was hard to keep up with him such was the speed that he barked out his denials and corrections, all of which he expected me to record verbatim. I did my best, allowing for the physical challenge of making any sort of written record when forced to stand. Despite my rather scrappy notes I was able to prepare the following paragraphs for counsel. For cross-examination purposes, George and Francis are laid side by side, as it were. Unlikely bed fellows!

Excerpts from statements from GOODWIN, FRANCIS and TOWNLEY, GEORGE extracted for defence counsel's use on 28th October 1863 by Samuel Leech Esq., Solicitor, Leech and Gamble Solicitors of Derby.

I, Captain Francis GOODWIN JP, DL, **WILL SAY** as follows:

I am a Gentleman and the freehold owner of Wigwell Grange which has always been in my family for living memory and beyond. I am grandfather to Elizabeth Caroline Goodwin. She came to reside with me a couple of years ago. I do not care to go into the reason for this.

I have been shown a copy of a so-called statement made by a certain Townley which purports to set out the nature of our meeting on 21st August 1863 and I have been asked to comment on this. I have to say that I do so with considerable reluctance as I regard his statement as abusive and arrant nonsense. It is no more nor less than a pack of lies from beginning to end. What more does one expect from a consummate dissembler like Townley? Still, I will do as I have been asked.

I George TOWNLEY **WILL SAY** as follows:

I was formerly employed as a merchant and commission agent in France. This assignment did not work out and the arrangements were terminated by mutual agreement. I am currently, through no lack of effort on my part, of no fixed occupation. I am fluent in French, Spanish and Latin. None of this matters now, I dare say.

This statement covers my interaction with Miss Goodwin's grandfather immediately after the incident. I put it forward as evidence of the terrible and unreasonable prejudice he has always held towards me – a solis ortu usque ad occasum. I will pick the story up from when he kidnapped me and held me captive in his library, awaiting my fate. I had just given him dear Bessie's letters to me. They were full of fond sentiments, professions of her love and promises of an idyllic future together – hers and mine.

GOODWIN

I can confirm that I accompanied Townley to my library on the afternoon of the 21st inst. I certainly did not coerce him into entering or remaining in my library as I understand has been suggested. We took tea and brandy at my instigation, hardly the typical behaviour of a kidnapper towards his hostage! It has come to my attention that this event has subsequently been the subject of some adverse comments, not to say expressions of astonishment, from certain quarters, in the press and elsewhere. The criticism, in a nutshell, is that I was far too considerate of Townley, far too civilised in my treatment of my granddaughter's killer, to the point of absurdity. I can understand this point of view. But whatever motives might have subsequently been ascribed to me I wish to state unequivocally that I did what I did for the sole purpose of detaining him – and most effective did it prove.

TOWNLEY

With a show, let's be clear, of self-conscious and mannered theatricality, the old man, the conspirator in chief, angrily hurled a packet of my Bessie's letters, that I had just given to him of my own free will, into the fire. Having then despatched the second packet into the grate with equal force he stabbed away at them both manically with a heavy poker. He then resumed his seat, glaring at me all the while. He clasped his bony hands together and half closed his eyes, pretending to be at prayer. It was a pathetic, and calculated, show of false grieving. As if he really cared. C'est l'émotion la plus facile à feindre, is it not?

Old Goodwin remained ominously silent. I was embarrassed by the silence, as well as by his self-serving and attention-seeking antics. I genuinely did not know what to say. I gazed out of the window looking for some inspiration. I had nothing to say to him – I had let my deeds do the talking after all.

Suddenly Goodwin gets to his feet again, eyes bulging, stares at me and declares, unnecessarily loudly, as I sat only a short distance from him and no one else was present, 'Now it is done. I have saved my grandchild from you. Now that is done.' To this day I have no idea what he meant by this. The ravings of a lunatic, I assume. And, by the way, there was no brandy offered. Tea, yes but no brandy. I would remember if there had been.

GOODWIN

Once we were ensconced in the library, he gave me two packets of letters clumsily done up with string which he led me to understand my granddaughter had written to him. I determined to burn said letters forthwith as I had no intention, whilst I still had breath in my body, that any foolish romantic ramblings, if such they were, were going to fall into the lap of the prurient readers of the *Derby Mercury*. The reputation of my family depended on me taking immediate action and I am delighted to say that I was not found wanting. I doubt that any responsible guardian would have acted any differently. I would go further and state that I know for certain that they would not. I watched intently as a brown stain spread agonisingly slowly across the packet of letters. To my relief, one by one, they did eventually succumb to the flames, finally egging each other on to embrace oblivion.

A second packet followed. This was even more obstinate, even less eager to perish and had to be encouraged by my judicious application of a heavy poker. I replaced the poker in its normal resting place and, relieved my task was successfully accomplished, resumed my seat.

I clasped my hands together, half closed my eyes and sought some kind of explanation of recent events from the Almighty, whilst knowing in my heart that there could be none. I wondered at my own pathetic willingness not to offend Townley at a time when no one could blame me if I had cast all social convention to one side and given the fellow a good hiding, at the very least.

I felt weary at the thought of any action on my part but somehow summoned the energy to speak. What then came out of my mouth was as unexpected to me as it doubtless was to him. 'Now it is done. I have saved my granddaughter. Now it is done.' I cannot be certain of the exact words but that was the gist of it.

I slowly turned my head to examine my guest. He, a much younger man than I, the unworthy object of the alleged correspondence, was indifferent to what had just occurred. What added insult to injury was that he was sprawled out on Bessie's favourite, the chaise longue which I had purchased for her for her twenty first birthday, sipping my tea and my brandy alternately and staring straight ahead through my French windows and out into my garden and my farmlands beyond. He avoided my gaze.

I was appalled by the lack of any expression of contrition whatsoever on his part and I told him so. But incredibly, there was still no remorse shown; far from it. He betrayed little or no emotion concerning the recent terrible and unspeakable events except, perhaps, a degree of irritation as to the position he now found himself in and a measure of 'ennui' as to what might or might not happen to him next. I made my views known to him, but he simply shrugged his shoulders.

TOWNLEY

He then has the bare-faced cheek to accuse me of being bored at the position I found myself in. Well, honestly, what on earth did he expect – in the circumstances? Could he not have acknowledged that I was upset too? Was that too much to ask? I had been through an ordeal too, after all. And I was injured too – a nasty deep cut to my hand. No medical assistance was forthcoming for me. I did ask for it. The grandfather treated my reasonable request with utter disdain.

We continued to sit there in silence, sipping our tea. We were like a pair of strangers trapped together in a station waiting room, each profoundly hoping that their train would arrive soon.

Thankfully, our Trappist-like silence was broken by the clanging of the front doorbell. Moments later one of the maids, Poyser I believe it was, knocked loudly at the library door, wanting to know if she should admit the visitor. In her distress the silly child omitted to say who it was. Despite this the Captain readily agreed. Anything, anyone to relieve the tedium. I was in agreement with him on that if nothing else.

Neither of us was at all surprised when it was a constable who entered. He was of average height with dark hair, solidly built and now rather short of breath. He entered the room slowly and cautiously. Addressing Goodwin, not me, he announced himself as Constable Parnham and asked for his permission to speak to me. I don't know why he felt that he required the Captain's permission to do so. He was not my keeper. All this time he was looking over to me and evidently sizing me up as to what my intentions were and whether my turning nasty was a possibility. Realising that I needed to put the poor man out of his misery, I leapt to my feet and declared fortissimo, 'I wish to give myself up for the murdering of the young lady.' Parnham asked me if I understood the gravity of the charge I was giving myself up to. I replied, without hesitation, that I did. He asked me what I had done with the knife I had committed the deed with. I took out a pocket knife from my trouser pocket. I noticed it was wet with blood: hers, I assume. I handed it to him, unwiped.

I then saw fit to add a comment which, in retrospect, would have been better left unsaid: 'I know I must be hanged for it. But I will go with you quietly. Only let me see her one more time first.' On hearing this request poor old Parnham was once more thrown into a state of indecision. He looked anxiously at Captain Goodwin for his approval. The old man nodded slowly whereupon the Constable grasped me by the arm and, after enquiring of Poyser as to Bessie's whereabouts, led me towards the kitchen where my recently betrothed was laid out on the table. She was too long for the table, I noticed. I found that most unacceptable. One has a right to dignity even in death. Then most of all.

I stood close to her still body and looked into her face, a face whose features I had venerated for so long. She was still beautiful and at peace at last. Parnham, believing I think that I was about to kiss her, (I was not – I would not have done such a thing) pulled me away with unnecessary force so that I staggered backwards onto him.

I was then conveyed by Parnham, with little ceremony and further gratuitous roughness, to Wirksworth Lock Up. On the way I felt obliged, despite his uncouth behaviour, to exchange some pleasantries with the Constable. We talked mainly about the late good weather, but I do dimly recall expressing the view that I felt happier now that I had done it than I

71

ever did before, and I trusted that Bessie did too. Again, I would have been better advised to hold my tongue, I suppose. I await the arrival of my solicitor, a Mr Leech of Derby, though, doubtless, there is little that can be done about my situation; il n'y a rien à faire.

GOODWIN

If my views count for anything, and they surely ought to, then it is my fondest hope, and my deepest desire, that Townley is despatched from this life as soon as the hangman is conveniently available. An eye for an eye, a tooth for a tooth. I would happily carry out the task myself, with my bare hands if necessary, so as not to brook any unnecessary delay. That would have been possible in my younger days but unfortunately, given my age and general decrepitude it is, sadly, impossible now.

XIII

A Kiss

⟡⟡⟡

15th December 1862

Despite the continuing inclement weather Bessie proposes to Will that they go on a midnight walk to a standing stone, which lies a short distance above the Grange, near to the Malt Shovel Inn. He readily agrees. She explains that John Greatorex, the landlord of the Inn, is notoriously strict about turning his patrons out at 11 pm sharp and so, provided they time their walk carefully, they need not fear an unwanted meeting with revellers slithering home to bed.

There is no grandfather to evade this time as he is again 'absent on business' but Bessie is still wary of attracting unwanted attention, especially from Reuben. She loves Reuben as an elder brother but knows from past experience that he would, like a real brother, not hold back as to any conduct of hers that he disapproves of. So, wrapped up in several layers to keep out the elements, they creep out of the Grange's gate just after twelve. Bessie has instructed William to be light on his feet rather than, as is usually the case, she says, 'clomping around like an elephant'. She has to stifle the giggles, though, as William adopts an exaggerated slowed down version of what he imagines walking lightly should look like. They make their way up the hill towards the field where the stone is located. The full moon lends the frosty road a reflective white sheen – there is consequently no need for the lanterns they have brought with them and so, by silent agreement, these are discarded at the side of the turnpike early on. It is a bit of a pull up the hill and William is somewhat short of breath. 'Come on old man,' Bessie says teasingly. 'Let me help you or you might not live long enough to make it as far as the stone and that would be a shame, would it not?' Bessie seizes hold of his arm and then holds onto it far longer than is strictly required. William makes no attempt to be released. So it is that, arm in arm again, they approach the stone.

Normally the field in which the stone sits is boggy and difficult to negotiate on foot. But the depth of the cold is such that all that was normally soggy is now rendered to ice. The field crackles with excitement as they walk slowly across it. They cannot mistake the object of their expedition, as the Stone also glows in the moonlight. Once they arrive, they admire the roughness of its surface and its crudely hewn form. William, ever the conscientious guide, speculates as to the origins of the stone. He calls it 'a menhir' much to Bessie's amusement.

'Why not a ladyhir?' she suggests. 'Are you quite sure it's not just an old gatepost after all? That's what grandpa thinks.'

Will shakes his head and then opines, rather speculatively, that it might even possibly be prehistoric.

'Like you then,' says Bessie, rather lamely. But instead of responding in kind, as he normally would, she finds that William is staring back at her intently. Without warning he pulls her towards him, and, without even asking her permission, kisses her. Bessie, though shocked, does not pull away and so William kisses her again. She laughs. The next time it is she who, recklessly, daringly, kisses him back. It is a wonderful, heart-stopping, sensational experience for both of them and they hold each other tight for several minutes, each trying to take in the momentousness of what has just occurred. They whisper that they love each other, and always have done. Eventually, reluctantly, slowly disentangling, they walk back to the Grange, this time hand in hand, gloves having also been discarded in the interests of greater intimacy, but stopping frequently to experience again their lips meeting and their bodies coming together. They are, by now, oblivious of everything, and of anyone who might be observing them, so wrapped up are they in their emotions. They forget to collect the lanterns from the turnpike, something that Bessie only realises during the night. She feels obliged to creep out again at first light to retrieve them. In any case she has been far too excited to sleep more than fitfully. Her dreams that night were all of her passion and love for William. They breakfast together next morning in a happy conspiracy of secret contentment. When alone they look so closely and deeply into each other's eyes that they each melt into the other's features and become one. They exchange whispered accounts of their respective dreams and are thrilled to discover that these too are pretty nearly identical. They also declare their love each for the other again and confess that they both had been wanting to do so since the Volunteers' Dinner.

Sadly, later that week, the snow and ice did relent, and it was time for Will to return home. Bessie insists on accompanying him to the station at Cromford. They choose this station rather than Whatstandwell on the basis that is not visible from the road and so rather more private and discreet, and also it is the prettier of the two.

'Come on old chap, time to go. You've outstayed your welcome already. By some weeks.' she adds, seizing hold of the carpet bag that was the sum total of his luggage.

'Yes, very funny Bessie, I'm sure. I know that really you will be missing me the instant my train crosses Cromford Meadows.'

'Not as much as you will be missing me, I'm sure of that,' retorts Bessie. 'You, Romeo, will be pining for me like a lovesick swain, trapped in that dull old rectory of yours. Unless, of course, you have some special parishioner there you have not told me about? An older woman perhaps who has her eye on you? She does the flowers in the church just to curry favour with you, and also so that she has an excuse to be in your most holy presence on a regular basis. I know exactly the type – another Mrs Turner – I can imagine that you would be flattered by such attention, receptive to it perhaps?'

'I know you are joking, Bessie. But believe me there's no such amorous flower arranger waiting for me, worst luck! But Bessie, joking aside, I think when I am with you next, we should talk about the future I mean, our future, our future together.'

Bessie nods vigorously but does not get a chance to reply since, at that very moment, the train from Matlock Bath emerges from the Willersley Tunnel, spitting dirty smoke into the clean Derbyshire air. Bessie and Will quickly embrace, in a respectable enough manner, although really they would both like to have done more. But it does serve as an affirmation, Bessie feels, to the question that Will has just alluded to. Bessie remains on the platform as the train pulls out from the station and Will waves vigorously to her until he is out of sight. She does, as Will predicted, immediately feel sad and bereft. But also, at the same time she feels light and gay as she looks forward to Will's next visit and to continuing 'that conversation'.

Bessie's entry in her diary that evening reads as follows:

19th December 1862,
I have found the love of my life and he of his.
It is enough.

XIV

A Doctor

e⌒⌂⌒ɘ

My dear Frederick,

As you so rightly observe in your most recent missive, I should really have had my doubts from the outset about taking this case on. I see that now. Only too clearly. It is just possible that I was seduced by the whole notion of attempting to save a man from the gallows. It is not every day that a high street solicitor gets such an opportunity. The destiny of the man rested on my shoulders. I had the power of life and death over him. However, I was increasingly worried by Townley's erratic behaviour. He persisted in justifying his actions to anyone who would listen to him. He continued to maintain that he was, at all times, sane and that the steps he had taken had been entirely rational, indeed necessary. After a good deal of persuasion on my part, he agreed to see a doctor to 'confirm' that this was the case.

In November 1863 I instructed Doctor John Hitchman, a known expert in madness who happened also to hold a part-time position at Derby asylum. I personally attended the appointment, which took place at the gaol, but I will not spoil the impact of his report for you by an account of what I witnessed. I could not possibly do it justice. Having read the resultant report with some horror, and its conclusion with great disappointment, I decided that I was duty bound to share the contents of the report with George. I obtained the permission of the governor so to do. He agreed to arrange for a close watch to be kept in case of an adverse reaction to the contents. George was however, in the main, ecstatic at the author's conclusions. He returned the report to me with extensive foot-notes. I have included these and would urge you to read them if you wish to try and understand his motivations.

What I found most disturbing about these notes was the thread of truth that they contained, a thread of truth only, but one that George had then taken and twisted and weaved into his own perverted system of logic and belief. You may find this a distasteful thing for me to say. But it is undeniable that when it comes to legal rights and duties, all of the former rest with the male of the species and all of the latter with the female sex. Arguably, and you will have to bear with me on this point as I am sure you will initially find it obnoxious, arguably all that George had done, apart from the small matter of committing a capital crime out on the public highway, was to highlight the immorality and hypocrisy inherent in our laws. You may consider these to be dangerous and radical thoughts for your old father to express. But they are not really all that radical. The jurist Blackstone (whom we all venerate do we not?) wrote something similar in his Commentaries, mark it, nearly a hundred years ago – 'Man and wife are one person under the law, and that person is the man.' Maybe this is why the legal system itself found Townley so hard to handle? His lunatic ravings contained, at their kernel, some painful home truths for the rest of us – namely that wives are still essentially, and with limited exceptions, the property of their husband. This is not a proposition that I intend to test with your mother. Discretion is very definitely the better part of valour when it comes to any conversation of that sort.

Well, Frederick, I hope that this has given you some food for thought at least. Do please tolerate the ramblings of a senile old man, masquerading as wisdom. Incidentally when can we expect you to bring home your own prospective wife for us to meet? We long for that day to dawn!

Paternal greetings (and maternal greetings from your mother also, at her particular request).

Samuel

Encls.

Report of Doctor Hitchman dated 16th November 1863, (with annotated comments supplied by George Townley Esq.)

I John Hitchman MD, MBC, MRCPI **WILL SAY** as follows:

I am the Physician Superintendent of the Derby County Lunatic Asylum.

At the request of Mr Leech, the attorney for the defence, I attended Derby Gaol at 3 o'clock on 13th November 1863. Mr Leech also attended, along with Mr Sims, the Governor of the gaol.

I went there to ascertain to my professional satisfaction whether or not the prisoner palpably knows right from wrong. Given the notoriety of the case in question I hope that this humble contribution may not be out of place on the pages of the *Journal of Mental Science* and so I have, with all due modesty, as well as providing this statement also presented my findings to that august journal.

My interview with the prisoner took the following course.

Mr Townley entered the room with his hands in his pockets, he said good day to me and sat down to the right of me. He kept his head slightly depressed and had a confused, shy air. He assumed a composure he surely did not feel. He was tense, as indicated by a clammy state of his tongue which caused it to give a clicking sound when special circumstances were referred to, and by his grasping the bottom of the pockets of his trousers in which he kept his hands. On observation Mr Townley's general physical presentation was not prepossessing.[3] He was sullen in countenance and his eyes had a downcast furtive look; the contour of his head was not pleasing, it being deficient in the anterior superior portions of the skull in which the phrenologists allocate the organs of 'ideality', 'wonder', 'imitation' and 'benevolence'.

He had the aspect of one belonging to the upper middle class of society whose life has been passed in easy indulgence, and who has not been called upon to exercise his hands or his intellect in any useful occupation.[4]

After a few brief opening remarks, I began my examination.

What is your occupation Mr Townley?

---

[3] I am sorry the Doctor did not find my appearance prepossessing. I, for one, have no real conception of what a prepossessing countenance looks like. Possibly my confinement in Derby Gaol had done little to improve my presentation and/or my countenance? GT

[4] I would mildly remonstrate with the good doctor as to his assumption although it is true that I had done little with my life up to that point. And now I never will. GT

TOWNLEY

I have been doing nothing for a long time. I was in an office in London and elsewhere abroad for a short time but I did not like it. I couldn't stay.

DOCTOR

What induced you to leave?

TOWNLEY

I did not like it. I was unhappy. I was bullied.

DOCTOR

How did you expect to keep a wife if you had no occupation, no professional pursuit, no earnings?

TOWNLEY

Well I hardly know ... There was my father ... But yes, you are right, her family disliked me because I was poor.

DOCTOR

Did she say that?

TOWNLEY

She did not but then she has fooled me in every way. She had been actively deceiving me. I found out that there was another. I don't know his name, but he had replaced me in her affections. I don't ... I don't know his name. She wouldn't tell it to me. Nor would anyone else. There was a wall of silence, a conspiracy. If I thought that a man was sensible to our betrothal and I saw him, I would shoot him dead.

DOCTOR

Suppose he did not know of it? Suppose he had no reason to know?

TOWNLEY

I would tell him and then challenge him to a fight, if he did not immediately forfeit any claims to my bride to be.

DOCTOR

Suppose that he would not fight?

TOWNLEY

I would kill him just as surely as if he had stolen a picture from me.

DOCTOR

Surely you would not kill a man for the sake of a picture?

TOWNLEY

I would if I could not get it back. Or could not punish him more severely. If I were a Greek god, then maybe I could have turned her into a tree instead. She could have been Daphne to my Apollo. (He chuckles to himself). But sadly, that is not within my powers. Man-made law does not always give satisfactory redress and I should recover my own whatever the cost might be.

DOCTOR

This is what you, unhappily, have done with reference to Miss Goodwin?

TOWNLEY

Yes, she belonged to me, just like a picture, just as your question suggests, Dr Hitchman. She belongs to me. She is my property.[5] As a slave in America was the property of the white man, within living memory. Just so. It is the same thing.

DOCTOR

But a slave owner could not kill a slave with impunity.[6]

TOWNLEY

Don't you worry. She deserved all she got. No more and no less. She deceived me. They deceived me. Sure enough. She deceived me. She was mine, she was mine. And she deserved all she got, because she deceived me . . . She deserved to die, she who deceives me must . . .

DOCTOR

Must die. Must die. Is that right?

TOWNLEY

Yes, that's right. She who deceives me must die.

DOCTOR

So you went to Wigwell with the intention of giving her her just deserts . . . of killing her, did you?

TOWNLEY

No.

(He blushes slightly and pauses briefly.)

---

[5] As to the question of the legal status of the wife as the property of the husband may I refer the distinguished Doctor to Blackstone's 'Commentaries to the Laws of England' 1765 where it is stated that *by marriage, the husband and wife are one person in law: that is, the very being or legal existence of the woman is suspended during the marriage, or at least is incorporated and consolidated into that of the husband: under whose wing, protection, and cover, she performs everything; and is said to be covert-baron, or under the protection and influence of her husband, her baron, or lord; and her condition during her marriage is therefore called her coverture.* So I conclude that the wife is, in fact and in law, the property of her husband and my logic is thereby vindicated. See also my note below re the status of the betrothed. GT

[6] I would question whether either a slave owner or a slave would necessarily agree with Dr Hitchman's, to my mind, naive opinion here, though they would disagree for different reasons no doubt. GT

It was only when I found out how she was dissembling, when I talked with the vicar ...

DOCTOR

So how came you then to possess the means of killing her, how came you to have a knife on you?

TOWNLEY

(Awkwardly, with tongue click.)

I was determined to see her. I thought they would oppose me at the house, and so I purchased the knife, on the way, from Manchester. To defend myself, if the need arose. It was a beautiful thing with an exquisite carved pearl handle. I do not have it now. It was taken from me at Wirksworth. They handled me roughly you know –Parnham and his ilk. Not that anyone cares. I am treated like cattle. No, worse than cattle. All I want is to be put out of my misery. It's all I have ever wanted. To be put down, like a brutish animal, do you see?

DOCTOR

Did you mean to stab any person that opposed you then?

TOWNLEY

I meant to see her at any cost and in spite of my enemies: old Goodwin and others who wished to set aside our promises of marriage ... (Getting increasingly exercised) there was a conspiracy here and Old Goodwin was at the heart of it. He was the Conspirator in Chief. You will think me a brute when I say it but it is better to say what I think. I do feel sorry for the trouble I have given to my mother, and to my family. I do not feel sorry as far as Miss Goodwin is concerned or for her precious clergyman or for Old Goodwin. They were all conspiring to ruin me, touching me on my tenderest point by taking her away from me. Bessie ... I can't know what Bessie thought ... Never mind that; her family wanted to injure me personally and they used what was at hand to do so. Her. (Pause.)

DOCTOR

If it was Captain Goodwin's fault, then why do you blame Bessie? Why did you hold her responsible for things beyond her control? You stabbed her several times. You stabbed her from behind. Was that not most cowardly on your part?

TOWNLEY

(Standing, pushing back chair, shouting and gulping.)

No! I was mad with rage. She was a fiend and a devil from hell, sent from the underworld to tease and torment me; she was an adulteress and vile and bad and richly merited all that she got. The world is well rid of her. A revolting woman such as her, who flirts with another after she is betrothed is, more or less, a beast! I am well rid of her. As for the Captain he is no more or less than a whoremonger. I only wish I had disposed of him as well. I had the opportunity you know. I could have done it. I wish that I had.

DOCTOR

Calm yourself, sir. Calm down and sit down, sir.

(He sits, noisily and reluctantly.)

DOCTOR

You have informed me that you do not believe in hell, but now you say that Miss Goodwin was a devil from hell – how is this?[7]

TOWNLEY

She was an adulteress and vile and bad and merited all she got.

The interview continued in this vein for the greater part of two hours. George continued to give voice to wild and dogmatic thoughts. When challenged as to the logic of his pronouncements he did not recognise the difficulty but simply reiterated what he had said, using ever more extreme vocabulary. I noted that he relied upon a lack of personal responsibility when it came to his own actions, but, by contrast, when it came to the actions of Miss Goodwin, in apparently preferring another gentleman, he became enraged and called her by the vilest epithets imaginable such as fiend, devil and adulteress and worse. He did not recognise a distinction as to property as an inanimate thing – such as a picture – and a lively intelligent woman. Nor would he acknowledge a distinction between an act of adultery in a wife, and the change of mind by a betrothed lady attracting a counter-offer of marriage from a gentleman who was not their betrothed[8] – he awarded each a like penalty – death![9]

---

[7] Mere sophistry from the good doctor I am afraid. One does not need to believe in the Devil to believe someone has behaved devilishly. I would have thought that to be obvious. GT

[8] It is Dr Hardwick who proceeds from a false premise. In church doctrine betrothal is as binding as marriage, and, as a matter of strict theology, a divorce is required before God to terminate a betrothal just as it is for a marriage – there is no distinction. Betrothed couples are, to all intents and purposes, husband and wife. My reasoning is unexceptional, but sound. GT

[9] I would suggest that Dr Hardwick, despite his other merits, again falls into serious logical error here. Is Adultery, otherwise known as Lechery, not a Capital sin? Is not the commandment that thou shalt not commit adultery equal to the commandment that thou shalt not kill? As St Paul reminds us, fornicators and adulterers, just as certainly as murderers, will most certainly be judged harshly by God. GT

My conclusion

Reflecting fully on the conduct of Mr Townley I cannot discover in him any recognised form of mental disorder. Much though I would wish to find a fellow creature guiltless, great as is my anxiety to spare Derby the pain and uproar attendant on a public execution, I infer, primarily, as the criminal act arose from the perceived conduct of a second person, not from subjective hallucination or imagination, that Mr Townley was, and is at this time, a <u>sane and rational </u>person.[10]

ॐ

Whilst the good doctor's conclusions may have fortified George they most certainly did not suit me. Fortunately, doctors being what they are, it did not prove too difficult to find two distinguished practitioners of the art who were ready to violently disagree with the diagnosis made by Dr Hitchman and to assert exactly the opposite conclusion to that which he had done. Even so it was a bad start to the campaign to prove George insane that even our own doctors were divided on the issue.

I'll leave it at that for now, Frederick.

Father

---

[10] My underlining – the right conclusion even if the Doctor's reasoning, as I have demonstrated, lacks finesse. Never mind, he got there in the end. As per Ovid 'exitus ācta probat', the end justifies the means. More importantly, I am shown to be more sinned against than sinning. GT

XV

A Silence

❦

And then? And then there is nothing, only complete silence! Bearing in mind the joy of their recent encounter and the profound nature of their conversation upon Cromford Station platform, Bessie is astonished to hear nothing further from William after he has returned south. It is quite unbelievable. No letters at all, nothing, not even so much as a post card. Initially she thinks that this might be due to his professional duties overwhelming him, the life of a country curate being very much at the will and whim of his patron. Or maybe William is showing greater tact and diplomacy than she thought him capable of and is not writing for fear of her grandfather intercepting his missives and re-assessing his suitability as a consequence. She, on the other hand, writes at least weekly to William, keeping the contents affectionate but respectable lest they should, in turn, be read at his end. She records his silence in her diary by way of a simple question mark against each week.

As winter threatens to become spring she is not only thoroughly alarmed but increasingly bemused, not to say resentful, at his continued failure to correspond. She begins to doubt herself and wonder if her memories of that wonderful night near the Malt Shovel were real memories, or maybe just a very lovely, vivid dream. She has too much time on her hands and begins to wonder if Will is quite the man she believed him to be or whether she has been duped by his easy manner and ready smile. She knows that these are wild and ridiculous thoughts and yet she cannot hold them back, however hard she tries. So when it is George who writes to her in February, unexpectedly and unbidden, seeking to rekindle their engagement, professing his continued devotion to her and his indulgence of her, of his forgiveness, she does not immediately refuse him. She knows in her heart of hearts that this is the wrong thing to do – giving George even a sliver of hope when she is now as good as pledged to another, and so she should not give him any hope whatsoever – but she cannot immediately bring herself to summarily dismiss him for a second time. Might it be better to settle for George even though her whole being yearns every day not for him but for Will? But if Will was now, for whatever reason, unavailable, or had lost interest, then maybe it would only be prudent to do so? She hedges her bets and hates herself for doing so. At about the same time her grandfather becomes unhealthily interested in who she writes to, and who writes to her, and this also inhibits both her attempts to contact Will or, indeed, to clarify things with George. For some time she has had an uneasy feeling that grandfather knows more than he was letting on, as to her situation. It may be that one of George's earlier letters to her had been intercepted, despite the careful arrangements that Ann and she had put in place. Or maybe Bessie herself had been careless and left a letter on her dressing table. She shudders to think of it. She is reluctant to make enquires of her grandfather about William, feeling that it is wise to keep her grandfather at arm's length when it came to matters of the heart.

Eventually though, as March turns into April, she has no choice but to take him partially into her confidence and to ask what, if anything, he knows. She is astonished to learn that William is seriously ill and that this was something that her grandfather has known for quite some time but had deliberately chosen to keep from her. She now learns, via her grandfather, that William had been taken very poorly immediately after his return from his visit to Derbyshire and is now in a very bad state, he believes. He has no further details. He had not told her previously as he 'had decided that the news might overly distress her and he wished to see how things worked out first'. Being now thoroughly alarmed Bessie prevails on her grandfather to contact William's family himself to see how William is and eventually, after a further frustrating week when Bessie can only imagine that the worst had happened, or was about to happen, a letter arrives from William's father, dated 20th April. The letter, addressed to Miss E Goodwin, is, simultaneously, both soothing and terrifying. It begins thus:

Dear Miss Goodwin,

Bessie, if I may call you so? I write to you to try and explain what has happened and to seek your indulgence for my inept handing of the nightmare we found ourselves caught up in.

On Sunday 21st December I experienced one of the heaviest afflictions that can befall a parent – the sudden illness of my eldest son. Immediately after taking the service and preaching a typically thoughtful sermon he was suddenly complaining of pain all over his body and was most restless. My mind was greatly troubled by his state, conscious, as I was, of how many of my neighbours have been taken from us by that most pernicious of diseases which even now I prefer not to name here. You will know what it is I speak of. It is a disease that goes on and on relentlessly mowing down the young. The wild flowers in the cottage gardens, as well as the manicured blooms of the rose gardens of the rich and noble, submit equally and helplessly to the sweep of its scythe. It is truly said that, in these terrible times, there is but a small step between the ball-room and the graveyard. And so I feared terribly for my son. I was right to do so for his state of health deteriorated sharply. Soon I could hear such heart-rending screams of pain from him both during the day and at night that I was obliged to muffle my ears. Our Christmas was, of course, entirely ruined - who could celebrate in any way when we were facing such a dire situation.

Bessie can hardly bear to read on but forces herself to do so.

What mortal agonies he sustained, what dreadful, deep throated groans his immense pain compelled him to utter. And yet what have been his own reflections on his sorry plight? Self-pity? No. Resentment? No. Neither. Instead he takes personal responsibility for his condition and places himself in God's hands. 'If I am supported by God, I do not mind the pain,' or, again, 'All these pains must be the consequence of sin, of my own sins.' He exhorts me and his mother to increase our praying for him. He says 'Redouble your prayers for me. I would pray a great deal myself, but I can do little this way, only now and then.' We did as we were bidden even though we could not imagine what heinous sins he could have possibly committed that he entreated us so vehemently to pray about and which could have justified God in inflicting such terrible agonies on him. By this time I was more fearful of his bodily safety than I was the state of his soul. Though in pain he would often ask after his brothers and sister and say – 'Tell my brothers and sister how much I love them. Tell them, tell them I beg you, not to defer the work of repentance to their sick bed or their dying hours. Tell them how little can be done at such a time.' He also spoke much of you – enquiring as to your health and well-being and frequently reminding us of the very, very high regard he held you in. He was puzzled by the lack of him hearing from you. But he truly observed that he was in no position to reply anyway and that it might be better if you gave him up as a lost cause. You will be bemused, I am sure, by these statements as you and I are only too aware that you did write to him, most assiduously. And here I have a terrible thing to admit to you. I have to confess to you here and now that I took it upon myself to keep back all of your letters to him. I did not pass a single one on to him. I did not wish to increase his agonies by kindling his yearning for something that could not now be. With the benefit of hindsight, I know I was wrong to do this. I was so focused on my son that I did not consider the effect that his long and unexplained silence would have on you, nor indeed yours on him. I am sorry for my lack of consideration, and I only hope that you can pardon me, a father on the edge of despair?

For you can imagine, I am sure, the effect of his deteriorating state on my wife and myself. We were ground down. We daily feared for the worst and watched and prayed for him whom we were desperate not to be prematurely deprived of. It was at night though that our sufferings began in earnest. What fears, what terrors came upon us in the early hours, such mournful images. I imagined not only his ghastly death but details of the funeral that would follow. Focussing on the minutiae of his funeral was almost a relief to me. I had chosen the hymns and prayers as well as drafted the eulogy for my dear son's farewell a thousand times, draft after draft in which I extolled his virtues in more and more glowing terms – but, by the end, even I grew bored of my own despair – even this eulogising of mine had become common place, meaningless. Not just meaningless. I feared I might be bringing his death on more quickly by imagining its aftermath in such excessive detail.

Bessie, sick to the stomach and by now in floods of tears, reads on:

This dark cloud hung over us for weeks and weeks. But gradually, gradually we began to see some improvement in him. His sun began to shine again, weakly at first but then brighter and brighter. We held our breaths and scarcely dared to hope. We lived in fear and dread of a relapse and were apprehensive that this could just be his Indian Summer, a temporary reawakening rather than a real and sustained recovery. Yet it is true, dearest Bessie, if I may call you that, he is now far stronger than he was. Our prayers have been answered, thanks be to God. We only hope that the present improvement will be sustained. Pray for us, and for him, if you would be so kind. You will have to trust us to know best when and how we tell him of your kind and attentive and constant solicitations to him, the existence of which he is, as I have explained, currently wholly ignorant of.
Yours respectfully,.
Charles————————'

This letter is followed, in due course, by another. The second letter, which arrives on the 20th May, is briefer but much more reassuring. William has sustained his recovery and is now nearly ready to correspond with her, having spent several days in tears reading through her past correspondence which had, at last, been released to him by his father. She could expect a reply shortly. His parent cautions her not to expect too much at first as he was still weak, and certainly she could not expect a point by point response! Bessie is offended by the suggestion that that might have been her expectation – she would, by that time, have been deliriously happy if William had merely returned her letters marked with a cross, or some other slight indication that he had read them.

Then on the 29th May comes another letter. This one, she is delighted to see, is in William's own hand. It is shorter than she would have liked, more of a note than a letter, but he assures her of his continuing love for her, which was, after all, the only important thing. He rails against the appalling and deceitful behaviour of his father in previously keeping her correspondence from him. He hopes to have fully recovered in a few months. He therefore proposes a visit in the summer, 'if your GF permits it'. Bessie assures him that she was sure this would not be an obstacle. She suggests his forthcoming stay includes a return visit to the 'ladyhir' as he had 'appeared to enjoy their previous visit so intensely'. Her diary entry for 29th May 1863 reads as follows; *Hoorah, W has risen from the dead and should be back with me soon. Praise the Lord!*

This was to be her last entry.

✍

Postscript – Bessie's diary was discovered by her grandfather on the day of her death when he unceremoniously broke into the cabinet in her bedroom, having not been able to locate the key anywhere. Along with the diary, he took some cartes visite and a bundle of letters he found in the chest. It is not known whether he read any of the contents.

XVI

A Dream

❦

*Private note – I withheld the following note from Fred. It is too personal.
It was one of the documents I had in mind when I resisted handing him
over all my papers. I will leave it to posterity to decide its fate. By that
time I imagine that all of the players, both major and minor, will have
long since shuffled off the stage.*

5th December 1863

Mary, Caroline and I had agreed at our initial discussion back in
August that our regular meetings should continue up to trial. They invariably took place at the Midland Hotel in a small private room, the Dales
Room. The hotel kindly allowed us to use the room without charge. It was
situated at the front of the building and so looked out over the station
itself. The meetings were attended by Mary and I and, occasionally, by
Caroline as well. Both had now returned to home to Manchester and so
travelled into Derby by train just for our meetings. I usually had progress
of some sort to report – my meetings with Reuben and the Captain, for
example, or my frustrations at dealings with the prosecution. My account
of my torrid meeting with Goodwin amused them greatly as I was able to
illustrate it by imitating the Captain's demeanour as he had read George's
statement – complete with grunts and whistles and raised eyebrows. It
proved to be light relief in spite of the ongoing awfulness of George's situation. Anything that I had been able to do, any little step forward I had
been able to make, was always much appreciated. Inevitably some weeks
there was, however, little or nothing to report. This could have made our
meetings very stilted. We could have spent our time awkwardly staring
out of the window and commenting on the comings and goings from the
railway station for want of anything better. Or just not to bother meeting
at all. But in fact we spent the allotted hour in more general conversation.
This was not mere chit chat, however, as it soon became apparent that

Mary was not one for small talk. We talked about almost everything which matters – music – she favoured Mozart, then Beethoven; literature – she extolled the merits of Trollope and Dickens; then art – Raphael was her favourite. Sometimes we debated one of the current national issues. Mary was warm and funny ... and very opinionated. She had strong views about everything from child labour (Mary was passionately against) to further electoral reform (Mary was passionately in favour). These were neither just a reprise of views of *The Times* Leader, nor mere uninformed prejudices, for Mary felt things strongly and marshalled her argumets effectively. I began to look forward to our meetings warmly, and for their own sake. She was such a pleasure to talk to, so easy to get along with. We had the same ideas about things.

But as the trial got nearer there was less and less focus on the outside world by her and more and more focus on what might happen to George. Alongside this Mary began to confide in me that she was sleeping very badly and that she was bothered by intense dreams, most of which involved George. 'I need to tell you about one of these, Samuel, because it has really upset me,' she began one meeting, grasping my arm as she said this. I encouraged her to go ahead.

'Well, Samuel, the night before last I dreamt that I was on a train with my George. I did not know where we were heading for. He had not told me. This unsettled me but initially I did not like to ask him – I thought there must be a reason for his reticence. Eventually I became impatient to know. "Where are we bound for George? I hope that it is somewhere nice – the coast perhaps?" He did not reply. Then I raised the issue that was really troubling me. "So how is it, dear, that you have been allowed out of prison on your own? I am astonished that the governor has allowed it. It is very trusting of him." Again there was no reply.' She paused and took a deep breath.

'As the train began to accelerate and stations passed by in a blur I became more and more anxious to know what our ultimate destination might be. I repeatedly asked my son, but he continued to remain silent. The guard then entered our carriage to check our tickets. I did not, of course, possess a ticket. The guard, a smartly dressed individual with a neatly trimmed moustache and a personality that reeked of punctilious-ness, nonetheless was remarkably unconcerned when I revealed my lack of a ticket to him. He looked over to my son who produced two tickets from his waistcoat pocket. As he did so he said to the guard, "Kindly do not tell my mother where we are bound for – it is supposed to be a pleasant surprise." George then showed the tickets to the guard, whilst all the time checking that I was not trying to peer over at them. To my astonishment the guard actually colluded in this by standing directly in my line of vision. He also, at George's request, drew down the blinds. This disorientated me further.

After what felt like hours, but might have been much less, George suddenly got up and left the carriage. Assuming the train had reached our destination, I tried to follow him. But I found that I was unable to move. Even though there was nothing obvious preventing me from doing so. I shouted for the guard, who was with me almost instantly. He must have been loitering outside our carriage. Standing guard perhaps? I asked him where we were arriving, what the name of the station was. He declined to tell me, stating that it was something that I did not need to know. I remonstrated with him saying that I simply wanted to know, as his mother, where my son was going. He looked at me as if I were mad ... but did nothing to help me out of my seat even when I asked for help. He was not really all that interested. The train then sounded its whistle and pulled out from the station leaving me on the train and George on the platform, waving. I am not sure how I managed to see him through closed blinds and stuck to my seat but there we are. I did. That's the wonder of dreams, I suppose? And that's how my dream ended. If you were expecting some denouement, some dramatic climax then I am afraid I will have to disappoint you. I just woke up. But it has left me very disturbed all the same. Where was George going? Why would he not speak to me? Why was the train guard apparently in on the act? Suppose it is some sort of premonition of what is to come? I don't like it Samuel, I really don't like it. I'm so afraid of what the future holds.' She continued to grasp my arm tightly. I spoke to her firmly and rather abruptly, I'm afraid.

'Mary, is that it? Is that what you were fretting about? It is just a dream, no more and no less. I have to say I am a little disappointed at the content if I'm honest – it's all a bit lame, not very original, is it? We don't really need Doctor Hitchman or one of his ilk to tell us that you're wound up and worried that your son is on his final train to hell. I can understand you are anxious, naturally you are. But you are really going to have to do a lot better and be more creative. Otherwise I am going to have to declare your dreams banal and out of bounds.'

As soon as these words had left my mouth I realised that I had gone too far this time. I was apprehensive about how Mary would take my obvious contempt for the intimate account that she had just shared with me. I need not have worried. She looked at me quizzically for a few seconds and then suddenly, without warning, burst out laughing.

'Samuel, you have got a nerve, haven't you? Who else would dare to poke fun at me like you do? Is this what you are like with all your clients? But I have to confess that I find your honesty rather refreshing. You don't beat about the bush, do you? It makes everything more normal, somehow, even though there is nothing normal now. Is there anything else you need to get off your chest? Do I have any other faults you would rather like to alert me to? Or am I otherwise perfect as I am?'

There was such a temptation for me to respond. But I did not. Now was neither the time nor the place. I bid a hasty retreat. I could not get Mary out of my thoughts. She really is a quite remarkable woman.

XVII

A Confession

꧁ꕥ꧂

July 1863

It is July and William is back for a short while at Wigwell and so all, or nearly all, is right with the world again as far as Bessie is concerned.

The two lovers take up where they had left off and each day (regardless of the actual weather) is sunny, bright and full of exciting promise for both of them. It is like they have never been apart, but even more intense as they each have so much to catch up on. Even with her grandfather back in residence there are plenty of opportunities for the two young people to find privacy and to talk intimately as they love to do.

The teak bench at the very tip of the Grange's pleasure grounds has become a favourite haunt of theirs, a place where they can take tea, and exchange confidences in relative privacy, partly screened as they are from the Grange by a small hazel copse. But it is not without risk. More than once they are caught out. On one such occasion, just as Bessie has turned towards Will to kiss him Ann suddenly emerges from behind the trees to serve tea. The young couple remain in a tight embrace. Ann says nothing but she and Bessie exchange smiles.

꧁ꕥ꧂

Naturally they often go on long walks together in every direction from the Grange. Bessie is proud to show off to William the local landmarks that he has not already seen – the steep footpaths around Black Rocks, the panoramic views from Middleton Moor as well as pretty walks along the moody River Derwent.

Occasionally they do manage to venture further afield. A notable example is a visit to The Wardwick in Derby, the new home of the Derby Town and County Museum and Natural History Society. Bessie yawns at the prospect of this visit when proposed by Will, and yawns again on learning from Will that there are some 4,000 volumes and an extensive museum of 'mathematical and philosophical apparatus, specimens and fossils'. It all sounds rather reminiscent of grandpa's library writ large. Nevertheless, not wishing to dampen his endearing enthusiasm, she agrees to go along with Will and on the appointed day a coach and four duly arrives to take them there and back from Wigwell. As is commonly the case Bessie enjoys the journey as much, if not more, than the arrival at their destination. The pair joke and laugh all the way to Derby, even managing the occasional embrace and brief kiss when they are confident that no one can see them.

Wardwick House turns out to be a formidable-looking red-bricked residence – all marble stairs and oak panelling. It is like a more grown up and more handsome version of the Grange. In addition to the expected attractions, Bessie is pleasantly surprised to find that several paintings by Joseph Wright, 'Wright of Derby' as he is popularly known, have recently been acquired by the Museum and Society and are on display. Mostly these are on scientific themes, as befits the aims and objectives of the Society – there are orreries, philosophers, academics lecturing attentive audiences and even a depiction of an experiment on a bird in an air pump. The latter strikes Bessie as in rather poor taste – she appreciates the need to make scientific advances but cannot see why this has to be at the expense of a fellow living creature. But the picture that really catches her eye was painted by Wright in 1767 and shows a girl reading a letter, with an old man reading over her shoulder. That is, in fact, the title of the picture. The man in question is standing close behind the girl. He is holding his spectacles on with his left hand as he cranes his neck to better read what is written. His right hand is laid, affectionately, over the girl's right shoulder in a partial embrace of her. The girl makes no attempt to conceal the letter from her elderly relative; indeed, she is clearly rather proud of it, holding it up to the light and half smiling, no doubt at some clever phrase or witty remark. It is unclear whether the letter is one that the girl herself has written or if it is a letter just received from a relative, or even from her betrothed. The discarded quill and ink blotches in the bottom right of the picture rather suggest the former. Bessie sighs as she takes in the overall scene. In the half-light of the painting the old man bears a passing resemblance to her grandfather, though this gentleman has less hair, being almost bald. The young girl (she flatters herself to think) rather resembles Bessie herself. Yet that is where any comparisons begin and end. There is an evident closeness between the two subjects in the painting, a sense of warmth and familiarity that cannot be denied. This could not be much further from her own situation. Bessie has to try her best to conceal her letters from her grandfather, not to invite him to read them over her shoulder! The thought upsets her and she finds herself on the edge of tears.

Full of sadness she turns away and joins Will who is, at that very moment, studying the bones of an extinct woolly rhinoceros (Coelodanta antiquitatis) discovered by lead miners in the Dream Cave, in Wirksworth in 1822. He breaks off from his examination on seeing that Bessie is upset. She takes him to the picture and explains what has upset her. He listens patiently and then he takes her in his arms and holds her close for several minutes. Then he tells her that the girl is a less pretty version of her, and the old man looks nothing like her grandpa. He is far less haggard than the real thing, he says. And he also looks far less grumpy. Not that that would be that difficult. This cheers Bessie up considerably and she feels able to enjoy viewing some of the other pictures of Wright's that are on display, notably his landscapes – scenes of Matlock Tor and Dale Abbey – which are delightfully rendered, she thinks. His 'Arkwright Cotton Mills, by Night' does, however, resurrect her pensive mood when it dawns on her that the reason that the bright pinpricks of light are shown shining out brightly from each of the factory's windows is not artistic licence but rather because that was how the factory did, in fact, look like late at night. This betrayed the harsh reality that Arkwright's workers – men, women and children – were expected to work long and unpalatable hours. Perhaps that had been Joseph's intention in painting the scene – to emphasise the plight of the mill workers to pave the way for improvements to be made to their working conditions – but she rather doubts it. Richard Arkwright was one of Wright's chief patrons and he was hardly likely to want to risk upsetting him now, was he? Maybe Joseph was confident that his patron would not spot the covert message the painting contained? Or maybe Bessie was bestowing on Wright a more highly developed sensibility than he did in fact possess and his painting was really intended only as a pretty, decorative object. Certainly Will had to have the underlying message pointed out to him by Bessie, when she invited him to view the picture and to tell her what he thought of it. He was one of those who was lost in admiration for the painter's brilliant technique in his depiction of lights in the dark and so did not, initially see the full implications. Once Bessie had explained her reservations to him, he expressed himself grateful to have been enlightened and educated by her insightful analysis, as always!

Shining Cliff Wood, however, remains far and away Bessie's favourite excursion. And Will's as well, she thinks. One sunny day (the 15th July), early in the morning, Bessie and Will take the familiar path from the Grange over Nether Haslees to the Wood. Will, no slouch himself, struggles to keep up with Bessie's elongated stride, and finds himself having to very nearly break into a trot in order to do so. Bessie pretends not to notice but is secretly gratified. The bright sun is still low in the sky and so they need to squint to see the path ahead of them, except when they enter into a more wooded part, when the trees themselves provide a welcome screen. The wood is alive with birdsong.

Down in the valley sits the Hush-a-bye-baby tree, or 'Betty Kenny's tree' as it is known locally. As they walk Bessie explains to Will that a long, long time ago the Kennys – a charcoal burner Luke, Betty, his wife, and their eight children – had lived within the shelter of this ancient tree. To escape from her family's cramped living arrangements Betty would sit out in the birch-filtered sun of a summer's evening, gently singing her rhyme over and over as one of her offspring swayed from a bough of the yew.

Local folklore has it that on one such evening a wayfarer from the south, investigating the source of the quiet music he had heard from afar, stumbled across this most domestic of scenes. The stranger paused to listen to her entire song before wishing Betty a heartfelt 'Good night!' The rhyme had later found its way into print in London. Apparently, Betty had not minded the attention that followed. Indeed, she had rather relished it, even consenting to a portrait of her, her husband and their tree being painted by a Royal Academician and hung in the dining room of nearby Alderwasley Hall.

Bessie continues, 'I did wonder why the owner of the Hall, Mr Hurt, had been so keen to commission the painting. I do hope it was not to make Betty a figure of fun. We are kindred souls, Betty and I, you know? When I was young my mother sang her rhyme to me as I settled down for sleep.'

She begins to sing:

'Hush-a-bye Bessie on the treetop.
When the wind blows then Bessie will rock.
When the bough breaks, poor Bessie will fall.
And down will come Bessie, cradle and all.

I so loved that song and loved the moment that my beloved mother would tickle me vigorously to simulate my sudden dramatic fall in my cradle. But I don't want you just to feel sorry for me, Will, so we are not going there today – maybe another time. I have something else to show you now.'

She purposefully leads the way down a steep hill riddled with tree roots. Will swears an oath as he stumbles over one such root and almost ends up on the ground. Bessie makes no comment and pretends not to have heard his profanity. She really cannot be bothered to be shocked by anything he says now. As they turn the corner by the cliff a not unimpressive, but obviously neglected, house comes into sight. It is surrounded by fir trees which are gradually advancing on the house itself. The setting, and the house, are almost continental in character. The latter is built in the gothic style, complete with a turret, balcony, pointed arches and even some stained-glass windows. Some broken windows at ground level give away, however, the lack of a current inhabitant. The house stands on the cusp of an uncertain future; it is still grand, or at least has pretentions to be considered so, but it could easily tip over into irreversible decay and then oblivion. It exudes a sense of impending doom.

'Look, Will. We could easily be in the Swiss Alps,' Bessie says. She does not explain her reasons for saying this and William does not press her as he still has Bessie and the abandoned rocking tree on his mind. Bessie begins to explain the history of the house and attached forge, relishing taking on the role of tour guide herself, for a change.

'Before you, William, stands Oakhurst. Or, more accurately perhaps, a pale reflection of what Oakhurst used to be. William, meet Oakhurst. Oakhurst, meet William.'

'An ironmaster, Charles C. Mold by name,' she goes on, 'built Oakhurst from scratch with the help of generous funds from a sympathetic local landowner, a Mr Hurt, the very same, to whom, as a result, he felt he was forever indebted. Mold lived and worked from it and then died within its walls. On his deathbed he bequeathed the house and forge to his only son, William H. Mold Esq, on condition that his son cared for and cherished what was his father's lifetime's work. He promised £1,000 as an annuity to help him to do so and commended the services of Robinsons of Belper to assist with any repairs that might be needed, for it was a house, as Charles knew to his cost, which swallowed up money and would continue to do so. But in the event the son made only the most basic of repairs, thus retaining for himself the majority of the annuity to spend on women and port. Despite these serious sources of competition for his attention Mold continued to occupy the house and forge, for the most part carrying on his father's business competently. As he got older the port came to trump other distractions and he more and more kept himself to himself, until suddenly and without warning he vacated the house and left it to take its chances.'

Will did not respond.

'I expect you will want to ask me why your namesake left so suddenly, won't you?'

'What? Oh yes. Sorry. Why exactly did William H. Mold leave Oakhurst so suddenly? Do tell.'

'Well, I am glad you asked me that, dearest William. The reason that he did so is far from clear. But local gossip has it that an incident had taken place earlier that year when William H had seen, or claimed to see, the ghost of his father stalking the garden, apparently inspecting the premises and seemingly none too impressed as to the state they had been allowed to get into.'

'Really? How interesting. And what precisely is the evidence for this unusual, and possibly unique, example of surveyor-haunting? Had he, perchance, been reading a little too much Shakespeare? He wasn't called William 'Hamlet' Mold was he, by any chance?'

Bessie ignored him.

'Well, apparently his father, or the spirit of his father, confronted his son and accused him of neglecting the house and failing to honour his promises, and this was enough to cause his son to up sticks and flee. Now ask me what the moral of this story is.'

'Yes, right, I will do so. What is the moral of your story Miss Bessie? Do tell.'

'I know you are making fun of me, Will. But pay close attention now, if you will. The moral of my story is this – just you take care, young William, lest you are seduced into failing to honour any of the fancy promises you have made to me. Hell hath no fury like a woman scorned. That might be Shakespeare as well? I'm not too sure. But I give you fair notice that, if crossed, I will be sending my spirit to frighten the life out of you. Or, better still, not a ghost at all but the far more frightening living fiend that is my grandfather, Captain Francis Goodwin. He'll sort you out. He'll take no prisoners, that I can promise you.'

Will acts out in front of Bessie the part of a man who has lost his mind with terror at the prospect of a confrontation with the devil, whether that be the spirit of Bessie or the human form of Captain Goodwin. Bessie ignores his facial gymnastics. For Bessie has moved on in her thoughts and even as William contorts himself in what he imagines to be a more and more manic phrensy she is lost to him, busy confronting one of her own internal devils that has suddenly popped into her mind . . .

Bessie knows with a new certainty at that very moment in her favourite woods that she must now urgently confront the inconvenient fact that could not be denied any longer, namely George. Ever since she finally found out the real reasons for Will's apparent neglect of her, Bessie finds herself wishing that George were dead. It would make things so much simpler and more convenient. She does not wish him a violent or a painful death though, just a gentle succumbing. Hardly a death really, more just a slipping away.

She would readily grant him a traditional farewell. His mother, Mary, and sister, Caroline, would be at his bedside. They would be distraught but, characteristically, stoic. Bessie would there also. On second thoughts, maybe not. She would be unavoidably detained at Wigwell by her grandfather, Captain Goodwin, who would expect her to read to him of the day's news as usual. The Captain, whilst he has his suspicions, would be unaware that Bessie was ever betrothed to George and Bessie would intend to keep it that way.

A few days later Bessie would receive by post a black-edged envelope. She would then don widow's weeds, as advised by her Ann. The Captain would be puzzled by this sudden wardrobe change, but he would ask no questions of her.

Bessie would think kindly of happy days spent in George's company.

Their betrothal had felt right at the time. But now she would, at last, be free to marry again. No, not again – to marry for the first time, Bessie would correct herself, hastily.

Bessie shocks herself by even having such wild thoughts. Indeed, she reprimands herself in the strongest possible terms for her casual immorality. But that makes no difference to the strength of her desire.

Bessie knows that not only is she certainly a very wicked person who should go directly to hell for even imagining this sequence of events but, also, that things are never going to happen in the way she secretly desires. The only death George might be susceptible to would be death arising from a broken heart, as a result of her finally terminating their betrothal, if it still persists, which she realises in George's mind at least, it very definitely does, and her revealing her love for another. Despite this Bessie knows this is the right thing to do. It cannot be right that George maintains any hope when she feels little or nothing for him. She knows that she has let things drift badly – not correcting George about their status straightaway. But she shudders when she thinks of what is required to resolve the situation.

Thus far George's name has scarcely even passed her lips in William's presence. She has mentioned a previous betrothal to George, but in such low-key terms that she has made it sound as if the so-called betrothal had never been very serious and indeed was more in the nature of a youthful indiscretion on both their parts, almost immediately mutually and heartily regretted. He has no idea as yet that there may be any current, resurrected arrangement.

Remembering how disastrous her interview with the Revd Harris had been on the topic a few months ago, she resolves not to prevaricate but to speak directly. She waits till after dinner that evening when they are on their own in the sitting room and then she begins thus.

'William, my dear, after such a long hiatus or delay I don't know how things stand between you and me – that is I do know but I don't know where things may lead, that is I do know where I would like things to lead. But if they do still stand, as I believe they do, as they did, and still may lead where I think they might lead, then I need to discuss something serious with you. What I have to say will shock you and you may fairly decide that you will have nothing more to do with me. I would not blame you if that were the case, but I cannot let things drag on in the way they have done. I cannot keep leading you on in that way. Or him. I should have told you more before now. I have to let it out.'

William replies that he is all ears. But Bessie's serious demeanour acts as a silent rebuke, and he therefore focuses all his attention on what she has to say.

'I have not told you the whole story – about George that is – you know of his existence, but we have never really talked about him, have we? Not properly? I suppose I wanted to keep things separate, did not want George to affect us. And you never ask me about him, do you? You don't even refer to him, by name. I am not blaming you, but I realise now that those kinds of different worlds can never be kept separate for long. I was wrong to ever think that they could. Because the thing is matters are a lot more compli-cated, less resolved than I have led you to believe. I need to tell you the whole story . . . from the beginning.'

Will settles back on the chaise longue – it is not the most comfortable piece of furniture to recline on, it is too short for him and, to compensate for this, he props himself up with a cushion.

'A long time ago now I visited my dear uncle, Dr Francis Goodwin, who resides near Manchester. That was where I met George. He and I were only 20 then. He was only a boy really, certainly not yet a man, let alone one of any real achievement but I . . . I saw some promise in him. He is an excellent pianist as well as having a knack for French and Spanish. Or so he told me. He is . . . distinctive-looking, rather than handsome, but tall. Like you! Tall, and with an extensive soft beard and mournful grey eyes. I got a sense of him being vulnerable, of needing me . . . We met again in Chester later and, well, then we became fond of each other's company. I felt safe with him, or at least I felt I could keep him safe. I felt that that might be my destiny. There are worse ways to spend a life than protecting and nurturing a wounded fellow human being. Inevitably, he soon made me an offer of marriage and, although it was all very sudden, I accepted. On my 21st birthday!

Papa was out of the country but agreed to the match in absentia and, as far as I know, without making any enquiries at all as to George's suitabil-ity. As for grandfather, I don't think grandfather was aware of . . . of what had happened. I am fairly sure that he was not. I did not intend to marry until I was at least 25, after all, so I felt that it was premature for him to be involved. It was better if he remained in the dark.

George went away and we wrote to each other regularly after that. Ann and I had an arrangement that his letters to me would be separated out and passed to me directly rather than bothering grandpa with them! To be honest, and despite the excitement of the subterfuge involved, I soon came to find George's letters a little dull ... But they were sweet, full of affection and expressions of his love towards me, and reminding me of my duty to him, of our attachment. George was away in France. Even if he not been it would have been hard to see him without grandpa becoming aware of the betrothal and opposing it, and bringing it to an end. I wasn't sure he was worth fighting for. It all began to feel pointless ... stupid. I felt bored, frustrated. By the time he got back from France at the end of August, incidentally not as the successful merchant he had promised me he would be, I had already decided to break off our betrothal.

And I did break off my betrothal, then, just as I told you. I wrote to him last August and said as much. I wrote to his mother as well to ask for her pardon for the whole wretched mess. I thought I had done an adequate job of letting him down gently. I remember that I said to his mother that I didn't care for myself so long as George was all right in body though I feared that he would not be all right in his mind until he got something worthwhile to do. But then, earlier this year, things became more ... ambiguous. George wrote to me in late February. He sought to rekindle things again, he assured me of his continuing love, again. He said that he forgave me for having tried to break off our earlier attachment the previous summer. He vowed that he would ensure that he had the means to support me, again. He asked if we could renew our promises, to become betrothed again, I suppose. He said that in fact that was barely necessary as really and truly we had never ceased to be betrothed. You were not here. I could not make contact with you, you know? You were not answering my letters. I know now why you were not answering them, because you were lying mortally ill, a reasonable excuse I do accept! But I did not know this at the time. I did not know whether you were still ... were still interested in me. Maybe you had found someone else and lost interest in me, had second thoughts. I rather assumed that you had. We are all entitled to them after all. And so, although I did not say yes to George, I did not say no, either. I fear he took, has taken, more from this than he really should have, and in his mind at least feels we are still pledged to each other – and maybe we are. Maybe I acquiesced, if one can do that. I don't know. We did begin to correspond again for a while. I more or less stopped about the time I knew you were getting better and, this time, I was never as enthusiatic as he was. I blamed grandpa for my reticence to write back to him, which was also wrong of me. But as you see now my dear, contrary to my intentions and my desires, I may be accidentally spoken for already and not able to entertain the delightful future with you I had imagined. Certainly Revd Harris, when I sought his counsel, thought so. He was pretty clear on the subject. Not that I told him the whole story, mind. He told me, in so many words, that there is no escape for me and that I need to buckle to and do my duty. That my duty comes before my happiness. If it is, after all, true that I must marry him whom I do not love then I feel I may not marry at all. I am sorry but there it is. It is truly a wretched mess. A mess of my own making, largely.'

William does not look as shocked as she had expected him to do though he does furrow his brow. For a moment she suspects that the Reverend Harris might already have spoken to him on the subject of her marital status.

He reacts calmly enough.

'Bessie, you must marry whomsoever you choose, if you choose, and when you wish to, and no fusty old priest should lecture you to the contrary. If he does then you should feel free to take your spiritual advice elsewhere,' he said. Even in her distressed state Bessie feels slightly embarrassed for him that he is, apparently willing, in his own blatant self-interest, to malign their mutual mentor, Harris, quite so readily and comprehensively.

'But what about those adulterers in that beastly mural in that beastly church of yours? You said they should get their just deserts – that is what you said? And I am hardly better than them, after all, am I?'

Will begins to give her his stock reply along the lines of 'We are all sinners Bessie and your sin, such as it is, is hardly a capital one. I hate to disappoint you, but you do not qualify for the fires of hell just yet.' But then he has second thoughts. He starts to explain to her that what she was confessing to him now was certainly more than a trivial transgression and could indeed be a capital sin. Bessie looks alarmed. He then backtracks on this as well and tells her that there is no point worrying about what cannot be changed. The crucial thing now is to put things right, or as right as they could be put, as soon as possible.

To put him out of his misery once and for all. He adds that he almost admires his rival's patience! He is not sure that he could have put up with so little contact for so long. He says nothing further and instead takes her in his arms and hugs her tightly.

As he embraces her, Bessie is aware of a huge burden lifting from her shoulders. It felt as if, having confessed, and despite the confusing response from Will, she has been absolved there and then from her sins and handed a new future that, moments ago, she felt was on the point of being snatched from her again. She hugs William back, hard.

William hastily changes the subject. Bessie is gratified when he tells her that he has been given leave of absence for most of August to complete his convalescence and that he hopes to spend most of the time in Wirksworth in general, and at Wigwell in particular, 'If you will have me, that is, and if that will not cause problems for you?' Bessie understands that this is really a reference to her grandfather and any opposition that may emanate from that source, rather than to George. Bessie assures Will that it will not. But she announces that she will go and see her grandfather anyway, to 'take the bull by the horns', so to speak.

The next day, after reading her grandpa selected classified advertise-ments and then the latest news of the American War, Bessie, summoning up her courage, decides to seize the moment and to broach the issue of Will with the Captain. She waits until coffee has been served in the library and Ann has left the room. She makes sure the door is firmly closed. The Captain is seated behind his desk. He looks at her quizzically.

'I wanted to talk to you about William,' she begins. 'You know we are friends don't you – William and I – and you know how distressed I was when you, eventually,' (she emphasises the word and raises her eyebrows) 'when you *eventually* told me about his grave and life threatening illness? And how happy I am that he is now well on the road to recovery? And how much I enjoy his company? And you like him, too, I think? Or at least you can tolerate him, can't you?'

Francis raises an eyebrow. 'What is it you wish to say, Bessie? Do I perhaps need to expect a visit from William shortly?' He places emphasis on the word visit. 'Does he have some special business he wishes, needs, to discuss with me concerning you … and him? I am certainly more than happy to hear his representations on the topic and to make my decision based on what he has to say on his own account. A country parson is not an ideal match for you, but it is perhaps, on reflection, not such a wholly disastrous one either. You could do a lot worse, I suppose. We both know that, don't we?'

Bessie suddenly realises that he has grasped the wrong end of the stick, and he is expecting Will to seek his approval to their marriage.

'No, it's not that,' she says.

'Oh, and what is it then?' says Francis, looking, Bessie was amazed to see, slightly disappointed.

'It's just that William has been allowed some time to convalesce by the bishop and would like it, we would like it, if you are agreeable, to it being spent here.' Bessie had made up the bit about the bishop's involvement on the spot but thought it must be true. 'Just so that he can get better, somewhere comfortable, where he can be looked after. By me,' she adds bravely. Grandpa says nothing, but nods. Bessie is very encouraged but feels she needs more than a nod to the arrangement.

'So I can say yes to him, can I? But what about the title tattle that it will encourage amongst local people. You know there was more than a whiff of scandal when he stayed last Christmas.' Before she has time to think about the likely impact of what she is saying, she adds, 'Reuben, in particular, was quite outspoken on the topic.' She then wishes she had not identified Reuben by name and tries to soften her words. 'Well, not outspoken perhaps, but concerned. He always has my best interests at heart, I do know that.'

Francis looks at her pityingly. 'Do you really think so little of me that you imagine I am to be so easily swayed by public disapproval? I am undaunted. It may come as a shock to you but even the good opinion of Mr Reuben Conway carries little weight with me. It is a damn impudence for him to even express a view. He should know his place. I know, Bessie, that you would do nothing to disgrace the family name.' Bessie nods. 'And that is good enough for me. So yes, William can stay for as long as he pleases. And if Reuben, or anyone else for that matter, has a problem with my decision then by all means suggest they come and discuss it directly with me. I would be delighted to discuss it with him.'

Bessie feels herself well up with tears and feels like hugging her grandfather in gratitude, but does not do so.

'But tell William from me that I expect a request for a special interview from him in due course, and not to leave it too long.'

Bessie swears that she sees a twinkle in his eye when he makes this last remark. She doesn't remember ever having seen a twinkle before. She is ecstatic to share the news immediately with William. She sensibly decides, given his response to the question of George, to omit the reference to grandfather's expectation about an imminent special meeting.

Bessie leans towards Will, hoping for a reassuring kiss. But Will initially turns away from her before turning back and kissing her on the cheek. Bessie does not comment on this show of petulance but, as on previous occasions, she stores it up, for future reference.

XVIII

A Trial

⌾⌁⌾

1st July 1872
Fred
And now, at last, we get to the nub of things – sit tight, it will be a rocky ride!
Papa
I was only too keenly aware of Derbeians' visceral excitement as the date of Townley's trial – 11th December 1863 – approached. The tolling of the cathedral bells had, in accordance with tradition, announced the beginning of the Derby Quarter Sessions. This had heightened the already febrile atmosphere in the town. Usually local residents, if they had nothing better to do that day, stood around as a matter of good manners to greet the judges and lawyers making up the High Sheriff's procession from the cathedral to the court. I had, in recent years, participated in the procession, though I was placed well to the rear. But now even this ritual occasion was not considered sacred so far as the more partisan members of the public were concerned and an appeal to the judges, actually more of a demand than an appeal, to 'Hang Townley' was shouted out, initially by scattered individuals, but soon taken up by many in the crowd. This most unwelcome and intrusive chant reached its climax as the judges entered St Mary's Gate, which led directly into the Court environs.

You won't be surprised to hear that the number of public applications to secure seats at the Assizes for the Townley trial far exceeded the capacity of the court. The majority of the applicants were ladies. Tickets were under the control of B.S Currey, Esq., the Acting Under Sheriff. His task of allocating tickets was not made any easier by the fact that a large proportion of the seats available had been reserved in advance by representatives of the metropolitan and provincial press. A small number of m' learned friends who had no pressing briefs and therefore had some time on their hands, also wished to attend, expectant as to the interesting point of law that they hoped would arise. The case was reported for *The Times* by N E Cave Esq., Barrister-At-Law.

With due respect to my esteemed correspondent, you did not need to be a fully qualified barrister to have a firm view as to how Townley's defence should be conducted. I was acutely aware that barrack room lawyers frequenting the saloon bars of Derby had for weeks been strongly, and sometimes violently, divided as to whether madness should be pleaded. The case for and against Townley being mad was argued with equal passion on both sides – the majority 'wolves' citing the presence on Townley's person, when searched in the Wirksworth Lock Up, of the receipt for a mother of pearl pen knife, purchased in Manchester en route to Wigwell, as well as his frank confession immediately after the murder. The minority 'lambs' also pointed to Townley's extraordinarily compliant conduct after the murder but interpreted it more charitably. Needless to say, no man shifted, even minutely, as a consequence of their ale-fuelled debate. What I heard of their discussion did nothing to assist me based, as it was, on a complete ignorance of the law and/or a scandalous disregard of the facts.

On the day itself I got to court early and nervously pushed my way through the assembled crowds – of course as the defence solicitor I had no fears that I would not be able to access my appointed place on the benches immediately behind the barristers. My relief that things would finally get underway was tempered by the frustrations of my non-speaking role at the trial itself. Whilst I have always enjoyed litigation and relished court work usually, I hated it when I had had to agree to instruct both learned and junior counsel to be the advocates in court. Present correspondent excepted, I especially resented employing junior counsel who are barely out of school but who think, as here, that it is their prerogative to send me off on a series of pointless errands. I hated the loss of control of proceedings that having barristers involved at all meant. There was always the risk that, despite my meticulous briefing of them, they decided to pursue their own path and present the case as they thought at the time, not as we had agreed in conference. In legal parlance you will appreciate to 'go on a frolic of their own'. This was markedly the case where leading counsel was involved. Mandatory in murder trials, Queen's Counsel, as we both know only too well, are invariably men with an advanced sense of their own worth. More accurately perhaps, with a greatly inflated sense of their own importance. If such a colossus of a man went on a frolic, there would be little I could do about it except tug at his gown, which was unlikely to have any impact. I sat in court chewing at what was left of my fingernails and hoping against hope that the trial would proceed as we had planned.

There was a buzz of excitement as Townley entered court and was escorted to the iron-barred wooden dock in the centre of the room, especially highly polished for the occasion. The assembled spectators strained to catch a glimpse of him. There was a murmur, not exactly of approval or disapproval, but of animated discussion between neighbours as to whether he looked like the killer he indisputably was. Disappointingly from the point of view of these observers, George presented as quiet and respectful, yes, just as I had instructed him to do. He was not unduly alarmed or anxious. I envied him his composure, in fact. He was dressed neatly all in black, his beard having been severely tamed for the occasion. He was escorted by what seemed like half the police force of the county, overseen by the chief constable no less. George nodded to me but was not the least fazed by the majesty of the law as exemplified by the imposing gothic courtroom he found himself in nor by the crowds packing out the public galleries, nor by Judge Baron Martin, nor by the no less formidable presence of Counsel for the Crown, Mr Charles Boden, QC.

In advance of the trial George had requested that he had the facility to pass notes to me as and when he had any observations to make on the conduct of the defence as it proceeded. This had been canvassed before the start of the trial with His Lordship and prosecution counsel who had agreed to it despite the novelty of the request, no doubt wanting to close off any possible avenue of future appeal. I was to be the reluctant conduit to our barristers of any such messages from George. Since the prisoner's dock was not within easy reach of the defence benches a court official had been nominated to serve as a 'go between' delivering any messages from George to me, and also delivering my replies, if any. Bearing in mind my first meeting with George and the extraordinary law lecture he had favoured me with, it was with a sinking heart that I saw that George had brought into court a small, but thick, notebook, and a pencil, which he placed in front of him, licking the pencil to ensure it was fully ready for action.

XIX

A New Regime

◦⌒⌇⌒◦

13th August 1863

'I have been thinking our little problem over and I have decided that what we need is a proper plan, a campaign strategy, so to speak.' So William says on his return to Wigwell in August as he and Bessie sit together, side by side, on the chaise longue in the library.

'A plan?'

'A plan to extricate you from your unfortunate "arrangement" with him. Without giving too much cause for bitterness. At least no more than is strictly necessary. Give him an honourable way out. But the break must be clear and unequivocal this time, Bessie. There must be no more dilly-dallying. A clean break, do you see? We need to justify your change of mind. We need a reason, something that will pass muster with the injured party, something plausible?'

Though she loves him dearly Bessie hates Will's continued reluctance to mention George's name and to refer to him only in the third person, that is if he refers to him at all. But it does serve to make George feel more remote, less of a person and so less of an obstacle to their future content-ment.

'What about your grandfather – could he be the reason? It's not a total lie. Far from it – he is part of the reason, isn't he? There would be no love lost between George and him if he was furnished with the full story. Whereas your GF thinks I am, more or less, a gift from God – which in a real and truly theological sense, I am.'

Bessie nods. She does not respond to Will's attempt at levity. This is no time for his habitual flippancy. She is getting a little tired of his tendency to try and turn everything into a joke.

'Well then, the GF it is. I am sure the old boy won't mind taking the rap if it's in aid of your future happiness? And it is what you want, Bessie, isn't it? I am what you want, aren't I? You don't have any doubts about me, do you? You are sure? I don't want to be let down at the last minute, taken for a ride.'

Bessie, though upset, accepts the implied criticism without comment and both nods and shakes her head vigorously to signal her assent.

'Well then, there's no time like the present. Fetch some paper and let's have a go at a Notice to Terminate a Betrothal, shall we? I have always fancied myself as a bit of a lawyer, you know. Given more opportunity I am sure that I could have been a formidable one. But I never had the chance. I wasn't born with a silver spoon in my mouth, unlike some I could mention,' he remarks.

Again, Bessie does not appreciate either his self-pity, something that he was not usually prone to, or his persistent attempt to make light of things, which he was. Certain things should not be trivialised. But, at the same time, she is seduced by the notion that she might not need to attempt the letter on her own after all.

She fetches some paper, pen and ink and sits down at the small desk whilst William takes up position behind the ostentatiously grand desk with scufffed green leather top that is her grandfather's. William puts his feet up on the desk. Bessie's desk, by contrast, is a small knee-hole desk made of beautifully burnished walnut. It is not the most practical piece of furniture in the house. Bessie has to squeeze her long legs into the knee-hole, and even then she cannot get up as close to the desk's top as she would like, and has to write as if she is distancing herself from the letter's contents.

The words do not come to her straight away. She had hoped that Will might simply dictate the wording of the letter to her, to save her from vexing herself, but he does not offer to do so. Instead, he adopts the role of an encouraging parent who wishes to guide their child to the right answer rather than to tell them what it is. She finds his approach highly patronising. She becomes distracted, studying in detail the tapestry on the wall opposite, as she has before when subjected to one of her grandfather's endless supply of military anecdotes. Bessie is very fond of this tapestry. To be sure, it is in need of some restoration after two hundred years – who wouldn't be? But even in its current state of disrepair it is apparent that it is exquisitely sewn. It depicts Charles I and Henrietta Maria, his queen, along with a whole menagerie of exotic beasts and birds and allegorical figures. And then suddenly, just as one is preoccupied with working out the likely identity of these creatures and has been lulled into a false sense of security, one notices in one corner of this otherwise bucolic scene a man, the body of a man more accurately, who has just been beheaded. His spurting blood is shockingly, but beautifully and faithfully, lovingly even, rendered in scarlet silk thread. This is a representation of Charles too – intended no doubt as a harbinger of his eventual tragic fate. She feels a gnawing sadness for Charles – did he really deserve this ghastly end? Could he not just have been locked up in the Tower of London out of harm's way? But it is not just the content of the tapestry, and its willingness to tackle difficult and sad subjects, that fascinates Bessie. When she is sure she is alone Bessie likes to get right up close to the tapestry, close enough to breathe in its musky smell. As she does so she likes to fancy that she can detect the sweet-perfumed scent of the tapestry's creator behind the sour odour of old age. A delightful mixture of cardamom and sandalwood and vanilla, she guesses. She envies the seamstress not only her craftsmanship and imagination but also for having left something real and tangible and beautiful behind in this world.

This sad thought brings her back, with a jolt, to the job in hand and to her letter. Will is still looking at her expectantly. She begins to write, in large spidery writing.

Wigwell Grange
13th August 1863
My dear George,

She puts her pen down and looks to Will for inspiration. He is silent but impatiently gestures for her to go on. She speaks out loud the words as she writes them down to ensure that they are acceptable. The slowness of her delivery adds to the lethargic drama of the contents.

This is a letter I hoped never to have written to you. It is a letter that I never have dreamt that I would be writing to you. I will say it straight and clear to you whilst I still have the courage. I cannot marry you, after all. I have to ask you to free me; it is a great object for me to say I am not engaged. I am sorry that I did not say this to you sooner, and more finally and more clearly, my dear, but it is not that I was not, am not, deeply fond of you – I was, and I am – it is just that we cannot be married after *all. I don't expect that <u>I will ever marry now</u>* (she underscores 'I will ever marry now' with such ferocity that her pen penetrates the note paper and marks the desk underneath) *and so be it, even though I have met a wonderful person, a man of the cloth, who might just have been suitable. I am so sorry, George. I know my words will cause you pain and I am truly sorry for that.*

'What's all this about you not marrying after all? Where did that come from? And what do you mean just suitable? And what about your grand-father,' whispers Will. 'When does he make an appearance?'
'Yes, patience please, I'm coming to that bit,' says Bessie.

My grandfather has always approached my marriage as if he were select-ing a prospective business partner for himself. Maybe he was. And sadly, my dear, now that he has found out something may exist between us, he has made some enquiries of his own and he has found you badly wanting – I don't know why exactly. I don't know who it could be that has black-ened your name. I tried to stand up for you with him. But I am weary of the conflict. He has told me not to 'sacrifice my future', that he will not allow this to happen. I cannot take any more or I feel my head will burst. Apparently therefore I must take the easy route for my own sanity and marry or not marry according to another's whim, though I myself still feel I will not.

Will winces at this outburst and is puzzled by the further reference to Bessie not marrying at all which is just plain daft. He tells Bessie so, but she simply shrugs her shoulders and says nothing. He likes the reference to a mystery person having blackened George's name which, as far as he knows, is pure invention on Bessie's part. He acknowledges this to Bessie. He says that it is nothing less than inspired. It neatly deflects the blame. He also says that he has, modesty aside, no objection to being judged to be wonderful. Bessie starts to cry, and her tears moisten the words she has written, causing the ink to run on the letter. She worries what effect these blotchy words will have on its intended recipient. But she cannot face going back and starting again so she finishes the letter off as quickly as she can.

I hope you do not take all this too badly. I truly wish you every happiness
in your life. I am only sorry that I cannot be a part of it.
Adieu and God bless.
Yours affectionately
Bessie.

'There, is it done now,' she says. 'Do you think "affectionately" is all right, given the circumstances, I mean? Is it too cold? Or too warm perhaps? I don't know any more.' William says he thinks that it will do.

Having finished the letter and placed it in an envelope addressed to George Townley Esq. etc. etc., she surrenders the letter to Will. Bessie then announces her intention to walk down to the river to clear her head. She does not invite Will to join her, and he does not offer to do so.

⟍ফ⟋

Will has not said so to Bessie, but he does in fact nurse a niggling doubt that the recipient of Bessie's letter may not be as fully and finally deterred as they had jointly intended. The tear stains will obviously not help. But he is also still more than slightly irritated by the reference to Bessie possibly not marrying at all when, as far as he is concerned, she has already promised herself to him. Still, it is too late to object, it is done now.

Will stays in the library gazing out at the park and then, once Bessie has gone, pulls the bell to summon her maid, Ann. Handing her Bessie's letter he asks her to ensure that it catches the next available post, without fail. He repeats this instruction insistently and Ann hurries off. William remains in the library, gazing out over the extensive and rich farmland. If everything goes according to plan, and despite the wording of Bessie's recent letter he does not doubt it, he expects to soon have a substantial interest in the future of the Wigwell estate by virtue of his forthcoming marriage to Bessie, the Captain's lack of any ready heir and the latter's, on the whole, favourable disposition towards him. He is far from displeased at the prospect. He permits himself the hint of a smile.

Inwardly he is less inhibited. He rejoices at Providence having freed him from the yoke of having to please a benefactor for the rest of his life. He imagines having the time and the opportunity in the future to follow his own interests, with the help of the Captain's fine, extensive library and so to do God's work. He feels he has something to say which should be heard. About what he is not quite sure at this stage but feels sure that it

115

will come to him. He has so many interests and so many views on things that he is sure that choosing one, and expressing it coherently and trenchantly, will come easily. He imagines himself writing a tract, a published pamphlet perhaps, to make his point, and to make his name. He would have to pay the costs of its publication and it would only be produced in a strictly limited edition no doubt. But what of that? He will not be the first, or the last, who begins his writing career at his own expense.

All in all, things have worked out rather well. All that is needed now is to see George completely eliminated. He settles back behind the Captain's desk and makes himself at home. He contemplates the contents of the rather overcrowded desk – a circular pewter box, a teak tobacco box, a penknife and an apparently barely used pair of mother-of-pearl opera glasses. He is surprised, and frankly, rather disappointed, that the Captain had allowed his desk to become so cluttered. He believes in an ordered desk where everything has its place. None of these 'knick-knacks' would survive his new regime.

XX

A Prosecution

⊙⌒⌒⊙

The Bulkeley Hotel
Beaumaris
20th July 1872

Frederick,

I did not really expect you to agree with my provocative comments as to the role of junior counsel, but you certainly were not prepared to take them lying down, were you? Thanks for letting me have your thoughts, again expressed in characteristically forthright terms. Apologies for the delay in replying but, unbeknownst to me, your mother had arranged for us to go on holiday to Anglesey! She says that I needed a break. How very thoughtful of her that was. We are there now as it happens, staying in a smart guest house. Yesterday we visited the Lligwy burial chamber – fascinating!

Changing the subject, have you come across Charlie Boden of the Temple, by any chance? If so, I feel sure you share my dislike of him.

Charles Boden QC was a man whose frown perpetually dominated his face. It was as if my grandmother's oft repeated warning to me, never to frown lest the wind change and the frown remain forever (advice I may possibly have passed onto you?) had come true in his case and so what had originally been temporary creases had become permanent fissures. You may think this is an instance of 'the pot calling the kettle black'? But he was, by reputation at least, a difficult man to like. He lacked the common touch and favoured a patrician style, most of all, I have on good authority, in his dealings with his own instructing solicitors. What also did not go in his favour, with me, was his high-pitched voice. It does me no credit, I know, but I did not look forward to the prospect of enduring several hours of his self-important whining.

'May it please your lordship and gentlemen of the jury, it is my duty to bring before you the facts of these unhappy events; all of the facts, mind, whether or not they assist my case.' he whined. 'It is your duty, members of the jury, to sift those facts and, in due course, to deliberate upon them. I know that in so doing you will be ever mindful of the momentous consequence of your verdict for that unfortunate gentleman who now stands before you at the bar . . .'

From the outset it was clear that Mr Boden was determined to milk his moment in the Derby sun. He took pleasure in reading out loud, in their entirety, what survived of George's letters to Miss Goodwin, pausing to dwell on the more tender sentiments expressed, pauses that were just long enough to communicate his personal distaste, but not so long as to be likely to attract the judge's censure. He dwelt, disdainfully, on the contents of a letter sent by Townley to Miss Goodwin just before the two young people met for the last time and which had been found by the servant Poyser on her employer's dressing table.

'The prisoner says, and I quote verbatim here from his letter of 17th August – "Dearest you will always be to me; so to say that I am not terribly cut up would be a lie but, at any rate, you know I am not the sort of man to stand in your way".'

Mr Boden paused to allow the irony of this declaration of apparent cooperation and resignation to register fully with the jury. He fashioned his face into what I imagined he thought was a frown, but which was a frown on top of a pre-existing frown and thus looked faintly ridiculous.

He continued to read from the same letter with as much dripping irony and contempt as he could possibly muster.

'"I wish to hear from your own lips what your wishes are, and I will accede to them."' He placed an artificial stress on the word 'accede', entirely for the jury's benefit. He swept his right hand across his body as if he was physically underlining the word.

'And then he says, and here again I quote verbatim and without any embellishment whatsoever – "I have but to hear from you what your wishes are and they shall be complied with. I have sufficient 'savoir faire'," (he raised a theatrical eyebrow) '"not to make a bother about what cannot be helped".'

Boden, undoubtedly a frustrated thespian if ever there was one, placed one foot on the bench in front of him, to better survey his audience, the jury, and closed his eyes briefly as if to signal the end of Act One.

But it turned out that he had one more devastating line to deliver before the imaginary curtain fell and he received the standing ovation that was surely due to him. He built up to it slowly, but venomously.

'And then, members of the jury, the final insult, the final insult before the terrible injuries one might say, he says this … in his letter … he says "We",' Mr Boden fashions his face into yet another contortion, '"We" – he means by that himself and Bessie – hopefully the last time those names are ever conjoined, "We shall both be better in mind as well as in body after this last interview." We shall both be better in mind and body after this last interview – that's what he says. Unbelievably. Well, the prisoner over there may feel better, in mind and body, but that transparently does not apply to Bessie. Her soul has gone to a better place, of that I'm sure, but as to her mind and her body they are no more and for that she deserves justice and yes, I have to say it, she deserves righteous retribution.' This last comment hung like a pall of smoke over the proceedings.

Personally, I considered his behaviour most unbecoming of a member of the Bar. I am sure, Fred, that you would never stoop to such vulgar antics, however great the provocation. But, for some reason known only to himself, the learned judge did not see fit to intervene. George sent me the first of his scribbled notes via the assigned court official. It is unrepeatable here but suffice it to say that, amongst diverse libellous remarks, it questioned the legitimacy of Mr Boden's birth.

Having made the most of this correspondence, leading counsel began Act 2 by turning his attention to bullying, that is to say 'examining', his witnesses. I say his witnesses since he had petitioned the court at an earlier hearing to oblige Townley's immediate relatives – his mother and his sister – to take the stand, not as defence witnesses but as prosecution witnesses. Although irregular, and even though I would have like to have done so given the earlier disreputable conduct of the prosecution, I did not think I had any legal grounds to deny him his wishes. I was mindful that he would treat them as 'hostile' and so go straight on the attack but there was little or nothing that I could do about that. The giving of evidence by the prisoner's mother and by his sister was one of the aspects of the trial that had been most keenly anticipated by the 'hoi polloi' of Derby. But knowing the two of them as I did by that time, I was sure they would acquit themselves well.

His mother, Mary, gave evidence first. She was as tall as Townley but much slighter, and more gaunt. I was concerned when I saw her enter the witness box. I thought that she might be ill. She looked even more pale than she had been and more care worn, which was scarcely surprising. Anyone would be ground down by what she had had been through in recent months. I felt like intervening on her behalf, creating some sort of diversion perhaps, but I couldn't think of what I could possibly do that would achieve anything, apart from my immediate removal from the court, that is. But I need not have worried. She was remarkably poised as she confirmed her name and address to the court. I observed that Townley was already writing furiously in his notebook. She had not even started giving her evidence. The phrase 'full of sound and fury, signifying nothing' sprang to my mind.

Mr Boden began his examination in chief. His first question was typically disingenuous and, as he asked it, he leant forwards with his right hand outstretched as if he expected Mrs Townley to grasp it gratefully in recognition of the easy start he was allowing her … yet more amateur dramatics … from the very amateur actor.

'Mrs Townley, you are the mother of George Townley, the accused who stands over there in the dock?'

He waves his hand vaguely in the direction of George.

'Yes, I am.'

'May I say, Madam, to begin with, how much I, and here I am sure that I speak for almost the whole court, we all regret your sad loss.'

Mrs Townley looked momentarily confused but maintained her composure.

'Sorry Mr Boden – I am not sure which loss of mine you are referring to. George has not even been found guilty yet. I hardly think it's right to assume that George will be …'

Mr Boden then sprang his trap, with undisguised glee.

'I refer, of course, not to your living and breathing son but to the sad passing of your prospective daughter-in-law. That is why you wear what you wear, I assume?'

He indicated her silk mourning dress by an opening out of his palms.

'Yes, I see, Mr Boden. Yes indeed. Miss Goodwin's, Bessie's, death has brought me and my daughter much sadness and we mourn for her. But she was not my prospective daughter-in-law, as you know, Mr Boden, not by then anyway.'

'Yes indeed. We will come to all that in due course. That you and your very fine daughter were upset I do not question for one moment. But not your son, I think? Her death has not brought him much sadness, has it? Quite the opposite, in fact. Even though he was the one who brought it about?'

Mrs Townley, rightly in my view, regarded Mr Boden's question as a rhetorical one which should not receive a reply from her lest she thereby dignify it. She therefore remained silent.

Mr Boden continued, undeterred.

'No, in fact your son has revelled in her death, has he not? "She who deceives me must die." That's what he said, wasn't it? He has justified his actions to whoever will listen to him. No self-doubt, no equivocation, no compassion, no mercy. She who deceives me **must** die – that's what he proudly declaimed, after he had butchered her to death on the toll road in broad daylight. How does that make you feel, as a mother, the mother of a self-confessed, cold-blooded, butcher?'

Judge Martin intervened. 'You are on dangerous ground, Mr Boden. I am sure jury members are quite capable of seeing for themselves the effect of these tragic events on Mrs Townley and we don't need you to underline them for us in this rather crass manner. She is not on trial here and I would thank you to remember that.'

'Very well, My Lord.' Mr Boden endured the judge's trenchant rebuke with characteristic fortitude.

'Allow me then to approach the matter from a different angle.'

'By all means: that is, if you feel you need to approach it at all. But please do not try this court's patience any further.'

'Very well, My Lord. Would it be fair to say, Mrs Townley, that your son George grew up without the steadying influence of a father?'

Mary bridled, sensing no doubt, a further trap being set for her.

'He most certainly did not grow up fatherless, Mr Boden. It is true that his father, my husband, was often away from home on business. But, despite this, he was still very much present, just somewhat intermittently.'

'Very well, Mrs Townley. So how would you describe the character of young George as he grew up, blessed as he was with your full-time guidance and the "intermittent presence" of his father? Was he what you and I might call a good Christian boy?'

'He grew up in a Christian home, if that's what you mean, Sir – he grew up humane and kind to animals. He loves his sister and me with a fierce and loyal love. He did not enjoy his schooling much. His school pals did not really understand him, and he certainly did not understand them. It was a relief to me when the time came for him to leave school. But the question then was, what was he to do next? His father, my husband, tried to "pull strings", I suppose you could say, to find him gainful and stable employment. But it was soon apparent that he had no head for business or indeed any other occupation.'

'You have run ahead of me, Mrs Townley, but no matter.' (Mr Boden looked slightly exasperated – maybe this witness was not proving quite the pushover he had expected her to be.) 'How then would you describe his outlook on life as he grew up?'

'He was drifting through life aimlessly, up until the time he met Miss Goodwin. I had always feared for George's future far more than any of my other children. He had certain accomplishments, to be sure, but he had no core, no solidity, nothing in his character which equipped him to meet the vicissitudes of life head on. His first inclination, whenever things got difficult, was to run away and bury his head in the sand. So, as his mother, I worried greatly for his future.'

'And what do you say changed on the occasion of his alleged betrothal to Miss Goodwin?'

'I don't know why you use the word "alleged", Mr Boden. There was, and is, no doubt that my son and Miss Goodwin were fully "betrothed",' she asserts defiantly. 'Not once, but twice,' she added. George nodded vigorously in agreement with his mother's assertion. A note arrived with me from George via the court official emphasising the point and referring to a letter he had written to Bessie at the time celebrating their God-witnessed attachment. I do not consider that it requires either a response or any action on my part.

'But coming to your question directly, Mr Boden, on becoming betrothed to Miss Goodwin everything changed – for the better. George showed a new zest for life. It was most wonderful for me as his mother to see. He was full of energy and optimism as to what life might hold for him, after all and in spite of his disadvantages. It was as if he was suddenly transformed from a chrysalis into a butterfly, fluttering in the sunlight. I should perhaps have known better, but I myself shared in his elation as an exciting and positive future with Miss Goodwin was dangled before him, and me. But though I liked her, Miss Goodwin, I always feared that she was not as keen on George as he was on her. I was not sure that she was quite serious about him, quite reliable. To be fair she was perhaps too young to be so. It was all too good to be true.' This last comment caused a murmur of agreement in the court.

'And then what happened, Mrs Townley?'

'I feared that it could all be short-lived, and so it did indeed prove to be. Out of the blue Bessie told George, in a letter of 31st August last year, on his return from France, that she did not wish to marry him after all and that was that, from her point of view. It was a disastrous finale. I find it difficult to understand exactly what happened after that but from what I could make out, at some point over the winter Bessie relented. She changed her mind again. This was in the early part of this year. Before I knew anything of it, they were apparently betrothed again. And George's optimism and zest for life returned and burned as brightly as it had done before, more so if anything.'

Mr Boden looked rather uninterested in the detail as to any renewal of the ties between the two and forged ahead with his next question.

'Tell us about the letter that came to George from Bessie in or about the middle of August of this year. When she broke things between them off – as she was surely quite entitled to do.'

'On 15th August this year an unexpected and, from my point of view, another most unwanted letter came for George from Bessie. It was a further cruel twist of fate. I read the letter before forwarding it to George. From what I recall Bessie wrote that she had a good deal to say and that it had better be said at once and she should have said it before now. She spoke of a clergyman who had been at Wigwell. She spoke of the clergyman as the most engaging and nicest man she had ever met. Her grandfather thought that he would just about suit her but Bessie herself said that she was not so sure that he would do. She said that her grandfather had found out that George and she had been corresponding and he would be wild if he thought there was anything in the way. She said that she wanted George to release her formally so that she might say that she was free. She said that he should not take this too hard in pity for her. At one point she wrote, "I still shall not marry if I can help it".' That was underlined, twice. It was signed "Yours affectionately".'

'What did you understand by the letter, Mrs Townley?'

'To be honest, Mr Boden …'

'That is what we expect here. Mrs Townley, honesty, at all times . . .'

'To be honest, Mr Boden, I found it a very confusing and muddled letter. It faced in opposite directions at the same time. She now liked the vicar more than George, but she also said that she did not intend to marry him, or anyone else, or so she said. Anyway, I felt obliged to forward the letter to George. I dreaded his reaction on reading it. I was sure that it would greatly distress him and, sure enough, it did.'

At this point, without being requested to do so she turned and addressed the jury directly, face to face. The impact of her words was magnified a hundredfold by this simple gesture. I myself was very much affected and had to hide my face behind a file. Mr. Boden, clearly put out that the witness was delivering a monologue out of his control, did not seem to quite dare to intervene.

'The effect on my George was instant, and terrible for me as his mother to behold when he returned home later that day. He behaved as if he were a dog which had been fatally wounded – he whined and whimpered. He said he felt as if his brain had been battered to a mush and he could not think straight about anything. He did not sleep at all for nights on end and he ate and drank nothing but a little tea and brandy which I had pressed upon him. I feared for his life. He was not safe to be left alone, I thought, and so I asked one of his acquaintances, I will not say friend as he did not really have friends, his acquaintance Washington Arrowsmith, to sleep in his bedroom with him. Washington is a kind boy and so he readily agreed to do this. He reported back to me that George was utterly despondent – indifferent as to whether he was dead or alive, preferring death to life if he was permitted to make a choice. It broke my heart, as his mother, to see him in such a terrible state. I was angry with Bessie – I know it was unworthy of me and I am sorry I must speak ill of the dead – but I . . . I was angry with Bessie for snatching George's future away from him, again, so brutally, and by letter, again – but what could I do? Nothing. She had spoken, again, and now we, his family, must try and pick up the pieces, again. I just hoped the trauma would pass without George becoming a permanent casualty of it – I hoped he might find a way through, a distraction or a venture in South America perhaps – but it was not to be, was it.'

Her statement was greeted by a hum of sympathy in court. George had suspended his furious note writing during the latter part of her evidence.

He was staring at his mother. The penny has dropped: at last, I thought to myself. I believe that I saw him wipe away a tear, but I cannot swear to this. He was certainly upset. I wondered whether or not the jury members had noticed – I rather doubted it. They had, like George and I, been transfixed by Mary's passionate declaration of love for her son. Not surprisingly perhaps, Mr Boden had no more questions. George quickly recovered himself and resumed his angry scribbling.

George's sister, Caroline, then stepped into the witness box. Like her mother she was dressed in deep mourning. I was nervous for her also, but she too began her evidence with firmness and composure. Mr Boden began again with the same strange hand gesture that he had used with her mother. It was almost like an offer of benediction!

'Miss Townley. I believe it is true to say that you were intimately acquainted with the deceased?' he asked in an oily manner.

'I would not necessarily say we were intimate but yes we became close; we were on good terms, for a while.'

'But she would confide in you, would she not? That is what I meant by intimate.'

'Yes, she did confide in me at one time. I do not think she had many other sources of advice.'

'And how did you find her?'

'It's a hard question for me to answer now, dispassionately, given all that has happened since.'

'Do your best. We cannot hear from Bessie herself, sadly and you are the nearest we can get.'

'I think that she meant well; she was kind, and she was generous to those who had little. But when it came to standing up to her peers, she could be less reliable. She could rather blow in the wind, blow hot and cold. She was wary of her grandfather, that I do know. She wanted to please him. Or at least pacify him. But at the same time, she wanted to live her own life, she wanted to live a meaningful life, not just a leisured and respectable one. He was more concerned that she did the right thing and did nothing which might compromise the family's reputation. So there was an in-built tension there between them which, at times, was palpable.'

'You had a falling out with Bessie, when she broke off the betrothal to your brother?'

'I would not say we had a falling out, Mr Boden. Bessie was a difficult person to fall out with. Rather, we drifted apart, things became cooler between us. And the second time she became betrothed to George I was a lot more wary. Once bitten, twice shy, you might say.'

'Tell us then about the letter from Bessie in August. What did you make of that?'

'When consulted by Mother about it I also found the letter to be contradictory and confused. Its contents reeked of coercion and a lack of free will. It indicated a change of heart again but at the same time felt contrived and distant, as if it had been dictated to her by another – her grandfather, perhaps? He was criticised in the letter but maybe that was just a bluff – he is cunning enough for that? That's what I thought at the time, leastways.'

She is, gently, ticked off by the judge for her speculation as to the author.

She continued thus. 'I knew Bessie could be contrary, as I have said, but even so her letter did not ring true to me. That was why I encouraged George to visit and meet Bessie and to have it out with her. To find out the truth. I thought that George visiting Derbyshire would at least resolve the position, one way or the other. Like Mama I feared for my brother's welfare if the matter came out on the wrong side.'

A further note duly arrived with me from George – 'If Bessie did not compose that letter, then who did? This is evidence of the conspiracy I have long spoken of and **MUST** be exposed at all costs.' I passed the note to junior counsel. He read it and shrugged his shoulders. He did not show the note to his principal. Meanwhile I could see out of the corner of my eye that Mr Boden from the parallel benches was craning his neck to try and read what George had written. Accordingly, I retrieved the note and laid it face down on the table before me. Mr Boden immediately looked away red-faced and proceeded to study intently the plaster reliefs decorating the court ceiling.

'But yes, I think, in retrospect, I did wrong in pressing George to meet Bessie. I suppose that is to state the obvious, given what happened. The tragedy. But what I mean is this – and I will choose my words as carefully as I can out of respect for the dead – I think perhaps Bessie was not as straightforward with me as she might have been – about George I mean, where he stood in her affections, and about the person she now carried a torch for. She did not even mention him to me. Had I realised at the time the true state of things I do not think I would have recommended the interview take place. I know I would not have done. And had I opposed the idea George may not have travelled to Whatstandwell but stayed at home with Mama and me and we could have protected and comforted him – just as we have done before. And maybe we would not all be here today trying to pick up the pieces. So you can see, Your Honour, that it was all my fault. The whole sorry mess is my fault. I will always blame myself. I was too trusting, too naive. I let George down and for that I am truly sorry. Now it is all out of our hands. We cannot protect him any further. His fate is in the hands of the jury. I only hope that you can find it in your hearts to treat him as gently as you would your own kin if they were to be as terribly afflicted.'

She became visibly upset at this point, looking with desperation across to her brother, who did not even acknowledge her but instead wrote another furious note which, however, never reached me. The ever-gallant Mr Boden reluctantly decided not to pursue his questioning of the young woman further and she was released, sobbing, directly into her mother's arms.

XXI

A Visitor

෴

18th August 1863

Unfortunately, in the event, Will's carefully thought-out strategy fails. It becomes clear that George is not going to give Bessie up without a determined rearguard action.

A reply arrives in the post on the 18th and is brought to her by Ann. Bessie, with a heavy heart, recognises George's handwriting and anxiously tears open the envelope, almost destroying the letter in the process. The letter states that George has plans to emigrate permanently to Cuba as he has an offer of employment from a Mr A.K. Thompson, a prominent South American merchant known to his father. It would mean that he would have to leave England. But, before he does so, he wishes to see her once again and for the last time, *'though God knows what misery it will cause me'*. He would, accordingly, arrive by the first or second train from Derby on Friday the 21st instant, staying at the Midland the previous night. She could meet him at the inn at Whatstandwell Bridge if she preferred this. Otherwise, he would come to the house either directly or after he had been to the vicarage to see the Reverend ... *'as I have some unfinished business with him'*. The letter writer concluded that it was undoubtedly better for both parties that the matter was settled once and for all.

With a rising sense of panic, and on advice from William, Bessie writes straight back to George.

GV Townley Esq.
Hendham Villas, Hendham Vale, Manchester
Immediate.
18th August 1863

My dear George,
I write this in the greatest haste to tell you not come on any account. I leave here today and can't tell when I shall or can be back again. I do not wish to see you, if it can possibly be avoided and indeed there will be no chance now, so we had better end this state of suspense at once and say 'Goodbye' without seeing you. I feel sure I could not withstand the meeting. If you write back to me by return, I may get it but not later than this time without it being seen, for my letters are watched, and even opened. God bless.
Yours truly
Bessie

No reply is received to this letter and therefore Bessie is left in the dark as to whether or not George might or might not visit Wigwell on the Friday. She has, despite what she has said in the letter, no intention of leaving Wigwell. Besides, where would she go? She prays George does not come, but she fears that he will.

She awakes on Friday morning to a fine summer's day. Ann delivers her breakfast to her on a tray, complete with a pretty vase containing a garden posy of pink roses and purple and white petunias she had picked at dawn. She proceeds to open the curtains, a little over enthusiastically perhaps, so that sunlight invades the room and momentarily blinds Bessie. After a brief feeling of euphoria at the beauty of the morning, and pleasure at the flowers that Ann has so thoughtfully picked for her, Bessie remembers what the day could hold for her and is left to contemplate the possible arrival of her visitor with a feeling of dread. Will had offered to stay on with her and to chaperone any meeting but she had said that it was better to meet George alone, should he visit her. Will's presence was likely only to provoke and excite him. Will did not press the point quite as much as she had hoped that he might. She had seen Will off from Whatstandwell yesterday when they both had been reduced to tears. There was an unspoken assumption between them that once the 'George problem' had been finally resolved there should be no further obstacle to their betrothal. She had, by now, disclosed to Will that her grandfather was not entirely ill-disposed to the idea, indeed he expected to be asked the question.

Their earlier differences having long since been forgotten she had also visited the Reverend Harris to tell him that he might expect a visit from George shortly. He had grimaced but had said nothing and asked no questions of her as to why she thought this likely, or what she expected him to say to George.

After picking at her breakfast Bessie dresses, with the help of her maid, and then heads downstairs to the drawing room, expecting to read, as usual, from the *Derby Mercury* to her grandfather. Not being at all interested in local news unless he himself was mentioned, he generally prefers that she begin with the classified advertisements on the front page and expects her to select for him some of the more interesting and/or amusing ones. She finds it hard to enter into the spirit of this, on this morning of all mornings, but she gamely selects a few, including an advertisement for a 'miracle' gout medicine which she, teasingly, offers to purchase a lifetime supply of for him. Her heart is not in the task, however, and her grandpa, noticing that she looks tired, suggests that she retire to her room for a rest for an hour or two rather than carrying on reading to him.

Bessie gratefully agrees to this suggestion and retires to her bedroom but is unable to rest. She spends the next couple of hours imagining what her final exchanges with George might be like. As was her habit she rehearses her responses in front of her mermaids but, again, they are not interested. She tries to cheer herself up by imagining what it will feel like in a few hours' time, when she has finished with George and she is able to settle down for the evening, having unburdened herself of him once and for all. It will be such a relief. It will be bliss.

XXII

A Captain

❦

5/8/72
Fred, the trial continues . . . stormy waters!
Brace yourself!
Father

It was the appearance in the witness box on 11th December of the apparently frail Captain Francis Goodwin, questioned on George's behalf by defence counsel, Mr Macaulay QC, retained by me at considerable public expense, which caused most excitement to counsel, to myself and to the county as a whole (when rendered word for word in the papers the following morning). It is not necessary for me to repeat much of the content here as Captain Goodwin largely expressed the same robust views as he had in his statement – I will say here only that he came 'fully up to proof' as we lawyers say. A short extract only is sufficient to illustrate that the tone was menacing on both sides and that it more resembled a gladiatorial combat than the calm and respectful cross-examination expected in an English courtroom.

Mr Macaulay:

'I will go straight to the point: Captain Goodwin, during your discussions, exchanges with him on 21st August, the prisoner handed you some letters, did he not?'

Captain Goodwin replies, 'He did, yes.'

'They were letters addressed to the prisoner, were they not?'

'I believe they were, yes.'

'How many letters?'

'Two packets with about 8 to 10 letters in each. But I did not count them, Mr Macaulay.'

'Quite so. But the letters, they were in your granddaughter's hand, in her handwriting?'

'I think … yes, well the envelopes were. I cannot speak for the letters inside them.'

'Quite so. Do you have the letters now? Can you produce them here, to the Court?'

'You know very well that I cannot.'

'Why not?'

'Because, as you are also very well aware, Mr Macaulay, I burnt the letters in the grate at Wigwell Grange.'

'You burnt them? Can I ask you why you burnt your granddaughter's letters? They would have been of such assistance to us here, to understand her actions, her side of the story, to know what she was feeling at the relevant times.'

'I am afraid I cannot very well explain it to you. And I do not feel that I should have to. It is family business. It is private and confidential.'

The judge intervened again.

'I am sorry, Captain Goodwin but you must answer counsel's questions. Yes, Mr Macaulay?'

'Thank you, My Lord. Perhaps I can assist the court by putting the question this way. You sought to protect your granddaughter's reputation, perhaps? You were worried she might not come out of this whiter than white. Or you burnt them to protect your own? I wonder if you have perhaps burned any other documents either then, or later, that might have been of interest to this court? I would remind you, sir, that you are currently on oath.'

'I beg your pardon – what are you saying? I most certainly did not burn anything else that day.'

The Captain was, by now, white-faced with anger.

'And what about on any other day?'

'Certainly not. What sort of documents do you have in mind, Macaulay? Do enlighten me, please. What do you take me for – a pyromaniac of some sort?'

Captain Goodwin turned to appeal to the judge.

'This is an outrage, Your Honour. Do I have to stand here and be insulted by this snipe of a barrister? Here is a man who thinks nothing of seeking to exculpate that fiend over there who murdered my granddaughter in cold blood, a man who is only concerned with the size of his own fee, who seeks to defend the indefensible and who think it is fair game to make some pathetic insinuations about my actions and my granddaughter's honour? I have done what any guardian or parent would do in my situation, no more and no less. He keeps saying, ad nauseam, that he is not wanting to cast aspersions on her. And then he uses his weasel questions to malign her all the same. Mr Macaulay says, "Far be it from me to say anything which would be calculated to be in the least disrespectful respecting the young lady herself" but then he goes on to do precisely that by suggesting that "the same poor young lady was given to deception." Your Honour, this is disrespectful to the dead, my late departed kin; it is not right, and it is not just and I will not tolerate it—'

The judge intervened yet again.

'Calm yourself, Captain Goodwin – allow me to decide what is just and what is not in my own court; that is my responsibility here. But I do think you have gone far enough on this tack, Mr Macaulay, further than I should have let you go, perhaps. Kindly withdraw your last remarks and apologise to Captain Goodwin immediately.'

'Very well, I happily withdraw them, My Lord and I do so apologise …'

Captain Goodwin's behaviour can be excused on account of the trauma he has recently endured. The conduct of defence counsel cannot. It was not the strategy he and I had agreed in our pre-trial conferences. I could not for the life of me see how impugning Captain Goodwin's motives in destroying Bessie's letters would work to our advantage in terms of our long-term objective of preserving George's life. What was he thinking of? Maybe, in this instance, I should defer to leading counsel's over-sized brain. But I don't think so. It was a case of a dog not being able to let a bone go. I had tugged furiously on Mr Macaulay's gown but he did not desist, or even acknowledge me. It was humiliating. I felt like a helpless bell ringer whose bell, lacking a clapper, made not a sound despite his furious efforts.

XXIII

An Apology

❦

22nd August 1863 one am

Grandfather lies awake in bed at Wigwell, rigid with despair.

It is not a state that I am used to seeing him in but there again yester-day's tragedy, I suppose that I, of all people, may fairly call it that, is beyond anyone's comprehension.

Grandpa is reliving the ghastly sequence of events again and again in his mind even as he tries, in vain, to rest.

He relives that macabre procession coming round the corner of the turnpike carrying a wrapped-up body which was then, unbelievably, revealed to be my own.

He relives instinctively and desperately grasping hold of Poyser's hand to seek some comfort. It was unthinkable in normal circumstance that he should do anything like that. How kind Ann had been to him then, as always.

He relives George confessing and of his instant decision to escort George to the library, a brief stopping off point on the way, he devoutly hoped, to the scaffold.

He relives his bitter exchanges with Townley whilst they waited for the constable to arrive.

Most of all he frets over lying in his comfortable bed in his comfortable bedroom whilst I lie downstairs in the kitchen on a hard table normally used for the preparation of vegetables. He is fully aware of the absurdity of his concerns. And yet he still feels a deep desire to do something about it. He is not sure what. I am not unmoved by his dilemma.

He resolves to go downstairs and see what he can do to help me. This, in itself, is not straightforward. He is not used to creeping about his own house at the dead of night, or to frequenting the kitchen at any time. He lights a candle lantern from the bedroom fire's embers and makes his way slowly downstairs, trying to avoid any creaking stair that might give him away. Reaching the bottom of the stairs unscathed he then feels his way down the corridor towards the further set of steps which lead down to the kitchen, successfully negotiating also the library to collect a cushion on the way. In exiting the library, he bumps into my chaise longue which he swears at.

All this takes a lot longer than, he feels, it should do – it must look a lot easier, he supposes, from above and his progress must look painfully slow. It does, I can assure you of that. I observe his clumsiness with amusement and would, in normal times, have teased him for it.

He tries to restrain his emotions but cannot stop himself from uttering a deep and unworldly sob as he recalls how I became as I now am. I am surprised to observe that he is then powerless to prevent a further loud moan from escaping his being.

Eventually he finds his way into the kitchen. He puts out his candle, which has very nearly expired in any event. It is unnecessary now. For moonlight penetrates the kitchen with unusual vigour, as if it is determined to locate and highlight my corpse. I am astonished to see that I glow white in the dark. He approaches me slowly, half dreading, I think, that I may suddenly burst back into life and reprimand him, or, worse still, rise up to pardon him. I cannot do either since I became as I now am. But I notice that he does not dare turn his back on me, just in case. He gently lifts my cold stiff head. He places the cushion under my head with some difficulty. He stands back and gazes at my smooth staring face trying to make out whether any vestige of me remains, but he can identify none.

'I wanted to come down and make you more comfortable, my dear,' he says. 'That's of no consequence now, I know. You may feel that I have done you a terrible wrong,' he whispers. 'If I have, and I don't really know whether I have or not, then I have only done so out of kindness and concern. Yet that does not excuse any mistakes I may have made. I know that.' By this time I am amazed to see that he has lowered himself to his knees before me. I am sure that the combination of his old bony knees and the hard tiled floor make this a not inconsiderable ordeal. 'I am a crusader,' he murmurs, 'kneeling before an unknown foreign altar, seeking absolution before battle. But it is too late for the battle. And much too late for any absolution.' Then, unsurprisingly, he becomes more truculent. 'I only wanted to protect you, to help you make a good marriage. Was that so wicked? I have been so catastrophically punished and for what? Being a conscientious guardian to you? Don't forget it was I who took you in when your feckless father announced, on the death of your mother, that he could not care for you and, what is more, he did not wish to do so. It was I who brought you up as a good Christian girl. It all feels most unfair. I wish now that I had not tried to interfere so much, that we had not had such secrets between us, that you had not felt it necessary to keep so much from me. It was your secrets that killed you, wasn't it? Things might have played out so very differently. You would have married Will, I expect, and hopefully lived here with him, or somewhere within striking distance. That way I might even have got to see my great-grand-children play in my gardens, climb the trees, play croquet. How I wish that that could have been. And now what is left to me? Very little. But more than there is for you, I know. Not for you even that terrible consola-tion prize of virginal garlands and well-laundered gloves proclaiming the innocent and blameless death of their owner, though you richly deserve both garland and gloves and more. I must hang on. I will still defend your honour, and that of our family and do whatever it takes to do so. You would expect no less, I am sure. You might be interested to know that I made a start on that yesterday, as a matter of fact. I will still seek justice for you and will do whatever it takes to get this. That will be my crusade from this moment on. I will gain strength from knowing that there were those who loved you. I will love you more now than I ever showed you I did in your lifetime, before you became what you are now.' The Captain fell silent. Having delivered his valedictory speech, to so little obvious appreciation from me, he felt empty and hollow and spent and unable even to cry.

I, for my part, could not deny that most of what he had said was true. Now was the time for love and not for revenge. I had done what I could to help – before I became as I now am.

XXIV

A Defence

❧

10th August 1872

F
The last instalment of the trial, no rest for the wicked!
P
The prosecution had wrapped things up by lunchtime. In the afternoon Counsel for the defence, Mr James Macaulay QC, learning from the amateur dramatics of the prosecution, also deployed the pause to some effect. But first he ticked off the prosecution for not, as they had promised they would do, presenting all of the facts and not just some of them. They had presented the facts that favoured their case only, he said. They had called the witnesses that, they felt, would further the prosecution case but had not called those who might not. In short, they had played only lip service to the rules and not lived up to their own grand promises. This last assertion caused considerable consternation to Boden, who snorted noisily. The judge silenced him with a single look.

Mr Macaulay then announced that, in order to compensate for the serious deficiencies of the prosecution case, he intended to call a waiter at the County Hotel to give evidence. He would give evidence, in particular, as to Townley's demeanour when he had seen him there in the days prior to the murder, particularly as, and here Mr Macaulay paused for effect . . . 'particularly as he will help prove to you that the unhappy young man who stands before you was then and is now, by the mysterious dispensation of Providence, wholly deprived of his reason. This means, as you will know, according to the jurisprudence of this country, and of every civilized country in the world, he is not amenable to the processes of the criminal law, least of all to its ultimate sanction . . . In short he cannot, and should not, be hanged.'

These last remarks of Mr Macaulay caused such excitement in court that even His Lordship was not immediately able to subdue the hubbub. He was only able to do so after threatening the main offenders with a night in the cells. The reaction was understandable, however, as now the cat was well and truly out of the bag. George sat bolt upright in the dock but did not otherwise react to the suggestion by his own barrister that he was, indeed, mad. However, a close observer sitting reasonably near to him, as I was, might have detected, as I did, a flicker of anger cross his face and the merest hint of a clenching and then unclenching of his fists.

The head waiter at the Midland County Hotel, Mr John Alexander Grew, was called. On being asked to confirm his name and occupation he was so busy grinning broadly in turn at his inquisitor, at George, at the jury and at the court in general that he had then to be reminded to do so. He was evidently a rather jovial character of the 'hail-fellow-well-met' school, dressed smartly but with rather too prominent a pin stripe in his suit and sporting a handlebar moustache, extravagant sideburns and a larger than average bow tie. He wore his suspiciously jet-black hair slicked back. He was asked to explain his first contact with George.

'Mr Townley stayed with us on the night of 20th August. He had not stayed at our hotel before, as far as I am aware. As soon as he arrived, he asked if there were any letters for him. I replied that there were none. At breakfast the following morning he again asked if there were any letters for him and I had to tell him again that, regretfully, there were not. He asked me where the smoking room was but then when I told him he turned round and said, 'I don't want to know where the smoking room is. Why are you telling me this when I know where it is already?' I took his reply in my stride, but I noticed that he looked extremely pale, as if suffering from a serious illness, and there was a strange, wild expression in his eyes. He was muttering to himself and throwing his arms about in a curious manner. It was all very peculiar. I wondered if he was not exactly right in his mind. In my own mind I felt that he might not be.'

'Did you share your concerns with any other member of staff?

'Yes, with another waiter, my subordinate, Mr Ellis. He, too, thought his behaviour was most odd. But as I'm sure you realise, Mr Macaulay, our clientele tends to be mainly gentle folk who are more advanced in years. So we get our fair share of eccentrics and have learnt to tolerate their odd ways and to be discreet as to their peculiar habits. So that is what we put it down to in Mr Townley's case. Not that he was old. He was, he is, a young man but the old do not have a monopoly of eccentricity, individuality, and a reluctance to conform, do they? So that's what we put it down to, at least until the events of later in the morning. Would you like me to describe these also? It is absolutely no trouble whatsoever for me to do so. I think you may find them of interest.'

There was a suppressed laugh in the court.

'Please do.'

'Yes, well, on his departure Mr Townley was presented with a small glass flask of brandy engraved with 'Midland Hotel, Derby' set inside a fastened belt round the edge of the bottle. This is something which all guests are offered by the hotel as a keepsake of their stay and to provide some spiritual sustenance for whatever journey awaits them. I say he was presented with it but in fact Mr Townley grabbed the bottle from me before I had the chance to do so. He must be thirsty, I thought to myself. He pulled out the cork and, without taking a second look, glugged down the contents in one go. He then demanded a further flask be supplied to him immediately. When this was done the contents met the same fate. He must very thirsty, I thought. (Laughter.) I felt obliged to decline his animated request for a third flask, which refusal he did not take at all well, cursing me and my staff in a most unnecessary way. I was not offended personally though his behaviour strengthened my view, our view, that he was not of sound mind.'

Mr Boden rose majestically, not unlike a cresting whale, to cross-examine Mr Grew. I imagine, Fred, that you can anticipate what his first question was. I am sure that even as an apprentice advocate it would have been your first question too?

'Mr Grew, could you please confirm what medical qualification you hold that has enabled you to come to such a firm view as to Townley's sanity, or rather lack thereof? Just your main qualifications will do.'

'I have no medical qualifications,' Mr Grew replied.

'Quite so, no medical qualifications at all. None?'

'Indeed. I have just said so, have I not. Perhaps you did not hear me? I thought I had spoken up.'

Mr Boden paused triumphantly. He thrust his hands into his waistcoat pockets and patted his not inconsiderable stomach. He then made the fatal mistake of asking one further question. I am sure, Frederick, that you would not have done so. Better to leave the jury wanting more than to overegg your cross-examination. Better not to ask a question that you do not certainly know the answer you will provoke. It was a schoolboy error.

'So when you say, Mr Grew,' (here he makes a show of consulting his junior's voluminous notes) 'that Townley was not of sound mind, when you say there was a strange, wild expression in his eyes, when you say that he was muttering to himself and throwing his arms about in a curious manner, when you say he looked extremely pale, as if suffering from a serious illness, you say all this from the standpoint of one who has no medical training or knowledge whatsoever? Am I right, Mr Grew? And if I am right, why should the jury take the slightest notice of your evidence?'

Mr Grew seemed unperturbed by the question and continued to grin broadly at his inquisitor. It was almost as if he had anticipated the jibe and was looking forward to delivering his counterpunch.

'You are right, Mr Boden, I have no medical expertise. But I know what I saw, and I have told you what I saw and, though I hesitate to boast of it, what I do have is a great deal of common sense and knowledge of the real world. These are virtues I myself value but which I imagine, sir, are not necessarily a key requirement of your own profession. They are, however, a necessity in my more humble station in life.'

This latter observation caused merriment in court. I observed that even the Baron smiled. Mr Boden, predictably, was not about to share in a joke made at his own expense and sat down grumpily. Thus the cresting whale, having reached the zenith of its leap, crashed back clumsily into the sea, spraying spume in all directions.

Then came the real doctors. In the only act of Providence that had favoured us in this case Dr Hitchman was sadly unable to attend to give the court the benefit of his views, owing to a vicious attack of the gout, and so the case for George's lack of sanity relied on the two doctors that I had previously ascertained were likely to provide much more helpful opinions.

Dr Forbes Winslow gave evidence first. He had examined the prisoner on two occasions – in November and just before the trial. He said that he found the prisoner to be thoroughly deranged on both occasions. His diagnosis was largely based on Townley's patently absurd belief that he considered Miss Goodwin to be his own property and so he had an inalienable right to deal with her as he had to deal with any of his property, such as the money in his pocket, the furniture in his house or the pictures on his walls. This last assertion brought gasps of disbelief from the large number of members of the female sex present in court. Townley himself had resumed his previous impassive state. During the second interview Townley had also claimed to have been the victim of a conspiracy with a chief conspirator at the head. He had alleged that there were six conspirators plotting against him, that this conspiracy was still going on. He had no doubt they would still go on with this until he was dead and buried. During this interview he became extremely excited with a wild maniacal aspect typical of an insane mind. The doctor had in fact stopped the interview prematurely because of this wild behaviour, which made it unsafe to continue. Townley had said to him that it was a matter of indifference to him whether he was dead or alive. A man so casual as to his own fate could hardly be expected to care much about the fate of others, including his physician. He was undoubtedly insane, but he was also a danger to himself and to others as well. But all that did not justify him being hanged. In his professional opinion. He was dangerous but he was also, in layman's parlance, barking mad.

The second doctor was Henry Francis Gisborne, surgeon to the county gaol. His evidence largely supported that of his colleague. He confirmed that in his view Townley was of unsound mind and that his mind had lost its balance at the moment of committing the crime, with a prior propensity to insanity lying dormant in his sorry family inheritance. The doctor went on to particularise this inheritance, being sure to include the episodes of the white hats and the unusual bathing apparel. This propensity was, he explained, as a sleeping serpent waiting to be poked. Once roused the serpent would strike with uncontrolled ferocity only to be calm again, though not contrite, once its quarry had been eliminated.

Mr Boden was offered the opportunity to cross-examine both doctors but declined to do so. He was probably still vexed by his failed attempt to intimidate the head waiter.

Then came a gamble. We decided not to call George to give an account of himself. He would not have been allowed to give evidence on oath in any case as this is not permitted of any defendant under our archaic and absurd procedural rules. Fancy letting the accused tell his own side of the story, Fred – what an outrage to justice that would be. The very idea! Yes, a defendant might lie on oath but so might any witness with or without a vested interest. The distinction the law draws offends against the basic principles of justice, do you not agree?

Even so George had wanted to speak, indeed he was desperate to do so. But in a rare example in this case of defence barristers and defence solicitor being of one mind we strenuously opposed it. We had weighed up the factors for and against and took the view that there was little or no advantage to be gained. I wonder if you would have followed the same strategy, Fred? Our thinking was, firstly that he would only have been allowed, at the discretion of the judge, to make an unsworn statement, if anything at all. That would carry little weight with the judge, the jury and, most of all, with Mr Boden, who would have mocked its status mercilessly, whatever the content. If George did make an unsworn statement from the dock he might speak well and cogently and therefore appear to be sane. Or (more likely) he might give full rein to his delusional beliefs concerning Miss Goodwin and her grandfather and his 'conspirators' in which case he stood to be roundly condemned as downright wicked, not just mad. I produced the classic example of the swimming of witches to try and bolster my argument with Townley. I am sure, Fred, you are familiar with this medieval trial by water, thankfully long since discredited? If, when subjected to a ducking in a river, a witch drowned, then they had not been a witch and were innocent. But if they did not drown then they must have deployed a witch's powers to survive and consequently deserved to be put to death. However, George dismissed my witches' analogy out of hand as strained and irrelevant. On reflection I rather tend to agree with him! He did eventually consent to remaining silent. He recognised that he had already made an unsworn statement of sorts, immediately after the murder out on the highway and look what a pickle that had got him into!

So the decision was announced, again to gasps of disappointment from those assembled, that George would not make a statement on his own account. Mr Boden will, of course, have welcomed any potential foreshortening of the trial. He would be relaxed at not being allowed to submit George to a devastating cross-examination, as he was surely dying to do, as the rules would not have allowed that anyway.

We had also considered calling the young Reverend – to illustrate to the jury the profound trauma that George had suffered as a result of the whims of Cupid. When I had eventually tracked him down, he was, it is only fair to say, prepared to be involved but only if he was really required.

He was not keen to do so, least of all as a defence witness. He stressed that he would only attend trial if his attendance was deemed as absolutely essential. He did not say so, but I formed the impression that he was (entirely understandably) very conscious of the risks that being a witness at such a public and well reported hearing might pose to his reputation. He wrote an emotional letter to me after I had interviewed him, in which he extolled Bessie's virtues, stating that it was from a desire to do what was just and right and honourable that she had lost her sweet life and that her beauty, goodness and kindness had endeared her to all who knew her. Her cruel and early death had plunged many into hopeless misery and had thrown a fearful shadow over his own life and prospects. Following Bessie's death, he had taken up the role of a country parson at Old Rode near Congleton. It had proved to be not such a bad life, to be sure, but 'it was far from the in every way glorious existence that he would have enjoyed as Bessie's husband'. Even if he had been more enthusiastic it is doubtful that the defence would have called him. The risks of calling him as a witness were just too high – it could easily look like we were trying to demonise Bessie and we could not afford to do that, nor did I wish to. Or, alternatively, he could break down in front of the jury and demand that his dear Bessie's death should be avenged. That would be the 'coup de grâce' as far as our chances were concerned. The odds were massively stacked against us as it was.

Mr Boden was cheered by Mr Macaulay's declared intention on behalf of the defence to finish the case by the end of the day and, even more so, the following morning, by the robust approach to the question of insanity adopted by the judge in his summing up. Despite Mr Macaulay's strenuous protestations the judge outlined this robust version of the legal test of insanity for the jury.

One – Did the accused know the act would cause death?

Two – Did he know that the doing of it would subject him to legal responsibility and sanction?

The jury retired. I felt honour bound to visit my client in the cells, thinking that George would welcome some company in his hour of need. I should have known better. I had expected to find him anxious and alone, contemplating his future and nervous as to the impending verdict. Not a bit of it. He was lying out on the bench in his cell with his hands behind his head, discussing cricket of all things with his gaoler through the open cell door. His gaoler was extolling the talents of a 15-year-old by the name of Grace who last year had played against an All England team and performed very creditably. George was expressing the opinion that the youngster would go on to bigger and better things. The gaoler agreed and then informed him that Grace had just been selected in the last few days to play on a forthcoming tour of Australia. George professed himself very happy to hear this!

Eventually I managed to get a word in edgeways.

'So George, how did you feel things went, did you think we managed to get your case across well, adequately?'

George's tone immediately changed. He became visibly angry.

'Since you ask, Mr Leech, no, not adequately, Mr Leech. Not adequately at all. Frankly I thought it was a shambles from first to last. I never agreed that I should plead insanity, so I was appalled to hear that being raised on my behalf. Is there nothing in your professional ethics which prevents you raising a completely fictitious defence on your client's behalf? If there isn't then there damn well should be. I don't agree with the Captain on much but he was right about my QC – or rather the QC you had instructed on my behalf – he is a thorough guttersnipe and a disgrace to his profession. I can't think how you came to employ him!'

I was spared any more of George's assessment of Mr Macaulay's short-comings by a junior court official who arrived rather flustered to say that the jury was ready to return. They had been out for only six minutes! It did not bode well but I remained determinedly optimistic, thinking that perhaps they had been so convinced as to George's insanity that there was no point in discussing it ad nauseam. They had been empanelled over night at the Midland Hotel and the desire to get away today as soon as they could, would be a powerful incentive.

All parties slowly reassembled in court, caught by surprise by the brevity of the adjournment. The jury members re-entered the court two by two. They avoided making eye contact with anyone. At the invitation of Baron Martin, the Clerk of Arraigns, Mr Coleridge, then addressed their foreman. The foreman bore a sallow complexion, was trussed up in tweed and betrayed no emotion. A farmer, I surmised. Perhaps a neighbour of Captain Goodwin, I speculated.

'Gentlemen of the jury, have you reached a verdict on which you are all agreed?'

'We have, Your Honour, yes.'

'Do you find the defendant, George Victor Townley, guilty or not guilty of murder?'

There was a pause.

'Guilty, Your Honour.'

The judge intervened.

'Guilty. Very well. And is there any recommendation that you wish to add to your verdict?'

The foreman shook his head. 'There is not, Your Honour, no.'

'I see – no rider, and that is the opinion of you all?'

'Yes, it is, Your Honour, my fellow jury members and I are all agreed that the law should take its course, as quickly as custom should permit.'

A tremor of horror passed through the court as the full implications of the absence of a recommendation of mercy dawned on those present.

The judge, the jury, the bar, even the reporters present, as well as the general body of spectators, were deeply affected. Mr Coleridge was scarcely able to put to the prisoner the usual question. 'What have you to say why judgment of death should not be passed upon you?' But Townley was unmoved and stood up with alacrity to receive the judgment of the Court.

Baron Martin slowly donned his black cap. Not a cap as such, of course, but a simple plain square of black velvet. It perched awkwardly on the top of his full bottom wig. It evidently took a good deal of concentration on his lordship's part to keep it there.

'George Victor Townley, the jury have found you guilty of murder and I am bound to say it is a verdict with which I concur, for if it were to enter the mind of young men that, because a young woman was guilty towards them of unfaithfulness by breaking off a betrothal, they were thereby justified in taking her life, the consequences would be dreadful.

'Now I have one more duty only to perform. I have no discretion in the matter. I must pass the sentence of death upon you. I would urge you to take the opportunity which will be offered to you to make your peace with God during the short time you have left to live ... I do not mean to make any gratuitous comment on the case which might distress those who love you; but merely pass upon you that sentence which the law prescribes. Whatever may follow, will follow.'

The Baron Judge spoke these words with great difficulty, and then passed sentence in the customary form, but he was compelled to stop in the middle owing to what would be described in the papers the following day as 'an outburst of pent-up feeling'. Amidst sobs from the bench and every part of the Court, the sentence was at length concluded and the final 'and may the Lord have mercy on your soul' was followed by audible 'Amens' from all parts of the court. The prisoner was removed as speedily as possible from the dock to prevent a scene developing. Before he left the dock George bowed deeply to the Baron Martin. He bowed also to the Chief Constable whom he happened to pass by as he was escorted from the court.

It was a truly humbling experience. Never in my extensive time in practice had I heard of a judge and a court being overcome in this way. I could not help but admire Baron Martin for his humanity and his final comments gave me some hope. On the other hand, I had not imagined that known, as he is, as a kind man and a competent judge, he would take such a perversely narrow view of the law. According to the Baron's ruling one could be as mad as a hatter but still sane and deserving of hanging so far as the law was concerned. All that was necessary was for the offender to know that stabbing someone might well kill them, and that one would be hanged for the doing of it. It was a very low threshold. It took no account, apparently, of whether the individual could stop themselves or no – whether or not they could control their impulses. The law was, self-evidently, mad. On my return to the office I said as much to Gamble, who observed that the Lord moves in mysterious ways. He declined to elaborate on what he meant by that.

I resolved to redouble my efforts to ensure that George did not hang. Not for George's sake – who, if truth be told, I still heartily disliked. But for that of his poor mother and sister, my admiration for whom had only increased. This was an easy resolution to adopt but one that was a lot more difficult to achieve. I passed more than one sleepless night turning over and over in my mind the events at court. Those silverfish of mine were, naturally, having a field day. I re-lived, in particular, Judge Martin's comments – 'You have far safer ground to go on than that, Mr Macaulay.' What did he mean by that? Did it mean anything? 'Whatever may follow, will follow.' What would follow? His Lordship had been cryptic to the point of absurdity. He could not be asked now what he had meant. It was too late to do so: he was 'functus officio' as we lawyers call it; he had outlived his purpose.

Immediately after the conclusion of the trial I had collared Mr Macaulay on his way out of the court buildings with a view to trying to interest him in appealing the decision to a higher court. He had dismissed my idea out of hand, waving me away for having the temerity to trouble him with such trivia. Having secured his fee of 150 guineas for his trial brief I suspect he thought there was unlikely to be enough uplift to reflect the considerable extra effort that an appeal would necessitate.

In the absence of any appeal the execution date was set for 31st December, less than three weeks away. The clock was now ticking and its tick-tock, tick-tock was oppressively loud. It was all down to me now. No one else could save George . . .

XXV

A First Quandary

Ꙭ

15th August 1872

Dear Frederick,
It's your father again!
We now come to the first of those difficult ethical questions which I
hinted at earlier. Please don't judge me too quickly, or too harshly. As I
said when we began, context is everything. In this instance I have not had
to mine my memory to recall what happened as the letter referred is, for
the reasons set out herein, still in my possession.
Your (mostly) reliable Father
Samuel

19th December 1863
As Christmas approached there were rumours that not only had the
scaffold begun to be erected but also that a hangman, William Calcraft, in
a former life a butcher in Smithfield and so, obviously, well qualified for
the role, had been retained and put on notice of a potential customer for
New Year's Eve. Meanwhile George remained impassive and apparently
indifferent to his fate. At the conclusion of a desultory interview at the
gaol two days after the conclusion of the trial, George had thrust into my
hands a letter addressed to his mother and demanded I give it to her as
soon as reasonably convenient. I should not even have entertained accepting the letter. It was a grievous breach of prison regulations to do even
that. However, I was alarmed as to the potential impact on Mary of any
letter from George, given his state of mind and her state of distress, which
I had seen for myself at our regular meetings. My thinking was muddled.
I wished to see what he had to say to her. I did not trust the prison to pass
it on without considering its impact on her. I fully appreciate now that I
should never have accepted the letter. It was madness to do so. But at the

time it seemed the lesser of several evils. I kept the unopened letter on my desk for a further day whilst I agonised as to the right course of action. I was constantly aware of its brooding presence.

Eventually I decided to open the letter, read it for myself and then, and only then, decide what to do next. I opened the letter and read the following:

14th December 1863
Derby Prison

Dearest Mother,

My writing gets worse and worse partly I suppose from want of exercising it in here and partly from the steel pen I am obliged to use it being the only one available here; but you won't mind I dare say. The beginning of my words are legible, I think, and the end of them, but what happens in the middle is in the lap of the gods!

Letter writing paper is only issued on a Monday but that is no great inconvenience to me as I do not have anyone else I wish to write to. I am writing to wish you a happy birthday for the day after tomorrow. But what can I say to you any more for your birthday Mum. Little I fear to the purpose in terms of hopes and wishes. There is still 'love' I think, whatever that may mean, but would that my love and gratitude were in any way sufficient to repay you all for all that you have gone through for me. Instead, I must sit here as Job's comforter. A pretty way indeed to wish you many happy returns is this, isn't it? The fact is, Mum dear, as is usual with me, I am muddled. I turn my brain inside out and there is nothing there – it is stagnant and turgid. I can only give you my best – and kindest – 'love', and tell you that I am just as usual   no difference whatever. No better, no worse. Well certainly no better.

You must not trouble yourself about me or my state or about my future, unexpectedly short though it may now be. In the meantime, however long or short 'meantime' proves to be, it is only for me to continue to make do with the lack of a few personal comforts and being dressed queerly, but otherwise this wretched bit of clay eats, drinks and sleeps, even though it is for no earthly purpose. But for you it is wholly different and far worse.

I have tried to put myself in your place and I now understand better I think than I did how you must suffer. Remember it is not with me as with other men. I have no one depending on me. I have no cause to take thought for tomorrow. Were it not for the trouble that my present position causes you there would, I think, be little to regret. I keep my own counsel in here Mum. By going on the opposite tack it only puts a stick into the hands of one's fellow yahoos – brutes in human form – to break my skull with. And they would not take much provocation to do that. They know I am Bessie's killer, and they take very grave exception to that and I must always watch my back lest one of them seeks to gain increased personal popularity by striking me down. But you must not trouble yourself about me or my state: what we are all doing and what's the object of it, we can have no notion of. It looks very nonsensical, but that's no business of ours, and, at any rate, we have had nothing to do with it, and perhaps we really do only see the wrong side of the carpet. Past and future is beyond our control. Never mind what happens to my body – as you know law and society are keen to vent their spleen on that – and in the meantime I am condemned to spend my remaining days with such terrible, disagreeable people. I have no wish for you to be exposed to them. I wager that there is not a man in this prison of any responsibility who would not be heartily glad if the stupid and cruel mockery of visiting were totally done away with. After all one can say nothing at such an interview – it must be barren as well as upsetting.

And so that brings me to the most vital point. From something you said in your most recent letter I fancy that you and Kate are thinking of visiting soon. It is good of you and I don't know how to thank you, but, it _must not be._ I have told the governor so in no uncertain terms and he has said that my wishes will be respected and will be 'recorded'. He has promised it in fact. I have told him also, in plain terms, what might happen were you or Kate to be allowed to do so. I am sorry to have to be so blunt and to have divulged what is really our own private business to the prison authorities but the very notion of you or my sister being within these walls or in contact with this place in any shape or way is torment to me and is infinitely worse than anything else I have to bear either now or am likely to have to bear in the future.

I would do _anything,_ to prevent it happening. So please do _not do so_ under any circumstances and however tempted you might, for the best possible motives, be. Pardon me dear Mum if this is abrupt. I would *have said more and said it more kindly but I have no space. After all one can say nothing of any value at such an interview even if we were to meet – it must be pointless or, at the least, unsatisfactory. It risks re-opening old wounds and I cannot face that. My fate will be what it will be and I embrace it but I do not wish to see your distress – it is selfish of me I know but I must shut it out of my mind if I am to remain sane. So please let us not speak or write of this again. In fact let it be as if I have never even written to you on the subject!*

To change the subject to something much more pleasant I want to thank you for the books the governor brought me from you- 'Gil Blas' and 'Silvio Pellico.' I am charmed with the latter. Do you know that he sometimes reminds me of you? 'Gil Blas' I have also nearly finished and laughed out loud over. Do please keep your books coming! I would say they are a tonic but really I have no need for tonics here.

I end by wishing my darling mother as many happy returns as is possible with such an unlucky wight as me as her son.

Yours, always

Your affectionate son,

George Townley

I read George's letter two or three times before replacing it in the envelope. I was sure in my own mind that this was not a letter that any mother should have to read from her own son, let alone a mother struggling to maintain her sanity, against all the odds. Even so I panicked, uncertain what to do next. Had it really been right for me to take it on myself to hold the letter back, given its contents? By that time my agonising was more or less academic – the reference to his mother's imminent birthday made it very difficult for me now to reseal the letter and present it to her and try and explain the delay, even if that was what I resolved to do. I was well and truly implicated. If I now returned the letter to Mr Sims, I was pretty sure that he would take a dim view of the letter and would block it being given to Mrs Townley anyway and so defeat its main purpose. He would find some flimsy reason for doing so. He might decide, for example, that it was written too closely, written between the lines (which it was). 'Prisoners may write as fully as they like but must confine themselves to writing only within the lines, not outside of them.' That was the rule. The letter fell foul of this rule. Sims would declare this a matter of principle and that would be the end of the matter. Townley would be informed, and penalised, and would know that I had failed him, at a critical moment. He would never trust me again. Mrs and Miss Townley would never see the letter anyway and would remain ignorant as to its contents.

But, in addition, Mr Sims would likely start an investigation into how the letter had passed out of the prison. The finger would point to me. There was no one else in the frame. This worried me greatly and sent me off into one of the downward spirals that I have told you about before. I would have a lot of explaining to do and the Law Society would, no doubt, take a dim view of the matter. As well as being struck off I might even find myself being prosecuted for a misfeasance. I shuddered at the prospect. That way led personal disaster and ignominy. Oh the irony! How much would Mr Boden QC relish my prosecution. He would positively slaver, labrador like, at the prospect. He might even waive part of his fee to take account of the pure pleasure of taking part in my humiliation. Mr Sims, normally a decent enough fellow, would be superhuman if he did not secretly relish the spectacle of me having to slop out. My incipient dream of one day becoming the Mayor of Derby would be history.

I tried to pull myself together. I drew comfort from the fact that retaining the letter should have no catastrophic impact given the formal recording of George's feelings on the matter of a visit. I therefore resolved to burn the letter in my grate at the office. There would then be no evidence of what I had done. George was never likely to be in a position to accuse me and who would believe a convicted felon anyway? It was the obvious thing to do. And yet. And yet. Even in my heightened state, I could not bring myself to do so. It was one step too far for a previously law-abiding solicitor. I could not bring myself to actually destroy evidence. Instead, I brought the letter home and secreted it away in the volume I have referred to previously. That is where it remains to this day. I try to forget that it is there. Most of the time I succeed. That is until you persuaded me to relive my experiences, when those silverfish became a writhing mass of recrimination and self-doubt. I have had to fetch out the letter and re-read it so I could relay the contents to you. I have felt ghastly all over again.

But back to my story. In the short term I now had brought upon myself the difficult task of dissuading Mary from visiting her son in prison but without explaining exactly why. This would necessitate exceptional dissembling on my part. The deception was not going to be easy as George was languishing in a condemned cell and a mother's strong and natural inclination would be to rush to her son and to do anything that she could to improve his situation. Logically, though, the only means of real improvement lay in my hands and not in hers and she was plenty intelligent enough to realise that. That thought provided me with the solution of what to tell Mary.

On 19th December, a few days after her birthday, I visited her at her home in Manchester, a smart, recently built double-fronted villa situated in the outskirts of the city. I wished her many happy returns for last Wednesday! She was pleasantly surprised that I knew when her birthday was! Pleasantries dispensed with I instructed Mary not to visit George at the present time. I forbade it. I stressed nothing must be done publicly to raise the dust whilst I was busy exploring what I mysteriously referred to as 'the usual channels' to try and seek the commutation of his sentence. Luckily Mary did not press me as to what these 'usual channels' were. Instead, she expressed her absolute confidence in me and so readily agreed to follow my counsel and not to visit. We both knew what kind of occasion any future visit would be unless I had managed to prevail. It was almost too easy to deceive her. It gives me no pleasure to say so, but it turns out I am a dab hand at lying to those I feel close to. It does not reflect well on me, I know. But my interview with Mrs Townley and her obvious distress increased the pressure on me to find a way forward. As if I needed to feel under any more pressure. I wished I shared her confidence in my ability to deliver a favourable outcome.

XXVI

A Second Quandary

e⌒⌢⌒o

19th August 1872

Thank you for your letter, sent by return, Frederick. I note that you disagree vehemently with my decision to retain the letter in question and that you express this view in the strongest possible terms. You have come disturbingly close to suggesting that you may have to report me yourself, retrospectively, to the Law Society. I admire the strength of your ethical standards, I really do. But I do think that you might show a little more compassion to those more error prone than yourself, i.e., me. I trust also that you do not have the gall to report your own father to the authorities. It would be tantamount to patricide!

I would say in my defence, as a defence is required, that I was there and you were not. There was a hard choice to make and, for better or worse, I made it. I am not ashamed of what I did, not this anyway. Is it condescending for me to observe that it is easier for the young to take the moral high ground when they have not yet had to experience first-hand the heat and chaos of battle? It's all very well for you sitting comfortably in your chambers, or down the road in the chop room of Ye Olde Cheshire Cheese, to pronounce as to what I should or should not have done. By the way I first wrote 'dine' instead of 'done' there! But there are human consequences to such decisions which cannot be ignored. I did warn you at the outset that not all my disclosures might make for comfortable reading. This is one such, but not the only instance I am afraid to say. The next one follows hard on and is just as serious, if not more so. I would suggest you gird your loins in anticipation of it now. By all means, sharpen your pen for another devastating critique of my shortcomings! I await your assessment with apprehension. Fortunately I did have the presence of mind to make a full note of what happened next, so I do not need to rely on my faulty memory!

⤳

On 22nd December, three days after my meeting with Mary, I received a most unexpected visitor to my chambers. I had wasted most of the afternoon wallowing in my continuing anguish at the Townley verdict and related matters but paralysed by uncertainty as to what I should do next. Anyway, just after 4 pm there was a knock at my door and Michael announced the arrival of an unscheduled visitor. He described the visitor as young and female and desperate to see me. He instantly had my full attention. He had not been able to find out from the young woman what her name was. She had refused to tell him. The most he had been able to prise out of her was that her visit touched on 'that dreadful Wigwell Grange business.' Although the lack of an appointment was most irregular I was, as you can imagine, intrigued both as to the identity of my caller and the reason for her visit.

'I will see her, Michael. In private,' I added as I could see he was more than slightly interested in our visitor and was angling to be asked to sit in.

I was most surprised to see that it was the servant Poyser who entered my office, dressed in what looked like her Sunday best.

Before I even had time to greet her properly, or to try and settle her down, as I could see she was nervous, she launched into the following monologue.

'My name is Poyser, Ann Poyser. You think you know me perhaps, sir? But you do not, least not as you think you do. This may come as a surprise to you, sir, but there are two of us Poysers at Wigwell: me, Ann, and my little sister Maggie, Margaret, who is 17. I am an old lady compared to her, having reached the ripe old age of 22, something she never lets me forget. She's the good-looking sister. I am the clever one. Oh and the kind one. So she says anyway! I can't really say if that's right or not. We are both housemaids at the Grange. No one, excepting Bessie, ever pays us much attention, or even knows us apart. We do look alike, as if we are twins some say, even though she is the better looking side of the coin, if you see what I mean? If you will allow me to say so, sir, we are both invisible to everyone, except dear Bessie. We are a part of the furniture, you might say. And not a very remarkable piece at that. Most like an old armchair, perhaps? A pair of armchairs, I mean. We just blend in. We are taken for granted. Maybe this doesn't matter too much normally. But it has maybe added to the confusion here, sir, and so I am here to put that right, or as right as it can be put, in the circumstances.'

I readily confess to not having appreciated myself until that point that there are two Poyser sisters working at Wigwell. I had not considered the possibility. There was no reason to do so. But I did now recall that this Poyser sister, Ann Poyser, had loitered after she had brought me tea at the Grange and before Captain Goodwin arrived for his interview. It had crossed my mind at the time that she might have a reason to remain. I kicked myself now for not having asked her then. At the same time I wondered what she could possibly have to say now that would be of interest and would justify her urgent need to see me. I had to bide my time but, as I am sure you can imagine Frederick, I was thoroughly impatient to know.

As if reading my mind Ann continued, at a faster rate than before.

'I say except Bessie. Bessie and I were more friends than mistress and maid. She confided in me. She talked to me as a person. She did not have a lot of choice in that. There were few people who she could confide in. Maybe George's sister, for a while. Bessie had lost her mother and never saw her father … Sorry I expect that you know all this, sir? As for her grandfather, well, you have met him haven't you, so I am sure you will realise why confiding in him was completely out of the question.

'We were more or less of an age, Bessie and me, and so over time we came to develop a close bond, a sisterly bond if you like. I am sure Maggie would not be too offended to hear me say that I felt closer to Bessie than I did to my own kin. You would know all this if you had bothered to ask. But you didn't, did you? Nor did anyone else so you should not feel too badly.

'So when it came to police and lawyers and evidence and such like it was Maggie, my younger sister, who was the only of us Poysers who was asked to make a statement and, later, to give evidence at the trial. I was not involved at all. No one came to see me to see what I had to say. I wondered why at the time. I thought, at first, it might have to do with Maggie and I being muddled up. But I now think there was another reason. A darker one. I'll come to that in a moment. Even Maggie was only asked, so she told me, what time the prisoner, George, had come to the Grange and what his demeanour had been at the time. She had said, when asked, that she had not seen anything untoward between George and Bessie and that was true, because she had seen scarcely anything at all. So how could she possibly answer this properly? But I could. I had. Had I been asked to go to the trial, or even to make a statement beforehand, there is a lot that I could have said. A lot I would have liked to have said. After all, Bessie could not speak for herself. Poor Bessie. One thing in particular. But I was not asked. Or even interviewed to see if I had anything of interest to say. It was not Maggie's fault that I was ignored. And now the verdict has been delivered and I fear it is too late. I wanted to tell you when you came to the Grange a few weeks ago. But I did not. You gave me no encouragement. Now I am fearful that I have not done right by Bessie, or by George either.'

She allowed herself a brief break, took a deep breath, and then continued.

'The fact is that, through dreadful worrying like you would not believe, I have had little sleep since the trial ended and George was sentenced to death,' Ann continued. 'I knew that that I must come and tell someone, soon. When we met at the Grange I thought you were a kindly and honest gentleman even if you too ignored me, and so I determined to make it my business to find you and to come and unburden myself to you. I was bursting and bursting to tell someone what I know. And now here I am.'

By now, as you will understand, Fred, I was pretty nearly bursting myself to know what it was that Ann was so desperate to unburden herself of. My thoughts ran riot. Had she perhaps seen George in the act of murdering Bessie? Was there someone else involved, an accomplice to the act? It seemed most unlikely. No one else had been spoken of by Reuben or by Bessie via Reuben. What could it be then? I was hoping I did not have too much longer to find out but equally Ann would not be rushed and would tell her story in the way that she herself wished to. The least I could do was to have the courtesy not to interrupt. Now that may sound just a little familiar to you, Fred? There is a lesson for you too here, I think.

I fetched her a glass of water. She thanked me and then continued thus.

'The problem was that Bessie just hated letting anyone down. She was just too kind. That was how she was made. So when it came to George and her change of mind she found it so hard. What she wanted, above all, was to help to reconcile George with his ... disappointment. She did not want to part from him on bad terms, if it could possibly be helped. She knew she would have to meet with him, face to face, to end it once and for all. I told her as much. She wanted to do it kindly though. Writing letters was never going to be the answer. She was dreading his arrival on the 21st. She was hopeful at first that he would not arrive, that he had got her letter and had thought better of it. But I was sure that he would come and so, I think, was she. It was my sister who answered the door to him, the first time. It was just as she said at the trial – no warning or indication of the trouble to come. I took them tea out on the croquet lawn. George was relaxed and was laughing heartily, mainly at his own jokes. He was even suggesting they played a game of croquet, which Bessie agreed to. When I got back to the house I rushed upstairs and I watched them playing from Bessie's bedroom window which overlooks the lawn – I suppose you could say I was spying on them, but it was virtuous spying, done for the best of reasons. I was pleased to see that they were getting on famously. Better than they had done for a long time perhaps.

George went away at that point and Bessie came backstairs to find me, to report back, I suppose. She was smiling and happy and saying that she felt it could all end well, after all. She told me that George would be returning at teatime for a final visit. He was going to see the Reverend Harris to say his farewells to him and would then return to the Grange, but just to say a final goodbye. I shared my mistress's relief at what was the best possible outcome. We even hugged in celebration! How foolish we were, looking back, that is, but I think, at the time, we really did think that the whole terrible nightmare was over at last. We should have worried more about the final goodbye. That's obvious now.'

Ann was on the verge of tears. She had been standing all this time but now I successfully manoeuvred her into the nearest available armchair and offered her my handkerchief, which she accepted. I encouraged her to go on. I was desperate to know the end of this story, wherever it might lead but was aware also that in order for this to happen I still needed to hold my tongue and to be patient, even though I must confess that by then I felt like trying to shake an answer out of her.

'And then? Well, then George came back in the early evening to see Bessie again, as he had promised that he would. It was I who went for the door this time as Margaret was otherwise occupied, fetching tea for the Captain, I believe. It was obvious to me straight away that, in a matter of a few hours or so, George was a changed man. And not for the better. His hands were thrust deep into his coat pockets and he was preoccupied, troubled, in a way that he had not been before. He was not looking at me but was staring past me into the house. Bessie, having heard the doorbell, came out up behind me. Immediately, without any exchange of pleasant-ries, he demanded to know from Bessie the name of the clergyman that the Reverend Harris had told him she was now engaged to. Bessie, upset and taken aback, refused to answer him. George repeated his question, this time with more menace but without raising his voice. He hissed it at Bessie. Again Bessie would not tell him. I said that he should speak more kindly and respectfully to my mistress. He ignored me and began to curse Bessie, and her kin. I did not catch much of what he said, and I doubt that Bessie did either. George asked her for a third time who the man was and, when he was rebuffed again, began to curse again. This time I could make out some of what was said, it was unpleasant in the extreme – I would not wish to repeat all of his foul-mouthed rantings to you – but his threats were now aimed more at the absent Captain than at Bessie herself. George accused him of aiding and abetting the sin of fornication by encouraging it to take place under his own roof. He said Bessie's 'pimp' must be prepared to pay the ultimate price unless he or his granddaughter were willing to divulge the fornicator's identity. He had tried, nicely, to get Bessie to spill the beans and she would not do so. Now it was time for the conspirator in chief to come clean. He started to move forward as if to enter the Grange, calling out, "Captain Fornicator, Captain Fornicator, Jezebel's Protector, a word, if you please. Don't you hide away in your precious Grange. Come out and speak to me, man to man."

At this point Bessie took charge of the situation. She remained in the doorway and, by so doing, blocked George's way into the house. Putting a hand on his arm she asked him to walk out with her down towards What-standwell so that they might talk further. Otherwise, she said, her grandfather might hear George's raised voice and come to find out was wrong. George reluctantly agreed, though he did express himself to be perfectly indifferent as to whether her grandfather was disturbed or not. He would be pleased if he did disturb the Captain as he wished to have it out with him man to man, and whatever the consequences. He was, however, pacified by Bessie's gentle tones. She did manage to calm him down, to some extent. Maybe, in his own world, George still believed that his position was not hopeless? Or maybe he went with her for old times' sake. I do not know. Before they left, she asked me to fetch her summer shawl, and a pen and paper as well, explaining to George that she needed to write a note to her grandfather to explain her temporary absence. I was worried that the reference to her grandpa might have excited George once again but thank heavens it did not do so. I fetched Bessie her shawl and a pen and paper. She put her shawl on. Then she scribbled on the piece of paper, folded it and handed that and her pen back to me. She told me that she did not expect to be too long. I watched as the two of them set off down the drive and went out of sight behind the rhododendron bushes. Bessie had by now placed her arm into George's and this further calmed him. That was the last time I saw Bessie. As they went out of sight onto the turnpike, I took out her note from my dress pocket, intending to deliver it to the Captain as requested. I was puzzled to see that the message turned out to be a message which was addressed to me, not the Captain. When I opened up the folded paper what was written inside was just this –Luke 23.34 – nothing else, that was all. Just Luke 23.34.'

At this point Ann paused for a much-needed further sip of water.

'And the worst of it is, Mr Leech, that I only came to understand the full meaning of Bessie's message later that evening, after her tragic death. I did not immediately understand it, in the heat of the moment. I should have done, of course. I am sure you would have done Mr Leech. So I let Bessie down. I thought the note was odd and I was curious about its meaning, but it was not urgent – not a matter of life and death leastways. I was expecting to see Bessie again shortly and I would ask her then to explain her message to me. But I do know the meaning now. I looked it up in that huge Bible in the Captain's library. I have written it down so that I can be sure to get it right.' Here she fumbled in her pocket and pulled out a scrap of paper on which a quotation was written in a childish hand. She read it with difficulty as her hand was shaking so violently.

'Luke 23.34.

Father, forgive them, for they know not what they do.'

Ann paused for long enough for me to grasp the significance of this final message. I gasped.

'Yes, that's right, Mr Leech, I think these words show that Bessie knew what might happen out there on the turnpike, what might happen to her. She saw that things might not end well, after all. She walked down the drive at Wigwell Grange knowing that that was at least a possibility. I have found it difficult not to be angry with her over this. In fact, I was furious with her and I still am. What possessed her to leave with George even if she only slightly suspected that he might end up doing her harm? Why did she offer to go with him, persuade him to go with her indeed, if she really thought that she might be putting herself at risk? The Constable could have been summoned instead? Why, when her life was all before her, more than ever, did she take any risks at all? I have turned these questions over and over in my mind. I have come to an answer, at least one that satisfies me. There are only two possibilities. Either she wanted to avoid something worse happening, to us, to her grandpa, especially to him, or she went with George to atone for breaking off the betrothal, prepared to pay the ultimate price. I do not believe the second one for one moment. She felt guilty, yes, but not to the point where she would have, in effect, committed suicide. Why would she when she was about to secure exactly what, and whom, she had wanted for so long?

But I saw the hatred in George's eyes. He hated Captain Goodwin more than anyone else in the world and Bessie would not have wished any harm to have come to her grandfather, at any price. The Constable, if he had been summoned, might well not have arrived in time to help. Even if he had arrived on time, and without wanting to be unkind to Constable Parnham, he might not have come out on top if it came to a struggle. Granted, George is not much of a physical specimen himself but he would have had youth, as well as anger, on his side. And think of the damage George might then have inflicted on the Captain – he may once have been a brave and courageous soldier, but his soldiering days were well behind him. He would have been like a coconut on a shy awaiting the blow that would shatter his skull into a hundred pieces. All this would have been as obvious to Bessie then as it is to us now.' She paused again, tearful now.

'We won't ever know the truth, I dare say. Some, not mincing their words, will say, if they ever get to know what happened, that Bessie's actions were stupid and absurd. Some will say that she was naive in thinking that she could ever part on good terms with George. I prefer to think of her acting on what she saw as the lesser of two evils. It was admirable in my view. To protect her kith and kin even when he had been so awful towards her much of the time. Blood is thicker than water, they say, don't they? And she knew there was something very wrong with George. She had to recognise that. The murderous attack on her was not bound to happen just because we know now it did. They could still have parted on reasonable terms. We need to be careful not to leap to judgment now. She acted for the best but the worse happened. That is how I have come to see it, leastways.'

With that she allowed herself another brief pause.

'Afterwards I kept expecting the Constable would come and ask me what I knew about Bessie's death, but he never did. I know I should have told someone about what had happened, about the message, but I didn't. I put it off, just for a few days. Then I became afraid that I would be criticised for not acting sooner. Or better. The longer I left it the more difficult it was.

Eventually a week or so after Bessie's passing, I plucked up the courage to go and see the Captain about it. I will never forget walking to the library to see him. Knocking on the door, knocking twice before there was a barking answer from him telling me to come in. I felt my stomach lurch thinking about what I had to tell him. And then, I didn't say anything at all. I couldn't. Words would not come to me. I gave him the scrap of paper Bessie had written on. I was shaking, much like I am now, even more so if anything. The Captain unfolded the paper, took one look at the contents, grimaced, and without speaking a word to me, or seeking any explanation of what it was, or how it came into my possession, he simply threw the paper onto the fire and then stabbed away at the ashes with a poker. I was shocked by his actions. He must have recognised his granddaughter's hand – her writing was so distinctive and so beautiful. His actions had only one meaning – that I was to keep silent about the note and its contents. Indeed, just in case I should be in any doubt about this, he told me so, patting me on the arm and telling me not to be upset and to forget all about the message as it could only serve to sully the memory of poor Bessie yet further, 'Which neither of us want, now do we, my dear?' He was not angry. He did not reprimand or seek to blame me. He did not shout at me. He was kindly in his manner and quietly spoken. He called me 'dear' which he had never done before. But he was also insistent that nothing further should be said about the note. He doubted I would even be asked to provide a statement, let alone to give evidence at the forthcoming trial. He said he that he would use his 'influence' as chief magistrate to ensure that was the case. That way I would not be placed in an awkward position. I need not worry my pretty little head about it any further.

I don't mind saying that, in a way, I felt relieved. I did not like his manner or feel easy about his instructions, but I felt that I was entitled to take the Captain's word for it and to do as he said. He was the master of

Wigwell, after all, and I merely his servant. I had told him, confessed to him and he had spoken. He had said that he would look after me. I was off the hook. At least so I thought then. And since then, I have kept my silence as I was told to do by master. I didn't even tell my sister about the note. I thought it was better that she did not know about it. She could not speak of what she did not know. My silence was made easier by the fact that no one official came to ask me anyway. My master had honoured his promise to me in that respect.'

At this point she was about to break down, so I offered yet another glass of water.

'But now, after what I read in the newspaper about the verdict the other day, I have been worrying about all this anew. I have hardly slept with worry. And I wanted to tell you, Mr Leech. Only you will know whether or not this has any bearing on Mr Townley's present fate. I am content to leave that to your judgement.' And with that and having tossed this metaphorical rock into the still pond, the young woman got up, shook hands with me, wished me good day and departed.

⁂

I was left alone to contemplate this strange and profoundly shocking turn of events. What were the implications for the trial that had just taken place and the verdict that was still so freshly baked? On the one hand her revelation was probative of nothing. It was evident that, even if Bessie herself believed that George had lost his mind and that she did not consider him responsible for his actions she is, she was, not medically qualified. The victim herself, speaking from beyond the grave, would have carried little or no weight at trial. No more than the opinion of Mr Grew could, or did. It was all speculation. Ann's confession did highlight George's anger towards his rival lover but that was barely news, was it? That had been the basis of the prosecution's case anyway. Certainly, he had a hatred for her grandfather – it was mutual – but again that had hardly been disguised by him or indeed by the Captain. It had been explored, rather too exhaustively in my view, at the trial. Even so every fibre of my being as a lawyer screamed that, this time, I must make a clean breast of it with the authorities.

But was that really necessary? I was outraged at the Captain's behaviour in destroying the message just as he had, on his own admission, done previously with Bessie's letters. And then to seek to influence a murder investigation. It was tantamount to contempt of court. No, not tanta-mount to, it was contempt of court. I got grim satisfaction, in retrospect, from Mr Macaulay's enthusiastic pursuit of the Captain in the witness box, even though it had irritated me at the time. If only we had known then what I knew now, then the Captain would not have escaped so lightly. I would have been the first to urge Mr Macaulay on in a withering cross-examination of him. It is a wicked thing for me to say perhaps but further aggressive cross-examination might have been enough to finish the old man off, with a bit of luck!

But now the trial was over, the sentence had been delivered. In analys-ing the evidence, as I now did, I was strongly inclined to sit on my hands and do nothing. It was the prosecution's own negligence that had led to their failure to identify that there were two Poysers who each, separately, might have something relevant to say at the trial. Bessie's message, like Bessie herself, had perished. Had the message survived it might have further stoked the fires of prejudice regarding George, but that is about all. He had been convicted, after all. In six minutes! Apart from Ann's word there was now nothing to say the message had ever existed. The Captain was hardly likely to disclose what had occurred, that is if he valued his liberty and comfort, and I was sure that he did. Weighing heavily in the scales for me was the fate of Ann. Whilst she might well escape judicial sanction herself there was no doubt that, on the basis of what I had just observed, she was close to being a broken woman and any public exposure was only likely to aggravate her mental state. The gentlemen of the press would turn on her without scruples. Perhaps we would then have another death on our hands. Having just seen her in such an agitated state I felt that this could not be entirely discounted. I could not inform on Goodwin without also implicating Ann. The very last thing that Bessie would have wanted was for any blame to fall on her faithful servant, Ann. I tried to look at it too from the position of Mary – she would be touched by Bessie's gesture but would it really change anything? I thought not.

And so I made my decision. I chose my bed to lie in. I gave way to temptation – if you want to see it like that. My decision to deceive the powers that be (even if by omission) would be bound to come back to haunt me in the middle of the night. But, for once, my worries were thor-oughly dwarfed by my respect for Bessie. This reached new heights, if that were possible. She really had been the most remarkable and most courageous of women. I felt at the time that I could never disclose this to another living creature but her scribbled message provided me with some moral validation to continue to work for George's relief. I resolved to redouble my efforts on his behalf – for Mary's sake – and for Bessie's truth.

Whilst significantly cheered as to the cause, an eased conscience, of course, butters no parsnips. I remained doubtful as to my means or prospects of success. Your mother, who is not normally taciturn when it came to making suggestions as to how I could improve myself, knew better than to try and buck me up. She rightly judged that any expression, even of concern, that she might be tempted to make was likely to be thrown back at her with interest, so to speak, so she chose, sensibly, to remain silent. She was unsurprised when I announced I was going into the office early, even though it was the day before Christmas Eve, and offered to make me a packed lunch to take with me as she 'assumed I would not have time for a lunch break'. I refused the lunch but made it clear that I appreciated the sentiment that lay behind the offer. Her sympathies had always lain wholly with Bessie and not with George. She did not know anything about Bessie's last message. That may or may not have altered her opinion. She still does not know, and I urge you, Frederick, to keep it that way. The information I have imparted to you is 'privileged' to you alone.

On arriving at my office, I began to leaf through the entire contents of the firm's law library, not really focusing on the job in hand. I discarded volumes, one by one, as I found their contents useless for present purposes. Law reports littered the desk and spilt out over onto the floor. Soon I too am crouched on the floor in the midst of this flotsam and jetsam of legal authority, searching for no more or less than George's salvation. In that moment I became a congenitally disorganised bird, a magpie perhaps, sitting disconsolately in the centre of the most chaotic nest imaginable whilst searching, ever more frantically, for the egg I was sure did exist somewhere but which I had somehow unforgivably mislaid.

I tried to think how I could possibly turn fate in George's favour. Time was short. There were leads of which I had briefly had hopes, but which soon turned out to be legal blind alleys. Every hour that passed I imagined that another piece of the scaffold had been put in place. How much more splanchnic must it have been for George who, on his daily exercise, could see for himself that preparations were underway for his despatch. Other prisoners no doubt ensured he did not forget what lay in store for him. But in spite of all this I persevered. I clung to the Latin maxim 'festina lente', make haste slowly, which a veteran QC had commended to me when, as a callow young solicitor, I had once rushed at a problem instead of taking my time to analyse it properly. His point was that I needed to take my time to avoid missing something in plain sight. The only trouble was that I felt that, with all due respect, there was such a thing as making haste too slowly ... or not at all. Making snail haste, if you like. With every hour that passed the cause became more and more desperate and George's fate seemed more and more sealed. The clock ticked on relentlessly.

And then an extraordinary thing happened. At home that night, when thankfully the rest of the family had retired for the night and I was still turning things over in my mind, I found, much to my own astonishment, that I had started to pray. Not an activity I had indulged in for many a long year – ever since religion had lost its allure and magic for me, when Good Friday had become just another afternoon, no longer an afternoon when I felt a mixture of terror and sadness – as if Jesus Christ was just about to knock at my door and remonstrate with me personally for my sins. Now I prayed, not half-heartedly may I say, but with gusto and without embarrassment. I actually knelt down, right there in the middle of the sitting room carpet. As a lapsed Catholic, an altar server no less, at least until that unfortunate incident involving another server's hair and a lighted candle, I could still confidently remember both my Hail Marys and Our Fathers (the edited Catholic version) along with a surprising amount of the catechism. I begin randomly quoting sections of the latter to myself.

'All things whatsoever you ask, in prayer, believe that you shall receive; and they shall come unto you.'

And again:

'I say to you ask and it shall be given to you; seek, and you shall find; knock and it shall be opened to you. For everyone that asketh, receiveth; and he that seeketh; findeth and to him that knocketh, it shall be opened.'

Despite my strong encouragement, however, God continued to decline to intervene on George's behalf. I neither receiveth, nor findeth, nor was a solution revealed to me. Perhaps He saw through my sudden and convenient re-conversion. I could not really blame Him for being sceptical as to my motives. I would have been, too! So I resolved to renew my close scrutiny of my law books at dawn break the following day and not to desist until I had found a human solution to the challenge that confronted me.

XXVII

A Revelation

❧

21st August 1872

Fred

I hope that a lack of a reply from you does not mean that you have gone into shock at my most recent revelation? Meanwhile – time and tide waits for no man – I will get on with my story. The moment of truth you have been patiently waiting for is nigh. I must thank you for holding back for so long. I know that forbearance does not come naturally to you.

Fondest regards

Father

It was Christmas Eve, and I was sitting in the silence of the office after everyone else had, quite reasonably, left for the holiday. I had been in situ since dawn as I promised I would be. It was only eight days until George was due to be hanged. Little more than a week stood between him and a premature, and I would suggest, extremely awkward, meeting at the gates of heaven with Saint Peter. He would not get past Saint Peter. I imagined Satan's assistants gleefully sharpening their knives and forks as I laboured. But, despite the terror of this and the urgency of finding a legal provision that would assist our cause, I felt a strange and unusual sense of calm. Perversely I felt more focussed, and more hopeful, than I had done since the conclusion of the trial. Maybe that praying the night before had helped me after all, I thought. I was now refreshed and relishing the challenge I faced instead of dreading the consequences of failure. I returned to the legal volumes which Michael had kindly rescued from the floor and replaced on the shelves. Forsaking praying this time I started to talk to myself, a novel habit and not one I would recommend to you Fred, certainly not in company.

'I need to find a law that puts us – me – in charge of what happens next.' (A statement of the obvious.)

'It can't be right for a mad man to be hanged. It just can't be, can it? It's not something that should happen in a civilised society. And George is surely mad? There can be no reasonable doubt about that?' I nodded to myself.

'There must be something that can be done and its down to you, Samuel. No one else can resolve things so you must buckle down and find out what.'

I began to comb methodically through the index of all laws in Halsbury. I start at the end, that is with those laws that our present Queen had seen fit to assent to thus far in her glorious reign. I focussed on the word 'insane'. It was a painfully slow business but – festina lente – if there is one thing I am known for, it is my powers of application. All those powers were called upon now.

There is a provision somewhere about people who become insane once in gaol and who pays for their transfer and detention. But I don't think that will help. It surely does not help those poor souls who are found sane before they are convicted and who are to be dealt with according to the law's sternest requirements! Otherwise, the loophole would be so gaping wide that almost anyone would be able to escape being hanged by leaping through it – our legislators would have abolished capital punishment without even having realised that they had done so!

I was not alone in that view. That was the accepted wisdom and had, without doubt, been the intention of our legislators, in all their wisdom. Insanity at the time of the murder can mitigate blame and punishment, even if is far from easily established, as we had seen. Insanity after the crime, by contrast, was a different kettle of fish. It was easier to establish and, in the public mind, more easily merited compassion and treatment – it followed the crime rather than being integral to it. The underlying presumption was I suppose more pragmatic – that, in the case of capital crimes at least, the hangman will usually have done his business promptly and efficiently and there will thus be no need for future provision of any kind to be made for the offender, other than burial within the prison grounds, that is.

But one thing we lawyers know, don't we, Frederick, is that the legislator's intention counts for nothing when it comes to interpreting the law.

There is so often a slip betwixt cup and legislation. It is the black letter of the law that counts, what is actually written down on the page, not what the legislators may, in their collective wisdom, have intended. So without much hope, but without wishing to prematurely abandon hope altogether, I fetched the relevant volume down.

I started to read the 1840 Act, clause by clause, line by line. One particular clause of the Act demanded my attention. Indeed, it grabbed me by the neck and threw me to the floor. You will, I am sure, readily appreciate its significance when I relay the Act's provisions:

> *An Act for making further provision for the Confinement and Maintenance of Insane Prisoners, 3rd and 4th Vic. cap 54*
>
> *Whereas it is expedient that further provision should be made for the confinement and maintenance of insane prisoners; Be it therefore enacted by the Queen's Most Excellent Majesty ... that if any person whilst imprisoned in any prison or other place of confinement under any sentence of death ... shall appear to be insane it shall be lawful for any two Justices of the Peace of the County ... to inquire with the aid of two physicians or surgeons as to the insanity of the person and if it shall be duly certificated by such justices and physicians that such person is insane it shall be lawful for one of Her Majesty's Secretaries of State, upon receipt of such certificate, to direct by warrant under his hand that such a person shall be removed to the county lunatic asylum.*

I re-read the clause several times. It was all as plain as a pike staff to me. With my excitement building, I checked to make sure that the Act had not been repealed or amended. It had not. I checked Hansard to see what I could discover about the reason for the legislation being passed. There had been little discussion about the proposed Act when the measure had come before Parliament for approval on 22nd May 1840. True the Duke of Richmond had objected to the provision on the basis of increased costs falling on the rates but his arguments had not impressed the Marquess of Normanby, the then Home Secretary, who stated that in his view the present bill did not contain anything which was either novel or difficult: its only new provisions went to codify the powers of having lunatics transferred to lunatic asylums, which powers already existed in any event. The marquess had therefore declined to alter the bill and the provisions had sailed safely into law, Her Majesty having also seen fit to assent to the provision.

I realised, in that instant, that I had found what I had been searching for – there was nothing in the legislation that prevented an application being made for transfer to an asylum whether the prisoner was sane or insane before conviction, provided he appeared to be insane now. I started to again talk to myself.

'You are a fool, Leech, a negligent bloody fool, but yet this might just do it, it might just do it, you think? I think it might. If I can only find two JPs and two doctors to agree. Not an easy task perhaps – these doctors can hardly agree amongst themselves about what they should have for supper – but not an impossible one either? And, if so, just think of the momentous consequences …'

Not only did I then answer my own question in the affirmative, but I am ashamed to admit that I allowed myself a little squeal of joy. I even, if you would you believe it, Fred, performed a little jig then and there in the middle of my office. Up to then I didn't know I was capable of such wild and flamboyant conduct. Just as well I was alone as otherwise my colleagues would have fairly concluded that I had, finally, lost leave of my senses and moved to pension me off as soon as possible.

I left my office still elated. I hurried home through the sleet and, reaching home and finding her alone, kissed your mother passionately under some strategically placed mistletoe. I appreciate you might not wish to know this. I also wished her a Happy Christmas. She was more than slightly taken aback. As you will recall we had a lovely Christmas that year once you children had all arrived from different corners of the country. I, in particular, embraced the joys of the season with gusto!

Returning to my office on Boxing Day with a sore head, the cold light of day began to bite. It dawned on me that, despite my pre-festive euphoria, I was still far from certain to succeed. My black letter lawyer-self began to reassert itself and nagging doubts began to resurface. In particular I was increasingly bothered by that phrase 'it **SHALL** be lawful for one of Her Majesty's Secretaries of State, upon receipt of such certificate to direct …' blab blab (my underlining and emphasis). It was truly a difficult phrase to pin down. Did it mean that Her Majesty's Secretary of State could issue such a warrant if he wanted to and was in the mood, but he did not have to if he was not, if he had woken up on the wrong side of his bed, for example? Was there a choice, a discretion involved? It could be disastrous if he could just pretend to hear what had been said, with his fingers in his ears, but then decide to ignore it, refuse to issue a certificate and press on with the execution. I needed some reassurance on this point, and the sooner the better, so I requested advice from the up-and-coming barrister, James Copewell, who also happens to be a friend of the family. So as not to take improper advantage of this I wrote to him at his Chambers, in carefully neutral terms, asking for his urgent opinion on whether were such a certificate to be issued then could the Secretary of State nonetheless decide to go his own way or was he bound to act on it. I quoted such case law as I could muster, which was very limited as most of the decided cases, were, predictably enough, concerned with who should pay for the confinement of any particular lunatic, not the process to be applied. I awaited counsel's reply with bated breath. I did not have long to wait. I received a note back from James by return. I hastily read his reply. I need not have worried. He did not disappoint. He answered my question in refreshingly direct and succinct terms. I have copied out his letter word for word as I thought you might enjoy it and also because you yourself, or a younger version of you, is mentioned in passing.

Gray's Inn
London
28th December 1863

Dear Leech,
In the matter of the Queen versus George Townley
& In the matter of the Act for making Further Provisions for the Confinement and Maintenance of Insane Prisoners 3rd and 4th Vic. cap.54
Thank you, as always, for your valued instructions. Compliments of the season and a Happy New Year to you and yours. I was amused to hear from a mutual acquaintance that Master Frederick is determined, despite your dire warnings, to embark on a career in the law. Mad fool! But I look forward to coming up against him one day and pitting my wits against the famous Leech intellect! Provided, of course, I have not entered my dotage by then.
And now straight to business. I have, in haste, considered the papers

that you have provided, along with the relevant statutory provisions, and am most happy to say that I am in a position to advise.

Your question

Were the Secretary of State (SOS) to decide to ignore a certificate of insanity validly issued under the Act and his decision were then to be challenged in the courts, what would be the likely outcome?

My advice

In that event, and please excuse my use of the vernacular, the SOS would most certainly be well and truly d——d! He would have not a legal leg to stand on. He would be putting his own neck on the block in place of Townley's. Costs would surely follow the event. In summary it would be an unmitigated disaster for him and might very well bring a premature end to a reasonably promising political career. If for that reason alone he will, emphatically, not ignore your presumptive certificate.

I would be most happy to assist further in the event that you find my advice ambiguous in any way, which, however, I doubt will be the case.

I remain, Sir, your obedient servant

yours sincerely

James Copewell

Barrister-at-Law

I was delighted that James had not sat on the fence, as many of you barristers might have done. His view was clear and unequivocal and positive. I did a little mental jig but this time managed to restrain myself from giving my pleasure any physical expression. There were other people around in the office and it would not have been seemly. What then gave me even greater confidence in the cause was that, also on 28th December I was (anonymously) sent a copy in the post of a letter that the trial judge Baron Martin had written to Sir George Grey, Home Secretary, on December 13th – the day after the trial, and a Sunday to boot! I also set out this letter in full below, partly because I feel I need to eat a large slice of humble pie bearing in mind my previous critical comments about his lordship. I do wonder why the letter had not been shared with me, as Townley's attorney, at a much earlier stage, i.e., when it was sent. I suppose, in view of the way these proceedings had been conducted hitherto, that I should not have been overly surprised.

He wrote as follows:

Judges Lodgings
St Mary's Gate
Derby
13th December 1863
Sir –
George Victor Townley was convicted yesterday before me at Derby of murder, and duly sentenced by me to be executed. I have directed a copy of my notes be made available to you, should you desire to have them: but there is a full, and reasonably accurate, account of the trial in The Times, emanating from the pen of their distinguished legal correspondent Mr Nicholas Cave. The conviction and sentence was, in my opinion, right, and in accordance with my directions on the law to the jury, which I am satisfied to have been wholly correct. Mr Forbes Winslow and Dr Gisborne, both distinguished medical men as you may be aware, were cross-examined at the trial and both deposed in the strongest manner that the prisoner Townley is of diseased mind and is now absolutely and thoroughly insane. I think it right to call to your attention at once to the subject, with a view to a correct opinion being formed as to the propriety or not of his forthcoming execution.
I am, Sir, your obedient servant
Samuel Martin
Baron

I found the Baron's letter extremely helpful. I do acknowledge that he had not left George's fate entirely in my hands, as I had feared. I still consider his observations at trial to have been enigmatic. But I must acknowledge that at the same time that I was traducing him he was putting pen to paper on George's behalf. Returning to the contents of the Baron's letter then. It was very helpful in terms of expressly stating that whether or not he had been insane at the time of the murder he was likely insane now. But it was also helpful in potentially creating the right climate for the Secretary of State to make the right decision. Most of all there was, I felt, a strong impression given by the letter that the Baron himself had misgivings as to the 'propriety' of any execution.

For now my focus was very firmly on seeing how best the certificate could be obtained, if indeed it could be. For it soon became apparent to me that this business of obtaining the certificate was not as straightforward as I had hoped. It was not just a matter of dragging two JPs and two medical men off the street, escorting them to the gaol and sticking George down in front of them. The simultaneous presence of four such individuals at the same time and in the same place would be difficult to achieve but also there were more subtle forces at play here. I realised I could not afford for either the selection or instruction of the men concerned to look pre-determined. It must not look as if I had recruited simple 'yes' men or had instructed them in such a way as to leave no doubt as to the outcome I expected. To do so would be to leave a loophole, one that the Home Secretary could, if he was minded, leap through and thus defeat us at the last gasp. One loophole was enough!

Another issue was urgency. Despite the Baron's helpful letter and the promising results of my own recent labours the execution was set for the 31st, only three days hence – it was not long to try to make legal history. The biggest potential problem of all was George himself – the Applicant. The application, if it was to be made at all, would need to be based on George's current insanity. Yet, as I was only too well aware, George loudly insisted to prisoners and prison staff alike, to anyone who would listen in fact, that he was sane. Frequent assertions to this effect by George might not defeat the application but they would certainly cast doubt on it were these wild assertions of his to be reported upwards. I would need to persuade him to restrain himself, if just for a few days, to take a 'pragmatic' approach to the question in order to avoid his own demise, even if only to avoid the grief that would otherwise certainly be caused to his nearest and dearest on whom he had already inflicted such unhappiness. Pragmatism and George were not well acquainted.

At least I was aware from the letter I had (criminally) intercepted that the future happiness of his mother was still a matter of moment to him. In conversation with George I therefore, without attribution and without shame, used sentiments and even phrases from his own undelivered letter to his mother to persuade him this was the right course of action – his love and gratitude to his mother, his desire to repay her for all that she had gone through for him, his own mental state and his feelings of helplessness and lacking any earthly purpose. The purpose he could avail himself of here and now was sparing his mother and sister the further grief that his execution would inevitably result in. It was essential therefore not only that he consented to the application but also that he stayed 'mum' about what his views were about it.

This impressed him. I did not (naturally) divulge that I was simply repeating what he himself had said in his own letter. The end justified the means. He did not recognise the phrases himself or, if he did, he did not let on. A last urgent visit to the prison finally did the trick. He agreed he would consent to the application being made and desist, at least for the time being, from making provocative remarks as to his own sanity. His mother and sister were most relieved when I told them. For my part I feel that my guilt over not passing on George's letter to his mother had now been partly assuaged. My silverfish went into (temporary) retreat.

As far as the Justices were concerned, I decided to start at the top, as it were, and call on Thomas Roe, the current Mayor of Derby. Fortunately for me Roe is not only a Liberal and a fellow lawyer but also, crucially, very much his own man. I visited him at his offices at the Derby Corporation on the 29th December. Our brief conversation, as far as I recall it, went along these lines:

Roe:

'It's always a pleasure to see you, sir, but I suspect your visit is not a purely social one. So speak your mind, Samuel, and tell me what I can do for you.'

Leech:

'My apologies for descending on you, sir, with no notice, especially at this time of year. It would be unpardonable in normal times, but these are not normal times. I need to speak to you about a matter of the utmost urgency. It is no exaggeration for me to say it is a matter of life and death. You may know that the prisoner Townley is currently languishing in Derby gaol awaiting his execution, which is due in two days' time. I believe that he is insane and that it would be unconstitutional and repugnant to all civilised men that a man in his mental state should hang, at least without further enquiry. My request is that you agree to visit him in gaol, along with a fellow justice of the peace and two medical men and to consider if you agree with me or no. I make it clear that there is no compunction at all on you or your colleagues to go, or having gone, to agree with me. Indeed, it is critical that you form your own view as to the matter. I also need to make it clear to you that by participating in this exercise, if that is what you choose to do, you may well find yourself the target of active public indignation and disapproval. I myself have recent bitter experience of this. But you are not the man that I believe you to be if you could be swayed by the prospect of adverse public clamour. I am afraid I must press you for a response here and now as we do not have the luxury of being able to delay. What do you say, sir?'

Roe rose from his chair, stepped towards me, turned and put his arm around me.

'What I say, Leech, is yes, I will willingly do as you request. It is a resounding yes! I am familiar with the case you refer to and I too am troubled, as are others here in Derby, by the uncivilised travesty of an insane man being hanged. I remember my Blackstone too, you know, Sir. It would be unconscionable to hang an insane man, even after he has been found to be guilty and sentenced for a capital crime. If I remember rightly, Blackstone's rationale is that an insane man, by definition, lacks the intellect or the memory to able to identify possible grounds for a stay of his execution. The danger identified is that he could be hanged by default, as it were. That must be so even when his attorney is as competent and capable as your good-self, Samuel. But I must not prejudge his sanity at this stage. Nor must anyone else involved. Samuel, I tell you what I will do. I will exceed your request. I will myself select the additional JP that you tell me is required and then the two of us will select the two medical men also. This will save you from any impugnation of the improper selection of stooges! Such an impugnation would be unworthy and groundless, but I do agree with you that we must seek to avoid even the possibility of such a challenge. As to the likelihood of the public clamour to which you refer, I find myself in agreement again with your prediction, but my shoulders are broad and I am more than willing to bear the brunt of any public disapprovals – I have spent my professional life deflecting the slings and arrows of outrageous fortune and I don't intend the prospect of controversy to deflect me now. Now tell me when we are required to attend, and I will make the necessary arrangements forthwith – there is no time to waste after all.'

Roe was true to his word and so it was that the Mayor and I attended Derby Gaol later that same day (the 29th) accompanied by Thomas Forman, a JP, Henry Goode MB, MRCS and Thomas Hartwood, Surgeon and Apothecary and Medical Officer of the Derby Union. Mr Sims, the Governor of the Gaol, also attended to ensure fair play. After the briefest of discourse with him the four gentlemen were more than satisfied of Townley's insanity. A memorial was accordingly drawn up by me which certified to this effect, signed by my 'accomplices', and despatched to the Home Secretary. Thankfully the Home Secretary shared the view of Mr Copewell as to the overwhelming legal constraints on his room for manoeuvre, if he wished to cling onto office. Or maybe, to be gracious, he too was uneasy with seeing Townley hang. Whatever it was that swung it, he gave his formal consent to the Respite. Accordingly, the following day, the 30th, a special messenger arrived at Derby gaol with a Respite signed by the Home Secretary cancelling the execution for the foreseeable future unless and until George was certified sane.

'The QUEEN commands that the Execution of Sentence on the prisoner be RESPITED until the further signification of HER MAJESTY'S pleasure.'

That was it. Just one sentence. But it was just in the nick of time.

The Respite was received with total indifference by George – he never even uncrossed his legs as he sat in his cell and received what should have been wonderful news. It was fortunate indeed that he was not required now to agree that he was mad because otherwise I fear he might very well, even at this late stage, have done an about turn and vigorously contested this. But, as it was, his fate was as cooked as a Derby duck and there was nothing he could say or do about it. The following day he was transferred to the Bethlem Hospital to start on his treatment.

XXVIII

A Funk

❦

25th August 1872

Fred

This was the moment of the greatest legal triumph that I had ever had or would ever have again. It was a once in a career moment. It was a personal coup. With all due modesty it had surely carved the name of 'Leech' into the legal history books in perpetuity.

And yet I could not bring myself to celebrate. The victory was tainted. By what I could not exactly say. The continued ungratefulness of my client maybe? The fact that it did not, and could not, alter Bessie's fate? The aching and worrisome thought that, at some future point in time, I might be found out if my brace of unethical chickens came home to roost? The galling prospect of the Captain escaping justice safely ensconced in the Grange? Whatever the reason the case of champagne that Mr Gamble had thoughtfully brought into the office to celebrate my victory – 'a masterpiece of persistence, perspicacity and perspiration in equal measures' according to his rather florid office tribute to me, went untouched, by me at least. I had intended to visit George's mother to try and celebrate with her, given that she and her daughter had played a such a critical role in supporting the application for the Respite. However, to my disappointment she was not at home when I called on New Year's Eve and so the intended rapprochement proved something of a wild goose chase.

Your chastened Father.

Note to Journal; Confidential
The account given above is not the whole truth. The following note, which I have not supplied to Frederick, is intended to set the record straight. Or as straight as is possible. I have placed it with my papers in a sealed envelope that is appropriately marked purely in order that, after my

death, posterity can fully understand what actually happened, should it be of any interest. Recognising that it will ultimately be a matter for my executors, I hope that they will chose not to share it with any living member or close descendant of my family. It would be misunderstood and could only do more harm than good.

Thursday 31st December 1863

It is true that, as stated above, I did intend to visit Mary at her villa to take tea with her and to at least mark our joint success. I made an appointment to do so. Without her presence any celebration seemed pointless and empty. But as I again approached her neatly tree-lined street I felt uncertain. What were my motives? What was I expecting from our meeting? Adoration? Certainly not. Gratitude? I don't think so. A recognition of our shared ordeal? Maybe. . .

Possibly I just wanted to be told that I had done the right thing and that it had all been worth it. For I still had my doubts. There was also the continuing problem of the undisclosed letter from her son. The reality was that George remained in detention, albeit of a different kind, and his current state of mind uncertain. I was caught in a web of my own deceit. As the Bard of Waverly has truly observed, 'Oh, what a tangled web we weave when first we practise to deceive'. I had kept back the letter and so kept back also the warning that was contained within it. The letter continued to burn at my conscience. There again, the authorities were aware of any possible risk that George posed. It was their problem not mine.

I imagined how the impending conversation with Mary might go . . .

'I want to say, Samuel, how grateful my family and I will always be to you for saving George's life, how grateful I am . . .' she would begin.

'I only did what anyone else would have done, in my position,' I would have responded.

'No, Samuel, I simply can't let you get away with that. You went well beyond what others would have done . . . It was inspired of you to find that legal loophole and tenacious of you to pursue it. And there will be a price for you to pay in the coming months, and years probably, I am only too well aware of that.'

'Do not waste your praise or pity on me. I do not deserve it. The truth is that I have behaved badly. More badly than you know,' I might have responded.

'What do you mean, Samuel? I cannot imagine you behaving other than with the utmost probity, especially where I am concerned.'

I would then hand her the letter from George, the existence of which I had previously gone to such absurd lengths to conceal. She would have gasped as she realised who the author of the letter was. She would have been full of questions for me; 'Why have you got this letter, Samuel? Why in God's name have I not seen it before? Have you kept it from me? I don't understand!' I would have responded, 'I should not have done so.' I would, no doubt, have hung my head in shame. 'Only read it, Mary, and I will explain my motivation, as best I am able.' She would then have read the letter slowly, maybe out loud. Her voice would have faltered at various points, but she would have made it through to the end. Further questions would have followed; 'It is a sad letter. But I still don't know why you kept it from me?' I would again have thrown myself on her mercy. I would have little choice about that, you might say.

'It is because it is such a sad letter that I concealed it . . . I could not bear the thought of you reading it. Just at the time when you most feared for your son's life. I was afraid it was too much. I cared. I care for you very much, you must know that, and I did not wish to see you any more upset than you already were. I am so in awe of you, for having survived as well as you have done. But I am sorry, it was the wrong thing to do. I was overly protective of you. I see that now. But at least you know all the facts now, it is no longer my tawdry little secret.'

Mary might have come over to me and grasped my arm. She might say that she forgave me for the omission. She might say that she quite understood my reasons. At least I had done it now, she might say. She would likely be crying by now, as would I. Then she might even have declared feelings for me. It would have required her to take the initiative, I'm afraid.

'I care for you too, Samuel. I am in awe of you and what you have done for me and my family. But it is not just that. You know that, don't you? There are feelings between us, on my side anyway, that can never come to anything but are strong and real, nonetheless. In other circumstances maybe it would all have been different. But then in other circumstances we may never have met at all.'

Her grip on my arm would have grown tighter as she spoke. In that moment I would have wanted to take her in my arms and to pledge my love to her or, maybe, I might actually have kissed her. The urge would have been so strong that I am not sure that I could have resisted. It would have been very wrong, but it would have felt right as well.

But none of this had yet occurred. Maybe it never would. I paused in the middle of her street to try and think what I should do now. I hesitated. I tried to think it through. My mind was befuddled by recent events; the abuse, the trial, the respite. All these had taken their toll. My emotions boiled over. I decided I could not face the ordeal, the consequences of my infidelity, the betrayal of my family. Perhaps, in truth, it was fear of the consequences that really decided me. I am not proud of that. I rapidly retraced my steps to the railway station without ever having got as far as her front door. I funked it, in other words. I am sure she was left puzzled by my failure to arrive. Whether that was only to my regret or to hers as well I will never know. I cried as I retraced my steps. Who, or what, I was crying for I am unsure, but it was probably mainly for myself. What a foolish excuse for a man I am. There's no fool like an old fool so they say. I am living and breathing proof of that. Who would have believed that I could sink so low?

XXIX

A Price

⁓⁓⁓⁓

(Undated note – S to F)

I braced myself for the public outcry, certain that there would be one. I was not to be disappointed. Once the news of Townley's Respite became public the reaction was both instant and vicious. I made the terrible mistake of reading some of my own 'reviews'. Not just reading them but methodically pasting each of them into a scrap book. The majority of these reviews were relentlessly hostile. Soon the scrap book was full to bursting with excerpts from the London and the Provincial press. There was a difference in tone between the broadsheets and the popular press but near unanimity in the general condemnation of Townley's reprieve and, expressly or by implication, my leading part in it. I found this hard to bear but did not flinch from preserving for posterity every last commentary, however mean spirited the correspondent may have been to me.

But there was official disapproval as well. The Derby Magistracy was quick off the mark in an open letter to the Home Secretary published in *The Times* shortly after the New Year.

The Magistrates Courts
Derby

An open letter to the Secretary of State January 5th 1864
We the undersigned magistrates of Derby write to condemn your decision to Respite Townley. We consider that the Act relied upon by his attorney was never intended for the purpose for which it has been misused. A great violation has been put on it. The Act was intended to allow the officials of the county gaol who in the discharge of their duties became aware that a prisoner had become insane to act to save him. The present situation is not that at all. The Act has been used to introduce into the prison a group of gentlemen who we will not name but who we

believe to already have had a strong opinion on the point which they were required to impartially decide. Concerning the Respite of the prisoner and the order for his removal to a lunatic asylum we would wish to comment in the strongest possible terms as follows.

The effect of this unilateral step being taken has been most disastrous. It has created a feeling much to be lamented – that is that there is one law for the rich and another for the poor and that justice has been turned aside for the power of money. Townley's professional advisors and friends have acted with all the energy and effort that money produces. If Townley and his friends had been poor, then he would most certainly have been executed by now. In our considerable collective experience, we can think of no precedent for insanity to have been found on such a flimsy pretext. We urge you to re-consider.

We have the honour to be, your most obedient servants etc. etc. (signed)

TW Evans, Chairman of the Derby and Derbyshire Justices and 42 other Justices.

Postscript: Many other Justices were anxious to sign the memorial but their intention was intimated too late. I append a list of these gentleman and you will see they include no less a personage than the Lord Curzon of Kedleston.

I must say I was touched to see my old associate Alf Curzon being given an honourable mention!

Mr Cave, in a leader in *The Times*, was also quick to pitch in, his criticisms having extra weight given that he had witnessed Townley's trial and had personally heard the evidence given, and also by the news that, shortly after sparing Townley Sir George had decided not to spare a Samuel Wright, a bricklayer, who had murdered his wife in a crime of passion.

He wrote as follows:

Public opinion will demand some unpleasant explanations from Sir George Grey. Whether it be the fatality of red tapeism or undue severity in the Wright case to make up for undue leniency in Townley's case, and not withstanding dexterous fencing by the Home Secretary, the nation will regard the execution of Wright as judicial murder and the saving of

Townley as an act of gross injustice. The People of England will not be able or willing to forget that it is gentleman Townley who has been saved whilst bricklayer Wright is thrust out of the world by official stolidity. Painful though it may be the punishment must surely follow the crime. To do otherwise will be to inflict a heavy blow as to the discrimination of the jury, the impartial verdict of the judge, and the fair administration of criminal justice of this great country which its People rightly cherish.

You have got to appreciate Mr Cave, Frederick, he is a veritable word-smith. I envy him the phrase 'thrust out of the world by official stolidity'. It is masterly! I wish that I had come up with it.

The most wounding rebukes of me were delivered, however, not by men of letters but via those familiar means of public revenge, namely ballads and cartoons. I will resist the temptation to quote these ad nauseam – it would be purely an exercise in self-flagellation. But this ballad caught my eye. It compares Townley's fate with another. For Thorley one could, I suppose, just as easily substitute Wright?

Poor Thorley killed his sweetheart dear
When his heart was jealous and sad;
To every man his guilt was clear,
Though his lawyer said he was mad:
A life he took, and a life he gave
To balance the scales of right:
No gold had he his life to save,
So he died in pitiless plight.

Rich Townley killed his sweetheart dear
When his heart was jealous and sad;
To every man his guilt was clear,
Though his lawyer said he was mad:
A life he took, no life he gave
To balance the scales of right:
For Townley's gold had weight to save,
And his victim's blood weighed light.

Oh! Shame on England's faulty laws,
And shame on those who guide us,
If gold can win the murderer's cause,
And gold can thus deride us.
Must loving woman's blood be shed
And the murderer go free Sir;
Must Justice bleed, and Law lie dead
'Cause madness is the plea, Sir?

By the way I don't know what you think but I hardly think that 'England's faulty laws' does my personal efforts justice?

Inevitably, however, whilst I tried to resume the humdrum of my normal duties, neighbourly disputes, breach of promise actions, charges of assault and of theft and the like, a war of attrition continued to be waged in the national press, and the public outrage that this both provoked and encouraged, ultimately succeeded. Further doctors were found, on the instructions of an embattled Sir George, to give opinions which, remarkably enough, accurately reflected their government paymaster's altered objectives. All this took time. The wheels of justice, as we know, Fred, normally grind slowly and it was not until January 1865 that George was finally declared sane after all and the Respite rescinded. It was far too late for the death sentence to be carried out, though I am reliably informed that this was seriously considered in the higher echelons of the Home Office. It was reluctantly concluded that it would have been inhumane and savage (sic) to do so! Instead, George was condemned to spend the rest of his days in the less than salubrious setting of the Modern Prison, Pentonville. Whether this was better or worse than Derby or Bedlam I could not really say. I am sure all three institutions have their merits.

All I do know is that George showed the same indifference on being informed that he was being moved from Bedlam to Pentonville that he had on being told he was to transfer to Bedlam from Derby. He did not even uncross his legs.

XXX

A Death, Another Death

꘏

1st September 1872

Fred

I have decided, after much (even more!) internal turmoil, to send you this further note. I know that it will upset you further, and I regret this, but you know so much of the story now that I wanted to include you in its conclusion. You will probably know the bare facts already of what happened next. What you will now be able to do, should you wish to, is to put two and two together and this will enable you to appreciate the true extent of my failings. Rather than give your response in writing, I suggest we meet to discuss once you have digested it?

Samuel

It turned out not to be an extended stay back in prison for George. On my way into my office on Friday 10th February 1865 I saw, out of the corner of my eye, the *Mercury*'s headline on the newspaper stand nearest the cathedral.

'WIGWELL MURDERER REAPS HIS JUST REWARDS.'

It was the headline that I devoutly wished I would never live to see. For a moment I was frozen to the spot. I was almost speechless through anguish of mind as to what might lie behind the headline. I just about had enough wherewithal to buy a copy of the newspaper and to hurry to my office grasping it tightly, as if my life depended on keeping hold of it and no one else getting to read the contents. On my arrival there I instructed Michael to cancel all of my appointments for the day. Having seen the strained expression on my face he had the sense not to ask me why.

I hurried up the stairs to my office and slumped into my desk chair. I opened the paper, hoping against hope that I was about to read of George's death from natural causes – a heart attack maybe – or even as a result of another prisoner seeking posthumous revenge on behalf of Bessie. Either would have been equally acceptable as far as I was concerned. But though George had indeed died, the paper reported with barely disguised glee that he had died not through the actions of others but by his own hand. Or, rather, he had 'leapt to the right conclusion' as the paper wryly, but tastelessly, observed.

Dr Lankester, the coroner, quoted in his report, re-printed verbatim by the paper, from an account of George's suicide from a fellow prisoner, as well as the evidence of the prison governor and a summary of the post-mortem report. I steeled myself for whatever was coming next.

A prisoner, George Bearman, says that he recollects that on Sunday last 5th February 1865 he was sitting on the right of Townley at chapel. Bearman says that Townley was silent till the last hymn was sung. Townley had then got up, opened his prayer-book, and sang out the two last verses very loudly. He had never heard him do that before. He thought it strange. Townley had whispered to Bearman, '319th hymn'. That was the right hymn. He said it to him as if it was a matter of great moment. He repeated two lines from the hymn to Bearman which, Bearman had assumed at the time, had just caught his fancy. They were 'Where is Death's sting, Where, grave, thy victory?'

George had snapped closed his prayer-book, and then, going a few steps in front of Bearman, walked out of the chapel. He made a full stop at the bottom step in the chapel, dropped his prayer-book, got hold of the rails which ran round the gallery and sprang right over, head over heels. Bearman said that as he fell, he exclaimed, 'Oh!' He had sprung over so suddenly that there was no opportunity for Bearman or anyone else to catch hold of him. He fell flat on his face below. Bearman, when asked, could shed no light on why Townley had chosen to end his life there and then. He said the gallery was 24 feet off the ground. He never spoke after he fell, other than calling out 'Oh'.

There followed an account of the evidence given by the governor of Pentonville. The governor was at pains to stress that the prison authorities had been unaware that George was a suicide risk. He had consulted the prisoner's record personally after these tragic events and there was no indication on the face of the record that he had been considered a special risk by any of the several penal and mental institutions he had passed through. There were no warning signs. Had they been aware then such additional precautions as were reasonably practicable would have been taken to try and ensure he served out his sentence in full. The governor speculated, for example, that he might still have been permitted to attend the service in question but would have been accompanied to the service by one of his prison officers. The prisoner would have been chained to his officer who would have sat alongside him during the whole of the service. Many, indeed most, of his officers held to strong Christian beliefs and so it would not have been difficult to identify a suitable volunteer. This, the governor opined, would have prevented the accident that had occurred as Townley would have been unable to leap over the balcony rail, in the way that he had done, with a prison officer tethered to him. But he reiterated that the prison authorities were not aware of any such risk applying to Townley exceeding that of any other convict and so no special precautions had been considered necessary.

In answer to questions from the coroner the governor was pleased to supply the following additional information.

On being asked about events the previous day he confirmed that the prisoner's mother had visited him the day before the incident and that he was aware that this visit had caused the prisoner some upset. He had initially refused to see her and had only relented after an hour or so. He confirmed it was the first time, to his knowledge, that the prisoner's mother had visited him. He did not know why there had not been a previous visit. He confirmed that it was not unusual for prisoners to be reluctant to allow their relatives to visit and that maybe, he speculated, this had been the case here.

On being pressed he again asserted that the prison authorities had no reason to think that George was a suicide risk. It was simply not reasonably foreseeable.

On it being pointed out to him that George's mental state had been the subject of extensive national speculation and legal proceedings which the prison authorities and the governor himself can hardly have been unaware of the governor simply repeated his previous evidence and added that, if indeed George was insane, then he would not have been placed again within a prison environment. That had not been his decision but one, he assumes, that had been made on medical advice, by 'the powers that be'. He declined to explain who he meant or whether or not he agreed with the decision.

On being asked why there was not a more substantial fence around the balcony so that convicts were not exposed to temptation the governor replied that there had been no previous incidents of this type, as far as he was aware, and therefore it was not considered necessary.

On being asked why there was no safety net to break any fall the governor referred the coroner to his previous answer. However, in the light of the recent event the governor conceded that he would most certainly cause investigations to be made as to whether or not it was feasible to do what the coroner suggested. The governor was very much obliged to the coroner for the suggestion.

The governor ended by saying that, whilst being only too aware of Townley's heinous crime, he had always found him a polite and unassuming man, a gentleman one might say, if that was not too much of a contradiction in terms. The governor was very sorry indeed that he had died in such a way whilst he was the 'captain on the bridge', so to speak.

The newspaper article reminded its readers that the 319th hymn was Abide With Me and, helpfully, set out the hymn in full:

Abide with me, fast falls the eventide
The darkness deepens Lord, with me abide
When other helpers fail and comforts flee
Help of the helpless, oh, abide with me

Swift to its close ebbs out life's little day
Earth's joys grow dim, its glories pass away
Change and decay in all around I see
Thou who changest not, abide with me

I fear no foe, with Thee at hand to bless
Ills have no weight, and tears no bitterness
Where is death's sting?
Where, grave, thy victory?
I triumph still, if Thou abide with me

Hold Thou Thy cross before my closing eyes
Shine through the gloom and point me to the skies
Heaven's morning breaks, and earth's vain shadows flee
In life, in death, O Lord, abide with me
Abide with me, abide with me

The newspaper went on to condemn even George's choice of hymn to exit to. It was wicked and malevolent. 'If anyone truly had experienced the 'pain of death's sting', the leader writer of the *Mercury* thundered, 'it was not George but rather George's innocent victim, Bessie. By adopting the hymn as his penultimate mortal utterance, his death bed message as it were, George was, even in his final moments, seeking to trivialise death, all deaths, including Bessie's murder. George was thereby seeking to justify himself and to minimise his own appalling crime.' The implication, went on the leader, was that George had done Bessie a favour by bringing her life to a premature end; he had just accelerated her arrival into a better place. The newspaper reminded its readers of some of George's reported utterances immediately after the murder itself. 'Had he not said that he was glad that he had done it and did he not say that he was sure that she was glad too, now that she was at peace?'

'So,' the paper went on, 'his recent suicide, far from being the tragedy that it is viewed as in some liberal quarters, was no more and no less than a pathetic attempt at ex post facto justification and should be viewed as such by all right-thinking gentlemen and ladies. His careless disposal of his own life was the final insult to her whose life he had so egregiously and deliberately snatched away.' Well, it was an inventive piece I suppose, compiled perhaps by a young Oxbridge graduate gaining some work experience, but I doubt even the more gullible readers of the *Mercury* were convinced by its logical twists and turns, which were worthy of Townley himself!

And then I noticed, contained in a footnote to the report, the final irony, almost an amusing one for those of a certain disposition. George had an above-average-sized healthy brain. Who would have thought it? How he would have loved discovering that this was the case whilst he was still with us!

Townley's brain 'above average' says medical expert.

Post Mortem Examination of George Townley
> *The body of the deceased man Townley presented a ghastly spectacle. A severe cut extended over the right temple and forehead to the right eye. There was a star fracture on the right temporal bone. The base of the skull was crushed and the brain completely lacerated. The substance of the brain was healthy – there was no evidence of any disease or abnormality that could be ascertained by a visual examination. The brain's weight was 55 ounces, which is above the average by some ounces.*

Every sentence of the inquest report had cut me to the quick, none more so than the evidence of the governor. His denial of any knowledge of George's state of mind was self-serving and likely untrue. Yet I could not get away from the fact that had I acted as I should have done then things might have turned out very differently. All my efforts on George's behalf to save his life felt meaningless, when measured alongside this abject failure of mine.

My thoughts were very much with his mother and his sister. I was desperately sad for them both, but sad also for myself. There was no point in telling Mary now. I could not even bear to meet with her. So I wrote her a rather stiff letter on 1st March expressing my condolences. She replied to me by return, equally formally but much more generously. She said I should not blame myself for anything. She must have been devastated and confused but her letter made me wonder if she had an inkling that I had been culpable in some way. I do not see that she could possibly have guessed how. She said that I always had done what I could for George and her, and that if mistakes had been made they were in the past and had better stay there. There was no use whatsoever in crying over spilt milk . . . it was better to let sleeping dogs lie.

She went onto say that she fully recognised her own grave mistake –

both in visiting George at Pentonville and not having visited him before, when he was in Bedlam. She had heard such awful stories about Bedlam. After all it was not so very long ago that people went there just for the spectacle of seeing mad men and women perform. Even if conditions and attitudes had improved, as she hoped and trusted that they had, when the hospital had moved, she could not bear seeing George confined in such a place. George had never encouraged her to do so or even canvassed the possibility that she might want to visit him in their letters. He never mentioned it. So, to her shame, she had stayed away. She just could not face it. She had let her letters to him and gifts of books, etc. stand in place of a visit. But then, when he was returned to prison at Pentonville, it felt like the right thing to do to go and see him, to make up for her past omissions. She knew that George might suffer further humiliation just by seeing her there in that place.

But it had been an error of judgement on her part. She realised now that she had really done it for her own sake, not George's. She recalled my earlier advice that she should not visit George whilst he was in Derby gaol. She said she wished she had followed the same advice on this occasion as well. It was a selfish act on her part – 'You always know what the right thing to do is, Samuel,' she had said. But, rational as ever, she also said she had resolved not to blame herself. George was never really fit for this world and so his early departure was 'well-nigh inevitable'. I knew that she was parading her own guilt to me as a distraction. The merest hint of her possibly knowing something but choosing to blame herself, not me, was typical of her generosity of spirit.

Still, mine was a secret I would have to carry to my grave. At least that's what I have thought till now. Your challenge, Fred, gave me the opportunity to confess. I am sure you cannot have imagined what you were letting yourself in for? You got more than you bargained for, didn't you? Perhaps I should have prepared you better? Or just refused to cooperate? I did try and warn you. Anyway, it is done now. I have confessed to you, and you alone, and so you will need, if you are still willing, that is, to share the burden of my guilt, which in itself makes me feel more guilty still. Maybe you will feel that you cannot bear such a burden. I could not blame you if that were so. In some ways I would welcome you spilling all the beans now and for me to receive whatever punishment I deserve.

By the way, Captain Goodwin died on 10th February of a 'natural' heart attack only five days after George died from his unnatural tumble. Francis' health had been failing for some time but no advance symptoms had been evident. This day he was seized by an attack of paralysis which proved fatal. Anecdotally, he had just been informed by special messenger from the Home Office of Townley's death. Although Goodwin's death was said to be the result of natural causes, and though he was of a good age, circumstantial evidence suggested the seizure may have been brought on by news of Townley's suicide. George, for one, would not have been sorry if that were the case. In fact, he would have laughed to hear of it. Compared to Goodwin, my trials and tribulations were as mere trifles. To make any more of them would be tantamount to comparing a minor cut on the hand to the slitting of a jugular vein.

I understand that considerable discussion took place as to where George should be buried. I was not consulted. I believe that Mary may have been. There were concerns expressed in Government that his place of burial, even if unmarked, might provide a rallying point for supporters of capital punishment, or indeed of its opponents. According to a newspaper report, he was in fact buried at Finchley cemetery, near London. The same press report said that the father and brother of the convict were mourners but, although it was known Mrs and Miss Townley were in London during the interment, it was not known whether or not they attended.

Postscript
8th September 1872
Fred,
I must admit that I am apprehensive not to have heard from you yet. I do hope that we can meet up soon? In the meantime, this question and response reported in *The Times* caught my eye at the time, but I only recently re-discovered it. Whilst trivial in its subject matter it confirms my long-held view that we are ruled by idiots and charlatans – by yahoos, in fact!
Your loving father
Samuel

Hansard
  27th February 1865
  In the matter of Prison Libraries – Question
  MR. HARDCASTLE
  Arising from the recent Coroner's hearing concerning the death of George Townley and incidental evidence given at that hearing regarding the deceased prisoner's access to certain popular works of literature, he would beg to ask the Secretary of State for the Home Department under what prison regulation George Victor Townley, sent from Bedlam to Pentonville as an ordinary prisoner under sentence of penal servitude for life, was there apparently allowed access to books of so-called entertaining literature such as Silvio Pellico and Gil Blas?

  SIR GEORGE GREY
  said, in reply, that by the Rules no books were allowed to be read by prisoners, except those contained in the prison library personally approved by the Director of Convict Prisons. However, it had been found, on enquiry, that a custom and practice had grown up under the then Governor of departing from that rule, and in certain cases allowing prisoners to receive books sent into them, if they were not actively disapproved of by the Chaplain. This practice was immediately put a stop to, and the services of the previous governor terminated with immediate effect, taking account of this and other matters revealed at the Coroner's hearing. A new governor had since been appointed who was expected to take a strong line on such matters and to rule the prison with a rod of iron more generally.

MR HARDCASTLE expressed himself very content with this reply and congratulated the Home Secretary on having taken prompt and effective actions. He had not always agreed with Sir George re his previous decisions relating to this particular convict, he had violently disagreed in fact, but here it was a case of giving credit where credit was due, and he was delighted to do so. He would seek a meeting with the new governor as soon as conveniently possible as it sounded like they would find considerable common ground.

An Epilogue

◦◦⌂⌂◦

Fred never did agree that I had done the right thing. Our correspondence had been tense in places and Fred had pulled no punches. He was still particularly upset by my concealment of 'that letter' which he considered ridiculous in the extreme and 'motivated by improper considerations'. That was fair comment I suppose. He never did report me to the authorities. Thankfully family won out over professional obligation. I always believed that it would, but I am sure that it was a close shave.

I don't regret my decision to share my case papers with him even after all the grief it has caused me. I hope that he now has a better appreciation of the challenges that beset me at the time. I, in turn, have been forcibly reminded of what it is to be young, a time when everything that is not black is white. How I wish that I could turn back time and be given the chance to act differently. To make better choices. But I cannot. Frederick, on the other hand, has his whole life before him. I am sure he will not make the same mistakes as I did. He will, no doubt, find his own mistakes to make.

⌂⌂

We agree it is time to draw a line under our differences and, to that end, we meet up in the Market Square in Wirksworth. Our meeting, in mid September, is an emotional one. We hug each other fiercely. Disengaging reluctantly, we leave behind the dusty highway which cleaves the town in two, and head, via the lonely lych-gate, towards the church of St Mary's. We pause only briefly to admire the sight of the horseshoe-shaped church close, framed by rolling hills. We then seek to enter the church, not a straightforward matter as it turns out. With the help of some reasonable force (applied by Fred) the forbiddingly large door eventually creaks open. We risk disturbing that gentle knight, Anthony Gell, himself a distinguished attorney, who rests here alongside his own father, Ralph. We come across the Wirksworth Stone, an ancient and worn sarcophagus. Cain, Herod and Judas (strange allies indeed) stare out at us, their mouths gaped wide in fear – with some justification since they are about to be roasted on a brazier by some unsavoury-looking devils.

Eventually we locate the object of our visit, a modest stone inset into the wall above the golden eagle lectern and to the right of the pulpit. Made of local alabaster on a slate background it is decorated with a few random scrolls and a Grecian-looking vase. Fred reads out the inscription.

In memory of
    CAROLINE wife of FRANCIS GREEN GOODWIN Esquire of Wigwell Grange who died August 9th 1858 aged 66 years,
    also of FRANCIS GREEN GOODWIN Esquire who died February 10th 1865 aged 85 years,
    also of CAROLINE daughter of HENRY & AGNES GOODWIN who died August 21st 1863 aged 22 years.

'We know Francis Goodwin died eighteen months after Bessie, yet Bessie is listed last – that is odd. Why is that do you think, Father – a matter of family hierarchy perhaps?'

His question is left to hang in the air.

He follows it up.

'Never mind that – why on earth is Bessie's name wrong? Look there. She was Elizabeth Caroline Goodwin, not just Caroline, was she not?'

I nod.

'So her better half, Bessie, Elizabeth, has been omitted. She has been stripped of her rightful name – the final indignity. Thoughtlessness? No, surely not an innocent error. No. I suspect her true identity has been deliberately obscured.'

'Unfortunate, yes. But not deliberate?' I say, rather judiciously.

But Frederick is not to be pacified that easily.

'You're wrong. You do always try and see the soul in people. That's typical of you. But it's not always a good thing, you know. I think we can see the hand of Francis here, scheming from beyond his grave. I'd wager that this was his wording, his bequest, his last-ditch attempt to protect Bessie, yes; but also to protect his precious successors from perpetual scandal.'

'It's a plausible theory, Fred, I grant you that, but that's about all it is – a theory.'

'Right, so tell me this – why is there no public expression of sorrow at Bessie's premature passing? Goodwin, whatever his failings, was not indifferent to his granddaughter's death, was he? She was only 22, for God's sake! So why nothing here to acknowledge the special tragedy of this loss. Surely she deserved some thing more?'

'Perhaps that was too much to expect? The public man giving way to the private one. The public man was always going to prevail, in public. The private man was always going to keep his feelings private. I can understand that.'

'Well, I expect you can – you who, it seems, let your own private feelings infect your public life so disastrously, concealing evidence and witnesses, contempt of court, that sort of thing! Need I say more? And you a lawyer! You and Old Goodwin have much more in common than you would like to think.'

It is a very low blow, and yet not an entirely undeserved one. I find myself in a sudden hurry to leave the church and get some air.

Unseasonal rain arrives as Frederick and I leave St Mary's. He kindly gives me his arm for support as we make our way to Bessie's grave, which is located a short walk away at North End, in a discreet annexe to the main churchyard. For Frederick, the obscure location of the grave on barely consecrated land adds further fuel to his fire concerning the deliberate severing of Bessie from her family.

As we proceed the rain becomes more persistent. We should really take shelter in the well-proportioned Georgian chapel that sits at the top of the graveyard – but we do not. I think we both relish the sensation of the cold water splashing our faces. For me it feels almost like a baptism – a chance to make a fresh start, my sins being washed away. I do not know what Fred is thinking but I am sure that he will not let me off the hook so easily. I am hoping that he is at least experiencing a slight pang of regret over his crushing remarks about me in the church.

After some searching, and with the help of a cemetery plan, we believe we have found Bessie. She is at the bottom of a steep slope. Her grave is unmarked and neglected, strangled by weeds and briars. We stand there together for some time without speaking. The whole enormous tragedy weighs down upon us and words became superfluous. I think we both sense the sad presence of Bessie.

⁊

I wonder about my own death and how and when it will come, and whether or not I will be prepared for it. Is there anything more I should do now to be ready, just in case? I remember reading somewhere that those on the cusp of life and death always feel that death has come too soon, sooner than they had imagined, and that they have unfinished business. They resent the calling of time, without more notice, or even the chance to appeal for an extension. I am sure it will be the same with me.

≈

Eventually Frederick and I retreat together back up the cemetery hill. Slowly, still silently, heavy in thought, still tearful, still arm in arm. Like our tears the soft Derbyshire rain continues to fall. It caresses both the flesh of the living and the bones of the dead.

Samuel Leech, Esq., Solicitor, Mayor of Derby.[11]
15th September 1872.

✱✱✱✱

---

[11]Samuel was Mayor of Derby from 1871 to 1872. He died on 18th October 1879. In his will he left his estate to his dear wife Lydia for the term of her natural life and thence to his four children Frederick Edward, Beatrice Mary, Florence Greenfield and Samuel Chiswynd. It is not known what became of his private papers.

Author's Historical Note

❧

This story is based on the Wigwell Grange murder of 1863. This is the first creative treatment of the events since a short story by Arthur Conan Doyle.[12]

There is a scrapbook in Derby City Local Studies Library, assembled in 1865 by an unnamed but concerned Derby resident, which includes extensive press cuttings and other material relating to the murder. It was a chance discovery of this album some twenty years ago which led to me thinking about writing about the murder.

There was a real Bessie and a real George and a real Samuel (though I have aged him) and a real Reuben. Samuel's partner really was a Mr Gamble – with his name though he should perhaps have been the litigator in the firm. There was also a real Captain Francis and there were two Poyser sisters who were employed as servants at the Grange called Ann and Margaret. The age difference between them was more in real life. Some of the other characters are an amalgam of more than one historical figure, for example, the Revd Harris.

The mysterious clergyman, 'Will', was later unmasked in the press, his real name being Francis Bryans and his real parish being Duddon, near Chester and then Old Rode, near Congleton. The circumstances of his discovery that Bessie had died bear recounting. He was passing along a street in Burslem, now part of Stoke-on-Trent, when his attention was caught by a placard of a Manchester newspaper posted outside the shop of a newsagent, announcing the commission of a dreadful murder in Derbyshire. He stepped into the shop and purchased a newspaper and was horrified to read the name of his betrothed as the murder victim. He was reported to have been 'almost speechless from anguish of mind' at what he had read.

My story draws freely on contemporary documents, in particular a

---

[12] Strange Studies of Life. II. The Love Affair of George Vincent Parker The Strand Magazine April 1901.

detailed contemporary account of the trial.[13] Dr John Hitchman's interview with George includes quotes from an article published by him in 1864. George's footnotes are invented.[14] The judge really did nearly break down even as he pronounced the sentence of death on George. Captain Goodwin really did burn Bessie's letters but not, so far as I know, her diary. He did invite George to tea in the immediate aftermath of the murder and he was the object of extensive press ridicule for having done so. He really did die of 'natural causes' only a matter of days after George committed suicide.

Some of the other historical material has been adapted e.g. the (undelivered) letter from George to his mother which caused such a deal of trouble. It was indeed undelivered but because it was written too closely and was therefore not allowed out of the prison. This was revealed at the coroner's inquest. It was in fact written from Pentonville, not Derby. The Prison Service was well aware of George's suicidal tendencies, despite the governor's strong denials in his evidence. Bessie's cryptic note to Ann is my invention but in character, I think. Ann is surely right to have interpreted Bessie's actions as indicative of her strength and courage and not of weakness or self sacrifice. Bessie's letter of 18th August arrived too late. George had already set off to visit Washington Arrowsmith in Bolton on his way to Wigwell.

The Thomas Gisborne book referred to at the beginning is genuine and was much admired by Jane Austen, amongst others, though not by Anna Seward.[15] Thomas was at university with William Wilberforce. Thomas became an MP and was a key figure in the anti-slavery movement as well as being a poet and prelate. His younger brother, John Gisborne, was also a poet. In my book Bessie quotes from John's epic poem 'Reflections' (1833) in response to Will's quotation from Byron. (Childe Harold's Pilgrimage – 1818).

The relevant legislation is, I hope, accurately quoted. The 1840 Act was repealed in 1864 to prevent a reoccurrence.[16] The *Justice of the Peace* publication of February 13th 1864, in covering the prospects of the

---

[13] Kemp, Henry Latimer (Robert Hardwicke, London 1864) *The Trial and Respite of George Victor Townley*, 1863.
[14] Hitchman, John, *Journal of Mental Science*, 1864.
[15] Gisborne, Thomas *An Enquiry Into The Duties of the Female Sex etc.* London 1801.
[16] Front page editorial, *Justice of the Peace*, February 13th 1864.

imminent session of the House of Commons, expresses the hope '*that this branch of the law will be put on some intelligible footing and that the reprieve or execution of a malefactor will be put beyond doubt and no longer left to uncertainty and caprice.*' The editors go on to mention that a Mr Ewart MP '*proposes to bring in a bill to abolish capital punishment altogether; such a measure may be desirable but whilst the law remains as it is at present let it be carried out whatever the position of the criminal*'.[17]

Townley was one of the last admissions into the Bethlem Criminal Department. From 1864 all criminal patients were transferred to the new state asylum at Broadmoor, built to hold 500 patients.

Wigwell Grange survives intact, though it went untenanted for years after the Captain's death as it was reputed to be haunted – by Bessie. The Grange can be seen from a public footpath that runs along the rear of the property. The standing stone near the Malt Shovel is still upright and in situ. The Malt Shovel welcomes walkers, with or without muddy boots! The Moot Hall and the Lock-Up also still stand in Wirksworth. The former is still the lead mining court for the Wapentake of Wirksworth and environs, though it meets only occasionally and ceremonially. The latter is now a bed and breakfast. The memorial to Bessie and other family members can be seen in St Mary's Church. The church is intact, save for changes made by Scott in his restoration of 1872. The Saxon sarcophagus is on show there.

Last, but not least, I must confess that the doom mural in Chaldon Church, which might possibly be the one mentioned in Chapter VII, was, in reality, only unmasked seven years after Bessie and Will's visit. It remains an extraordinary insight into the attempted manipulation of emotions of the poor by religious imagery. It is also part of my own childhood, as are the North (Farthing) Downs and Happy Valley, and Box and Leith Hills. I have lived in Wirksworth for the past thirty plus years.

Simon Hobbs

Wirksworth, Derbyshire, May 2024

---

[17] Justice of the Peace February 13th 1864, No 7, Volume XXVIII.

Note on text

The text is set in Garamond which given its historic roots, as well as its readability, seemed particularly appropriate.

Two other aspects of the text requires some comment. First the use of capitals. In modern usage capitals would only be used when part of a formal title. However, Victorian writers commonly used capitals in a freer way- Eliot's Middlemarch provides examples of this. So, in this text, both Bessie and Samuel adopt this freer approach. However, when it comes to his 'home patch' of legal titles, Samuel usually reverts to strict 'correct' usage.

The second issue concerns the use of italics. The structure of the novel is such that half of it consists of letters or other messages from Samuel to his son Frederick and this could feasibly all be in italics. However, it is conventional wisdom that italics are not so easy on the eye so I have used them more sparingly- generally to highlight quotes from external sources and letters from third parties.